THE
REDEMPTION
OF
RIVER

ELI EASTON

THE REDEMPTION OF RIVER – by Eli Easton

Sex in Seattle #4

The Redemption of River takes place in part at the Expanded Horizons sex clinic and is thus book #4 of the Sex in Seattle series. It features a brand new couple and can be read as a stand-alone.

River Larsen is a world traveler, truth-seeker, and tantric healer. He's a master of loving all—and no one. Both his past and his spiritual path warn him against attachment. When he falls for his surrogacy client and coffee magnate, Brent McKay, River tells himself it's a temporary idyll, a beautiful encounter they'll both enjoy and move on from like two ships passing in the stream of life. Except his heart misses that memo.

Brent McKay hasn't been interested in sex since his wife died two years ago. When he goes to Expanded Horizons sex clinic in Seattle for help, he meets River Larsen, a sex surrogate specializing in reiki massage and tantric sex therapy. Brent never expected to be interested in a man, but River's light-filled spirit, inner peace, and electric touch bring him back to life. Brent's loyal heart is ready to commit again. But how can he convince River that love can last forever—if you just have faith?

The Redemption of River features a widower who surprises the hell out of himself, a gorgeous hippy who thinks he's a dandelion puff, an age gap, midlife discovery of bisexuality, foodie Seattle, a houseboat, dogs, a trip to Mumbai, and tantric secrets. (You know, the ones that let you have sex for hours. Those secrets.)

Acknowledgements

My heartfelt thanks to my beta readers Veronica Harrison, Quinn Anderson, RJ Scott, and Eric McDermott, and to my editors Edie Danford, and Jason Bradley. The cover is by the talented Anna Tif Sikorska.

PART I: THE CLIENT

"Life is like a book. Some chapters are sad, some happy, and some exciting. But if you never turn the page, you will never know what the next chapter holds." – Buddha

Chapter 1

Expanded Horizons Clinic
Capitol Hill, Seattle
February, 2019
Brent

"How can I help you, Brent?" Dr. Jack Halloran asked.

Brent had heard that question a hundred times over the years—in clothing stores, restaurants, coffee shops. But he'd never really thought about it.

Could anyone help him?

Did he even want to be helped?

He closed his eyes and fought an urge to leave the room. When he opened them again, Dr. Halloran was patiently waiting. His pleasant face revealed nothing, but those blue eyes were understanding. Brent wondered how many people made an appointment at the sex clinic only to walk out again without speaking. It was so embarrassing.

Welp. Might as well get it over with.

"I've lost all sexual desire. And interest. And... functionality? Ever since my wife died. I guess that's to be expected for a while. Only it's been two years now. And... I don't know. A friend of mine thought I should see someone about it. He found you guys and said you came highly recommended. So. Here I am."

Halloran made a note on the pad in front of him. "It's been exactly two years since your wife died?"

"Two years and one week." The date was etched on his brain. Kathy had died the day before Brent's thirty-seventh birthday. And he'd just turned thirty-nine. Even thinking of that day caused his insides to ache with a dull, sickening dread. *Why did I come here? What is the point of getting my sex life back?*

It was Sean's idea. Brent had finally been honest with him, hoping to stop the constant attempts to set him up with one of Sharon's girlfriends.

Come on. It doesn't have to be serious. Annette's a fun girl. She'd be fine with something casual. Dip your toe back in the water, bro.

You don't get it, Sean. I don't have any interest in that anymore.

Jesus, the look on Sean's face—as if Brent had admitted to cutting off his own balls and preserving them in formaldehyde. It had almost been funny. Almost.

"Do you masturbate?" Dr. Halloran asked.

Brent felt his cheeks heat. "Not recently, no."

"Have you at all since your wife's death?"

Brent shook his head. "Or the last year of Kathy's life, really. She had ovarian cancer. It was slow and painful and—" He swallowed. "—messy."

Yeah. Somehow, the urge to jerk off just hadn't been there while his wife was in their bedroom dying.

"So it's been approximately three years since you ejaculated?" Halloran pressed.

Brent gave a sharp nod. "That's pretty unusual, I guess. For a guy."

"It depends. There are many things that can dull the sex drive. From injuries to depression to drugs to disease. I always like to rule out medical reasons first. I'd like to do a physical at the end of our appointment today. Take some blood, if that's okay."

"Sure. But I don't think there's anything physically wrong. I'm just... I can't seem to get over it."

Halloran looked up from his notes, eyes kind. "Have you been to grief counseling?"

"Went for three months. It was useful, I guess. Kathy's gone. I know that. I've accepted it. But the way it happened...." Brent trailed off, his throat dry.

Halloran put down his pen and leaned his forearms on his desk. "I know it's not easy to talk about. But the more you can tell me, the better I'll be able to help you."

Brent liked Jack Halloran. He was slightly built, probably weighed around one sixty. But he had an air of confident command about him, of inner strength and competence. He didn't seem like he'd judge. Hell, he was a therapist. He was paid not to judge.

Haltingly, Brent told him. He spoke about the things they don't tell you when a loved one is diagnosed with cancer. About the smells. About the incontinence as the cancer ate into her bowels. The unfathomable suffering. The way her personality changed under the influence of the medication. The denial and forced optimism that finally cracks open to reveal utter despair. The taste of hopelessness when you realize there's nothing you can do. Not a damn thing. The way you'd do anything to stop her suffering.

The guilt when you just pray for it to be over.

"It was like a horror movie." Brent's hands were over his face. He forced himself to lower them. "There was no dignity. No serenity." He swallowed hard. "It was the goddamn *Exorcist*." He blinked at the dry heat in his eyes. Even his tears were fucked up. Instead of ever crying for Kathy, the love of his life, his eyes became the Sahara desert.

"I'm so sorry, Brent," Halloran said quietly. "And I know you've probably heard too many people say that, and it means nothing. But no one should have to endure that. Not your wife and not you."

Brent said nothing. Because they had. They had endured it. Only that wasn't the right word. Kathy had endured. Brent had merely survived.

"You were her sole caretaker?" Halloran asked.

"Not exactly." Brent cleared his throat. "Kathy wanted to be at home, so we had nurses come in. But I was there and I helped. Through all of it."

"I'm sure that meant a lot to her."

Brent honestly had no idea anymore.

"How long were you married?"

"Nineteen years. Kathy and I got married right after high school. We were eighteen. Our parents weren't happy about it, but it worked out."

Halloran gave an interested hum, a slight frown between his brows. "Have you ever had a sexual partner besides Kathy?"

Brent blew out a breath. "Two girls before her, during high school. Wild and crazy guy, right?" He chuckled self-deprecatingly. "No one else after we got married though. I never cheated."

"Have you tried dating at all since she passed?" The calm, clinical tone of Halloran's voice helped, like he was asking routine questions on a survey.

Brent shook his head. "Friends keep trying to set me up. I've gotten really good at making excuses. You wouldn't believe the number of colds I've been getting over. I could be a plague ship."

Halloran's eyes twinkled with amusement.

"And, um, I own a bunch of coffee shops around town. Kathy and I built that up together. She jokingly called it *our empire*." He smiled. "Since she passed, there've been a few women involved in my work that have made it clear they're interested. I've also gotten really good at pretending I don't notice."

Halloran made a note. "Tell me about your sexual urges. You said you haven't masturbated in a few years. Have you gotten an erection, possibly in the mornings?"

"Honestly, pretty much zilch. I can't remember the last time I had morning wood. And if I do start to feel anything—" Brent hesitated.

"Yes?"

"Say I see a really attractive woman, or think about sex, and where in the past it might have gotten me going, you know? At least a warm feeling. But now I get a kind of nausea, like a nerve twinge or a bruise or something, and I feel..." It was hard to put it into words. "I just remember how awful it was. Those last few months.... Kathy's poor body. And that's... that's just the end of any sexy feeling."

The weight on Brent's chest became unbearable. He shouldn't have come here. Nothing was worth reliving this, not even his sex life. "It's really uncomfortable to talk about this."

"We don't have to talk about the past," Halloran said easily. "Let's talk instead about what we can do to help you."

"Do you honestly think you can?" Brent hadn't meant to sound so cynical, but he had doubts.

Halloran nodded. "Yes, I think we can. I'd recommend weekly

therapy sessions. We can discuss your positive sexual experiences in the past and explore what things you've found arousing. Discussing sex openly in a new context can help take it back from its negative associations, and it will give me a better idea of what to suggest you try. You might also consider seeing one of our surrogates."

Brent licked his lips nervously. "I saw something about that on the website. But if I can't even, you know, get it up—"

"That's exactly what a surrogate is for." Halloran smiled kindly. "Not necessarily right away, but when you feel you're ready for more intensive therapy. A surrogate provides a safe space and a trained partner, so that you can explore touch again, and relaxation and sensual play, with or without an erection or orgasm."

The idea left Brent cold. "Maybe at some point."

Halloran opened his desk drawer and took out a colored brochure. He opened it and laid it on the edge of his desk, facing Brent. Brent leaned forward to see it clearly.

There were four photographs with bios underneath. The first two were women, Andrea and Emily. They were attractive enough. The two photos and bios on the right were of men.

Michael Lamont

River Larsen

Brent sucked in a quick breath, then coughed as spit went down the wrong way. He hacked into his fist. Halloran watched him, patiently waiting.

"Sorry," Brent said, recovering. "I didn't expect.... I guess the guys are for female patients?"

"No. This brochure is for our male patients."

"Oh." Brent's cheeks flamed again. Well, duh. Of course the clinic had gay clients as well as straight ones. For fuck's sake, this was Capitol Hill. "Sure. That's great," he said lamely.

"We hopefully have an offering that suits everyone," Halloran said easily.

Well, *duh* again. Just because there were guys in the brochure didn't mean he had to pick one of them. His face burned hotter.

He stared at the brochure, reading over the bios without really seeing them. Certificates. Degrees. Soothing phrases like "incredibly rewarding working with clients" and "comforting atmosphere."

His gaze kept being drawn to the right side of the page.

The male surrogate named Michael had a thin, long face with thick, dark hair, bangs practically covering one eye. He was interesting. But it was the other photo that Brent could not stop staring at.

River. Like his name, the headshot had a hipster vibe. It was a black-and-white brochure, but it looked like his hair was blond and it was tied back. He was quite handsome, with a beard and very gentle eyes. They almost seemed alive, staring through Brent right from off the page.

Brent glanced at his bio. *Tantric massage and energy work. Certified massage therapist. Licensed Reiki healer. Trained at the Sacred Triangle tantra ashram in India.*

Wow. Interesting guy.

Brent blinked and forced himself to sit back. "I'm sure they're all very good."

"They are," Halloran agreed with feeling. "There aren't that many clinics that deal with sexual healing in the United States. So when I say we're able to hire the best of the best, I'm not exaggerating."

"That's great. I'll, um, I'll think about it."

That nervous, nauseous tugging began low in Brent's belly. Hell, even the *idea* of getting sexual with someone was uncomfortable. A wave of hopelessness washed through him. But he was so used to that feeling by now, it was hardly notable.

"Take the brochure home. And while you're considering it..." Halloran gave a reassuring smile. "I suggest you not discount the men automatically. Sometimes straight men find it easier, less stressful, to work with a male surrogate. Especially if there is any kind of performance anxiety. And River is really quite special. Some of my clients claim he's a miracle worker."

Brent chewed his lip. Halloran had apparently noticed Brent staring at River's photo.

"Think of it like this," Halloran continued, "when you go to a physician, it doesn't matter if that person is a man or a woman, only that they're good at their job, that they have the training and the aptitude."

"That makes sense." Brent had been to a male masseur before. In fact, he'd preferred them. "But, um, the tantric stuff… that's sexual. Right?"

"It can be. It depends on how the massage session goes. But ideally, yes, eventually your work with a surrogate would help you get back in touch with your sexual desire and, ultimately, achieve an erection and orgasm. It's a process, however. It can take time, and that's okay."

Brent's gaze fell once again to the brochure on the desk. To River's face.

"I'll think about it."

"Just one other thing…." Halloran leaned forward, folding his hands on the desk. "It's far too early to give you a diagnosis, but a few of the clients I've treated over the years have had reactions to witnessing physically traumatic events involving genitalia. One example is husbands who attend live births, but I also had a male patient whose husband had testicular cancer and afterwards my patient had difficulty not thinking about that during sex. It's not something people chose. It's not just them being assholes. But the subconscious is a tricky thing. Experiencing physical desire—or not—isn't something we can control."

Brent knew exactly what Halloran was talking about. "Yes," he said, his voice coming out a whisper.

Halloran tapped his pen on the desk. "The good news is, that sort of mental association can be treated. We can go over techniques to redirect your thoughts away from those memories when they come up during arousal. And working with a surrogate who understands those triggers can be useful. When and if you're ready, of course."

Brent swallowed. "I'll think about it."

Chapter 2

March, 2019

Brent

"Hi. I'm River Larsen." The tall, blond man held out his hand. It was a rare sunny March day in Seattle, and the stoop of Brent's Lake Washington home was bathed in sunlight, making the gold in River's blond hair glow.

"Brent McKay." Brent shook the man's hand as if it were a business meeting, as if he hadn't paid money for the guy to come over and try to help him get a stiffy.

Oh God. How is this my life? I'm only thirty-nine goddamn years old.

In person, River was even better looking than his photo in the clinic's brochure. Hell, he could have stepped out of the series *Vikings*, with his Nordic looks, complete with trim blond beard and long, dirty-blond hair twisted back in a casual knot at the crown of his head. Black gauges the size of dimes were in his ears, and a black tattoo of Indian script marched in a narrow band down his neck. He was maybe six foot one or two with very broad shoulders, long legs, and slim waist and hips. He wore a faded black T-shirt with some kind of Indian design on the front, and well-worn jeans.

Damn, but he made Brent feel old and pathetically stodgy with his black LL Bean shorts and short-sleeved blue button-down shirt. Not that he wasn't used to hipsters. Hell, a quarter of the staff at his coffee shops *were* hipsters. But River seemed more genuine, grounded, like he probably woke up in the morning and wound his hair back in a knot and didn't think about it all day, like he legit belonged on a beach somewhere. Or an ashram, like in his bio. He radiated a peaceful, light positivity that was appealing.

"I need a space to set up. Do you have an area in your home where you'd feel comfortable? I'll need open floor space."

"Oh, yeah. Sure. Um... Come on in." Jesus. Was he gonna make the guy stand on the porch all day?

Brent led the way up the stairs to the room he used as a home office. Even though he lived alone, he didn't want to get massaged on the main floor of the house with all its windows. His desk was in front of a window, which overlooked Lake Washington, but the office was on the second floor, and the angle would make it difficult for anyone to see inside, even if passing boaters cared to try. It was a large room, and it only had a desk and one small bookcase, so there was plenty of space on the carpet.

River's gaze lingered on the window for a moment, maybe surprised by the multi-million-dollar view, but he didn't say anything, just put down the things he'd been carrying—a large duffel bag and a big, black, square case that was probably a massage table. Too late, Brent thought he should have offered to help. God, he was off-kilter.

It's just a massage, he told himself. *That's all it has to be.*

"Would you mind giving me five minutes to set up? It's better if I do that alone," River said with a gentle smile.

"Oh. Yeah. Sure."

"Do you have a robe you can get changed into? Or a towel. Nothing underneath."

Brent swallowed and nodded. He left the room.

As he removed his clothes in his walk-in closet, Brent thought about his googled research. Tantric massage had looked very, uh, sensual, with the masseuse in one video even sort of rubbing their oiled body along the client's back. And then Brent had followed a link to *lingam* massage, and had found a video and, *holy hell.*

It was hard to imagine any guy in the world not getting aroused by *that,* by having his *lingam*—aka his penis—manipulated and massaged every which way. But Brent's body had responded with its usual weird nausea, an uneasy, painful tugging sensation low in his belly, and a nice dollop of guilt on top. He'd shut the video off.

He tried not to be pessimistic about his chances with a real tantrik, in the flesh. He tried not to think about it at all.

He'd already showered, so he put on a thin cotton robe in navy blue. He suddenly recalled Kathy had bought it for him for their last Christmas together. Brent pushed that thought from his mind too. Hell, he was getting so good at pushing thoughts away, it was a wonder his brain wasn't wiped clean.

When he went back into his office, he blinked in surprise. The space had been transformed. The blind over the large window had been lowered—probably for the first time since he bought the place. The room was dim but not dark. Light still filtered in through the semi-opaque blind. Candles had been set around the room and lit, and incense burned. The scent was dry and woodsy, like cedar or sandalwood. There was a futon in the middle of the floor—not the massage table Brent had expected. It was draped with a soft fabric in rust and red and browns, an Indian design. There was a thin pillow for his head at one end.

"Wow."

River straightened up from a little clay pot he'd plugged into the wall. An oil-warmer, Brent guessed. "Hey." He studied Brent's face for a moment. "Are you feeling okay about this?"

Was he? Not really.

"It's worth a shot, I guess." Brent forced a chuckle. "Just to be, um, open, Dr. Halloran said it wasn't necessarily going to be sexual right away. I'm not sure anything will happen."

River gave him a soft smile. "Then tantra is perfect. Because it's not about a destination. It's not about trying to get anywhere. It's just about being present in the moment."

"Okay. Good." Still, nerves churned in Brent's belly.

"The practice is aimed at reconnecting us to our bodies. There's no expectation or judgment."

"Maybe Dr. Halloran told you that I—"

"Your body will tell me." River's voice was fairly deep, calm and soothing, like nothing could surprise or perturb him. Brent relaxed a little.

"In tantra, we always begin by making a connection. Will you join me?" River sat crossed-legged on the futon. Brent suddenly realized he'd taken off his jeans and was now barefoot and wearing only dark shorts and his T-shirt. His long legs were golden brown and dusted with fine gold hair. They were nicely muscled.

River patted the spot on the futon in front of him.

Brent walked over. "Facing you, or...?"

"Facing me."

Awkwardly, Brent sat down on the futon. He had to adjust his robe so he didn't expose himself. River scooted a little closer, until their knees were touching. He reached out and took Brent's hands in both of his, letting them rest on their knees.

"Look into my eyes. If you have to look away, you can, but hold my gaze as much as possible."

Hum. This was out of Brent's comfort zone. But he was also curious. He stared into River's eyes.

River was a wee bit taller than Brent standing, but with both of them sitting on the futon, their eyes were exactly even. Lovely, kind eyes with soft, light-brown lashes stared at Brent. Seconds ticked by.

It wasn't easy to hold River's gaze. It was so intimate. Raw. Had Brent ever stared into someone's eyes like this? Maybe Kathy's, when they were first in love. But he didn't know River at all.

Brent took a deep breath and stared. He was paying for this therapy, and he was going to make the most of it.

Blue. Not a vibrant blue, more gray-blue, the color of a dull sea under leaden skies. But the openness in them was unnerving. There was a depth there that made Brent's head spin, like standing on a tightrope over a void.

"Now take deep breaths, all the way down into your belly," River said quietly, still staring into Brent's eyes. He demonstrated, breathing in long and deep, his inhale loud, his chest rising, then slowly letting it out. Brent mimicked him.

"Release your worry and anxiety. Just be present with your breath. Don't think."

Brent tried. With every deep breath, his head got a little lighter and spacier. Thoughts quieted. Was that a hyperventilating thing? Whatever. It worked. He relaxed.

At first, River matched his breaths to Brent, like they were two lungs in a body, all while staring into Brent's eyes. Then Brent became aware that River had switched the pattern—he inhaled slowly as Brent exhaled slowly, and vice versa. It was as if they were taking each other's breath, as if something vital were streaming from River's lungs to his and back again, in a never-ending circle.

Brent became aware of the smell of River, a warm scent of clove and cinnamon with something that smelled like the beach.

Those eyes. Jesus. Was he being hypnotized? Part of him wanted to lie down, he felt so relaxed, but there was an energy that hummed between them, too, causing his body to prickle with awareness even as his mind went numb.

When River spoke, it broke through the fog.

"You're doing great. You're so open." River smiled at him.

"I am?" Brent's voice was husky.

"Very open. Thank you for that. I think we're ready to begin." River released Brent's hands and shifted to kneel beside the futon. He picked up a white towel. "Take your robe off and lie on your stomach."

His voice was soft and low, and it took a moment for the meaning to sink in. Oh, right. The breathing had really soothed Brent's mind, because he felt no apprehension as he took off his robe and dropped it beside the futon. He lay facedown, with his head turned to the side on the pillow. The dense mattress was very comfortable. A moment later, River laid a towel across Brent's ass, reminding him that he had been, in fact, naked under the robe. Well, River had gotten an eyeful.

Brent took another deep breath. This was a massage. That was all. His head still felt floaty, but a touch of anxiety crept back in.

River moved to the foot of the futon and laid warm oily hands on Brent's calves. Just that touch made a tingle go up Brent's thighs, only to dissipate into unease in his belly. He must have tensed up because River spoke.

"Nothing has to happen or not happen. I'm going to do some

energy work on your body. Just relax and feel the sensations. Stay in the present moment. There is no right or wrong. We'll just assess where you're at. It's all good."

Nothing has to happen. Brent didn't have to get off or even get hard, he reminded himself. Dr. Halloran had told him that, but it was good to hear River confirm it. And he was such a chill guy, gentle and positive. Brent believed he meant it.

He was also so good-looking. He had nice hands. Brent didn't have any issue with being touched by this person, even though he was a guy. Not necessarily sexually, but a massage? Yes, please. It had been too long since he'd had any touch at all.

River moved to sit on his heels at the side of the futon and started with Brent's hands. River's hands were warm, and he rubbed oil into Brent's skin, threading their fingers together in a light, flowing touch, rubbing his thumbs into Brent's palms.

God, that was good. Brent sighed and closed his eyes.

"Take deep, slow breaths," River instructed quietly. "Pull the air all the way down into your belly and let me hear the exhale."

Brent slowed his breathing, deepened it, as they'd done when they looked into each other's eyes. Quickly, his head grew floaty again.

River massaged his forearms, biceps, shoulders. It was heaven. Oh, man. So nice. When he got to Brent's neck, his fingers slipped up through Brent's hair to the top of his head and cupped him there, his large hands surrounding the crown of Brent's head, palms down.

Jesus, his palms were so warm.

"This is your *sahasrara* or crown chakra. Breathe deep, and when you exhale, I want you to imagine pushing your energy up into my hands. Imagine you're filling my hands with light. See it in your mind."

It sounded weird. Brent wasn't even sure what River meant by "light." And yet, he found he was able to visualize it, to mentally push energy toward River's hands. It didn't hurt that River's large palms were so warm and alive, pulling Brent's awareness to them.

"Good," River said soothingly. "Very good. Breathe deep. Melt into the mattress."

Oh, he was melted all right. Brent breathed out and relaxed as River released the top of his head and carded his fingers through Brent's hair again. Mmm, that was delightful. The top of his head was all warm and tingly.

River cupped the back of Brent's head with one hand. "I'm going to gently touch your face. Relax." His other hand touched two fingers to the bridge of Brent's nose, between his eyes.

River held there for a long moment, pressing lightly from both sides. "This is your *ajna* chakra, your third eye. Breathe deep and mentally push your energy and breath into my hands."

Brent did. It felt like he was pushing his exhales into those pressure points, one behind his head and one between his eyes. The fingertips at the bridge of his nose seemed to grow hotter.

"Excellent. I can really feel you. Now relax."

River threaded luxuriant fingers through Brent's hair again, lightly scratching his scalp. Brent groaned into his loud exhales. Maybe he could just have River follow him around and play with his hair all day.

Next, River cupped the back of Brent's neck with both palms. His long fingers gently wrapped around as much of Brent's neck as possible with his head on the pillow. "This is your *vishuddha* or throat chakra. Breathe into my hands."

Brent breathed into River's hands. His neck grew warm. There was a weird sensation there, as if his neck was expanding. Which wasn't actually possible, but it sure felt that way.

Next, River placed both palms, side by side, on his upper back. "This is your *anahata* or heart chakra. Breathe into it for me."

Oh. This one ached a bit. Or maybe it was the weight of River's hands. Was he pressing down? His hands felt so heavy. His palms grew very hot. It was uncomfortable if Brent was being honest. For the first time, the touching didn't feel so great, and he wanted to squirm, but he managed not to. He was relieved when River moved on.

"*Manipura,* or solar plexus chakra."

This one was midback, right between his ribs on his spine. It felt okay. But Jesus, River's palms now felt like they were burning him.

Was that some kind of hypnotic suggestion? Was he going into an altered state thanks to all this heavy breathing and incense? Maybe his skin was just getting more sensitive, cooling in the air.

He breathed into River's hands, and he could swear he felt energy swirl between them. His back prickled like one of those weird physics experiments in middle school where you touch an electrostatic ball and your hair stands on end.

"*Svadhishthana*, or sacrum chakra." River's hands moved lower, palms spreading firmly on either side of his spine just above his buttocks.

A cry erupted from Brent's mouth, shocking him. He arched up.

River removed his hands at once. "Ah. Sensitive there?"

Brent shuddered and drew in a breath. "That was weird. I don't know—"

"It's okay. Relax and just breathe for me."

Brent melted back onto the futon. It wasn't difficult. His body felt heavy and slow, like he'd been deeply asleep. Only, that touch to his lower back had done something…. He had no idea what.

With a few deep breaths, he relaxed again. River ran his fingertips lightly up Brent's arms and across his shoulders. Brent sighed. The touch felt sensual, and that uneasy tug of want-not-want twinged low in his belly. He sighed.

"I'm going to place my hands on your lower back again. Very gently. Okay?"

"Yeah." Brent really had no idea why he'd jerked before.

River trailed his oily palms down Brent's back, on either side of his spine, slowly, slowly. They were literally radiating heat. It felt good.

He held himself still as those palms reached his lower back and paused there. He didn't jump this time. But when River gently reminded him to take deep breaths, instructed him to breathe up into his palms, he couldn't. He just couldn't. A terrible weight came upon him, a crushing sense of dread. Nerves twinged where River had his hands, sounding a warning through his lower back and belly.

"That hurts," Brent admitted, struggling with the sensation. "Christ, your hands are hot."

River let up with his palms, thank God. Instead, he massaged the area gently with his fingertips. It should have felt good, but it didn't. "Can you direct your energy into my fingertips?"

"Can't," Brent said at once. "It feels really weird. Like... like a sore tooth."

"Breathe deep." River breathed loudly in demonstration, so Brent could follow his breaths, match them. "Good. Now try to push your breath into my fingertips."

Brent tried. But he couldn't focus his attention there at all without feeling sick. "Can't."

River made a humming sound, as if he expected as much.

"Why do I feel so weird there? I don't have any old injuries that I—" Then it struck him like a ton of bricks. Not him. *Kathy.*

Brent swallowed hard. "Did Dr. Halloran tell you about my... my wife's illness?" His voice was choked.

"He told me your wife transitioned, and you haven't felt desire since."

"He didn't tell you how she...?"

"No. Can you turn over, please?"

Brent turned over, careful to keep the towel over his genitals. God, his limbs were so heavy. His body was so relaxed. Yet that tug of unease lingered low in his belly like the dull throb of an exposed nerve. He blinked up at River. The dim daylight and flickering candles made a halo around his hair, and his face was so serene. Jesus, he was a beautiful human being. River met his gaze, and it was too much suddenly. Too raw. Brent closed his eyes.

River stroked up his arms again and over his chest, a light sensual touch that created another want-not-want tug in Brent's belly. This time, Brent was very aware that the sensation was just where River's hands had been.

Those too-hot hands smoothed their way down to his lower belly, pushing the edge of the towel down a little. They spread out just below his belly button, wrists touching and fingers extended like bird's wings toward his hips. They rested there. Not pressing down, not hurting him. But not comfortable either.

Brent's breathing sped up.

"Your wife was sick here?" River asked.

Hot emotion welled up in Brent's chest, his throat tightening with tears. He nodded. *Oh God.*

River rubbed Brent's belly oh-so-gently, and he breathed out very audibly. Nauseous eddies swirled under his hands.

"You're holding a lot of grief here." River rubbed circles with his thumbs on either side of Brent's belly button.

"Ovarian cancer," Brent choked out. "Dr. Halloran didn't tell you?"

"No. Sometimes we take on the suffering of others, internalize it, store it in our bodies. It's a way of trying to ease their burden."

That made no sense. Brent had never tried to take Kathy's pain. Not like that. Had he?

"I know it feels blocked, but breathe into my hands as best you can, try to release the tension here. Sync your breath with mine. Ready?"

Even with his eyes closed, Brent could hear River's long, loud breaths, and he mimicked them. They breathed together—in, out. River pressed on his belly, or maybe it just felt like he did, or maybe Brent was crazy. Queasiness washed through him. Dark emotion rolled up as if rising from an abyss. He realized he was shaking all over. A sob tore from his chest.

"You're doing great. I know it's uncomfortable, but we've got to bring up that pain so we can release it," River urged softly. "Now imagine it's attached to my hands. We're going to move that pain and grief up your spine. Ready?" He ran his hot hands slowly up from Brent's belly to his ribs, then his chest, then neck. His hands felt so heavy. Brent could imagine that something dark and ugly was attached to his palms, that he was dragging it upward, something that had been inside him all this time.

"Now we're going to push that pain all the way up to the top of your head and release it, letting it leave your body." His hot palms pushed up over Brent's temples to the crown of his head where he opened his hands. He repeated this over and over—moving his hands from Brent's belly to his crown, pushing up wave after wave of dark emotion.

Brent just laid there and cried. It was the *idea* that struck him so hard, the idea that his grief and anguish had gotten buried inside him, wrapped around his bowels where Kathy's body had been riddled with all-too-real tumors.... He'd heard of men experiencing phantom twinges while their wives were pregnant, but... God. *Kathy.* Her poor body. Her poor, beautiful body.

He cried and cried until he was a mess of snot and heat.

At last, River removed his hands. Brent sensed him moving off. He returned and placed something in Brent's hand. Tissues. Brent cleaned up his face, too exhausted to even feel self-conscious. Then River helped him sit up using a strong arm behind his back. He handed him a bottle of water and urged Brent to sip from it.

When he was steadier, River sat next to him on the futon, one arm still supporting Brent. "How do you feel?"

"Like I've been hit by a truck." Brent half laughed. "Jesus, that was intense."

River nodded. "You released a lot of pain today."

Brent thought maybe he had. Though whether that was all of it or whether it would turn out to be an endless well inside him, like some kind of emotional ouroboros, he didn't know.

Except... he already felt a little lighter. There was an energy humming through him that was kind of good? He tried to joke. "That wasn't the outcome I expected. Kind of the opposite of a happy ending."

River's eyes grew amused. "We don't always get the ending we want. But hopefully we get the ending we need."

"So profound."

"To be fair, I stole it from Mick Jagger. But I think he stole it from the *vedas*. So."

Brent chuckled. "Is nothing original anymore?"

"Not much, no."

Brent smiled at River, and River smiled back. Something about the guy was so comforting, sort of light and chillax and just good juju.

Brent had an urge to lean into him, to be held in River's arms, to rest after what he'd just been through. But River didn't offer that, and Brent wouldn't presume. He was just a client—not besties, and not anything else either.

"It might take a few sessions, but I think the energy work can help you release that pain."

"Do you think that's what's been holding me back? Sexually, I mean?"

"Absolutely. The *svadhishthana* chakra is the seat of your emotions, your sensuality, and creativity. When it's constricted or blocked, it absolutely messes with your sexuality."

"Oh." Brent took another long swig of water from the bottle. "But it can get better?"

"Yes. That's what the tantra work is for." River sounded matter-of-fact. "It's important to release it for other reasons too. Holding grief in a part of the body like that, you can actually attract disease. In the same way that stress can cause heart disease or ulcers, a spiritual block can turn into a physical one. Tumors, for instance."

Holy shit. That didn't sound good.

River's gaze was kind. "Don't worry. You made a lot of progress already today. If you have the will to let it go, we can make it happen."

"Thank you," Brent said sincerely.

This time, it was River who looked away. "Tonight, try a hot bath and some more deep breathing. If you feel up to it, breathe into that chakra. Try to release the tension there, direct light and positive energy to that area. And if you want to continue with me, you can schedule an appointment through the clinic."

Brent kind of wanted to try again, right then. But their time was probably up. "I'll book another appointment."

"Great. Then I'll see you soon. Do you want to go wash your face while I get packed up in here?"

Brent took his cue and left River alone to clean up.

Chapter 3

"Hey, Mr. McKay!"

A chorus of hellos greeted Brent when he entered Adrenaline Junkie Coffee on Madrona's main drag. He wiped his face with his sweatshirt sleeve and smiled. "Hey, guys."

It had been, what, three weeks since he'd been in the place? Probably more like a month. Too long. His gaze swept the room assessingly. It was crowded at eight in the morning—as it should be. Dani, the manager, was at the register. A twenty-something woman, Lori or Laura, was making drinks. Beside her was a new redheaded barista Brent didn't recognize.

The storefront was clean, right down to the glossy checkerboard floor. The newspapers on the shelf by the door were today's. From the looks of all the people on their laptops or phones, the Wi-Fi was working, and the short line at the counter moved swiftly.

Brent slipped behind the register to grab a bottled water and avocado-egg wrap from the display case and held them up to catch Dani's eye so she could make a note of it. He took them to a seat at the long bar along the window and pulled a newspaper closer.

He didn't read it though. He watched the people passing by—an older man doing a morning walk with the dogs, a fit young mom with an infant in a jogging stroller. Across the street, there were peek-a-boo views of Lake Washington. The sky was overcast and dull, but it wasn't raining, and the air had a touch of warmth. For Seattle in March, he'd take it.

He noticed his own reflection in the plate glass, and for a second, he didn't recognize himself. He was smiling.

He surreptitiously studied his reflection. He'd slept hard after yesterday's session with River and woke up this morning feeling refreshed and with a restless energy. He'd decided to go for a run for the first time in ages. He'd only run two miles, and slowly, but it was still a win. He'd enjoyed it. The view of the water and the gorgeous houses on Madrona Beach Road, the feeling of his muscles being put to the test, the incandescent green of the trees and bushes at the park, even the overcast Seattle sky. The world seemed sharper, as if a dirty filter had been lifted from his eyes.

He bit into his egg wrap. The tortilla was soft and the avocado and lettuce inside were fresh. The scrambled eggs had the right texture and flavor. Good. It pissed him off when staff let food sit around in the display case for too long.

Dani plopped down on the seat next to him. "Hi, Mr. McKay."

Brent wiped his mouth with a napkin. "How's it going, Dani?"

"Good!" Dani was a little too animated, trying to impress him. She was in her early thirties, dark-haired and pudgy with a very pretty face that she wore completely au natural. She had a degree in restaurant management from UW and was good at her job. Brent was fortunate to have her. "Did you get the report from Roscoe last week? Business has been pretty good, especially considering the new Starbucks down the block."

Brent nodded, not wanting to admit that he hadn't looked over the report. And Starbucks... fuck. They'd be the death of him. He glanced around the room. "Decent traffic for a Friday morning."

"Oh, yeah! You should see it on the weekends. Even better."

Brent felt a pang of guilt at her words. He *should* see it on the weekends. He'd become too much of an absentee boss. But honestly, some days it was all he could do to get out of bed. And though he felt better this morning, the thought of how far behind he was threatened to put him right back there.

"Is everything okay? I mean..." Dani fidgeted nervously. "Did you want to talk to me or something?"

"Nope. I was just out for a run and thought I'd stop by."

Her smile was relieved. "Okay. Great! It's nice to see you, Mr. McKay. Want me to get you a coffee?"

"Sure." He and Dani both said, "Oat milk venti latte with cinnamon," simultaneously. He smiled. "You remembered."

She winked. "That's my job. Sometimes I swear I have coffee orders etched on my brain." She left him to go make his drink.

Brent pulled out his phone and looked at the time. 8:10 a.m. He brought up his contact list. What time did Expanded Horizons open anyway?

"Hey there, Brent."

Brent turned to see a familiar face. It took a moment for the name to come to him. "Chuck Cornish. How are you?"

"Never better." Chuck, a big guy in his fifties, grinned and held out a meaty hand. They shook. "I just happened to see you in the window. It's been so long, had to come in and say hello."

Cornish had been a fixture at the Seattle Restaurant Alliance events Brent and Kathy used to attend. He was the type of high-voltage salesman Brent didn't really care for. There was a lot of that in the hospitality business, but it wasn't Brent's style.

"Can I get you a coffee?" Brent offered.

"Oh, no thanks." Cornish's brow furrowed as he glanced over at the chalk menu board above the register. "I've had my coffee today. Just popped in to say hello. I'm opening up a place down the street. Jasmine Express. Asian fusion. My fifth one. Business has been hopping!"

"That's great, Chuck."

"Hell, the Seattle boom is making us all rich, huh? Of course, you can't sit still in this city. Ideas fall out of fashion quicker than the latest version of Windows. Innovate or die, amiright?" He glanced again at the menu board and frowned. "Gee, the coffee business must be tough. Didn't a new Starbucks just go in down the street?"

Brent gritted his teeth. "Adrenaline Junkie Coffee was one of the first serious coffee chains in town. We have loyal customers."

"Right. Right. Great location too." Cornish's smile felt patronizing. "So have you been out of the country or what? Haven't seen you and your wife at the Alliance dinners."

Brent's hands clenched on the counter. "Kathy passed away two years ago. I haven't been getting out much."

"Oh. Oh shit." Cornish's face reddened. "Sorry to hear that. She was a pretty lady. That's a shame." Cornish patted Brent shoulder awkwardly. "Well, uh, if there's ever anything you need, my place will be just down the street. Jasmine Express. Glad to be neighbors."

"That'll be great. Good luck with the new place."

"Thanks. Nice seeing ya, Brent." Cornish made his escape.

Innovate or die.

Chuck freaking Cornish. What did he know? Probably not that Brent's business revenue was down ten percent last year. And the year before that. Hardly surprising given how depressed he'd been. The Alliance wasn't the only thing he'd dropped the ball on. Thank God he had solid managers like Dani, and that he did, indeed, have loyal customers.

Still. A twinge of shame unsettled his gut. Guys like Chuck had been out there making deals while he'd been sleeping. It was time to get his shit together.

His phone was still lit up on the counter, still open to his contacts list. *Expanded Horizons Clinic.* He pressed Send.

"How did your session with River go?" Halloran asked the following afternoon.

"Besides the fact that I ended up sobbing on the massage table and nothing remotely sexual happened? It went pretty well." Brent chuckled self-deprecatingly.

Halloran leaned forward. "Really? What brought up that emotion for you?"

Brent told him all about it, about the pain and discomfort in his lower back and belly and River's explanation that he held his grief there. "What do you think about that whole *chakras* thing? Do you think it can really help me?"

"I absolutely believe the mind has a powerful effect on the body. And I think there are different ways of looking at the body-mind connection. Western science hasn't done a great job of examining it, so other traditions are worth considering. It's kind of like the blind men and the elephant parable. Do you remember that?"

Brent thought about it. "You mean the one where a blind man

feels the side of the elephant and says it's like a wall, another feels its trunk and says it's like a snake?"

Halloran's eyes twinkled. "Exactly. The idea of chakras is just one way of looking at the mind-body connection." Halloran tapped his pen on the desk. He hesitated, then spoke. "I was in the military, and I was wounded. I had therapy for PTSD, and we did breathing work and a little reiki to release internalized trauma. I found it helpful. At the end of the day, what matters is whether or not it works. Did you find the experience beneficial?"

Brent blew out a breath. "It's probably one of the most powerful experiences I've ever had in my life. I wasn't expecting anything like that, and then *wham*. I have no idea if it makes any logical sense, but it absolutely felt like some kind of... of blockage in my body. Like River found this cache of buried emotion. All of this stuff came up for me. And then afterward.... It was cathartic." A giddy bubble rose in Brent's chest at the memory. "River is amazing. He was thoughtful and gentle.... So professional. It's like you can really feel the energy in his hands. Incredible. He's got such a healing..." *Light? Gift?* Those sounded too cutesy. "... uh, way about him."

"I'll consider that a glowing review then." Halloran had a bemused expression, and Brent realized he was gushing a bit too much. "Would you like to book another session with River?"

"I, um, already booked two more through Loretta. I'm seeing him next week."

Halloran refrained from looking smug as he wrote it on his calendar.

Chapter 4

"Relax. Breathe into my hands."

Brent felt the silly smile on his face as he breathed in deeply and relaxed into the futon. It was only his third session with River, but already the smell of incense and oil, and the feel of River's hands, blissed him out in no time. Pavlovian response. It felt so good to be touched. It felt good to feel good. *God.*

And the staring into the eyes and deep breathing thing they did at the start? So incredibly intimate. Hell, Brent was a ball of putty before he even lay down.

Last time, they'd worked almost exclusively on releasing pain and grief from Brent's lower belly. It had been uncomfortable, and he'd felt sadness and despair rise up again, but not nearly as strong as the first time. Weirdly, he hadn't even thought about trying to get an erection or getting off until after River had left. The healing seemed more important. And that was fine.

It was honestly helping. He'd felt lighter and more energetic during the past week than he had for years. That was more valuable to him than sex.

Brent expected more of the same in this third session. But as River massaged him, rubbing warm oil into his palms, which were surprisingly sensitive, and his arms, and up his shoulders, the touch felt more sensual, teasing. Or maybe River's technique hadn't changed. Maybe Brent was just feeling it in a new way.

When River ghosted fingertips across Brent's shoulder blades and sank his fingers into Brent's hair, lightly scratching his scalp, a wave of desire went through him. River continued to massage his scalp, then lightly touched Brent's ears. Liquid heat pooled in his groin. His cock plumped against the futon.

In the past when his body had started to get an erection, that nauseous tugging sensation in his belly wilted him in a hurry. But that didn't happen. With a sudden thrill of nerves, Brent realized he was genuinely getting aroused. He forced himself to focus on his breathing, and on River's hands, and not think about it, afraid his head would get in the way, and he'd lose this feeling.

Maybe River sensed the shift, because he ghosted his fingertips over Brent's ears again—God, when had they become an erogenous zone?—then down his neck in a teasing touch. He got more oil on his hands and rubbed up Brent's spine with his thumbs, firmly, then followed with that ultra-light touch back down, nape to ass. Brent broke out in goosebumps.

He breathed deeply and licked his lips. "I'm feeling... um...."

"Awesome. Just focus on my touch and your breath. Let everything else go."

Brent did his best. The touch was nice. It was really fucking sexy, in fact. And his body was so relaxed. He wanted to push into the futon, nearly overcome with an urge to feel friction on his aroused dick for the first time in ages. Not moving was difficult.

"Would you like to turn over?" River asked, removing his hands.

Brent swallowed. God yes. And no. It was a little embarrassing. He put one hand on the towel on his ass and tried to keep himself covered as he turned and settled onto his back. He was tenting the towel a bit, but not as much as he'd expected. He closed his eyes, not able to look at River.

River moved Brent's feet a little farther apart, settling between his calves. His hands, warm with fresh oil, rubbed up both shins, ankle to knee, then his thighs, slowly, slowly, moving all the way up under the edge of the towel to the crease where his thighs met his torso. But then, somewhat disappointingly, they shifted up to his hips, then his ribs and over his nipples, slow and firm. He cupped Brent's neck.

Brent swallowed a moan. The towel shifted as he grew harder.

"Would you like to try the *lingam* massage today?" River asked, his tone as neutral as if he were asking Brent if he wanted cream with his coffee.

But hearing the words said out loud caused Brent's heart rate to pick up. "I guess." He swallowed. "Not sure how it'll go, but...."

"It's just touch. Let it feel nice. It doesn't have to go anywhere. Tantra is about enjoying sensation, energy—not reaching a destination."

Right. River had told him that several times, but it was difficult, as a guy, not to focus on getting off, especially since he hadn't in a long time. "Okay."

"All right if I remove the towel?" River asked.

Brent nodded, eyes still closed. He swallowed a mouth full of saliva as River pulled the towel away. His dick sproinged a bit. God, how long had it been since he'd had an honest-to-God erection? River gently lifted one of Brent's legs, then the other, and placed what felt like small pillows under each knee, tilting his legs slightly outward. Geez, he must be able to see everything.

Oh God. He can see everything.

As if encouraging Brent to relax, River placed his palms on Brent's quads and rubbed light circles on his inner thighs with his thumbs. The circles got a little higher, and a little higher, until they were close to his balls. Which River could clearly see. The idea, and the touch, turned Brent on. A gush of heat washed through his groin. He felt his semi enlarge and trace a path up his belly. A long tremor went through him, and he clutched the edge of the futon with one hand.

It had been so long since he'd felt arousal like this. Just as the thought hit him, queasiness stirred in his belly, a trace of that tugging sensation, and it terrified him. Oh, no, not now. Please. He wanted this. He *needed* it.

"Shhh. Relax." River rubbed Brent's hand until he let go of the futon, and then he returned it loosely to Brent's side. "Don't think. Just breathe and feel my hands, right here, right now. Breathe with me. Like this."

River's breathing became loud and slow, sounding like a breathing machine. Right. Right. Brent needed to get back to that hypno-state. He mimicked River, focusing on the sound. In. Out. In. Out. His head got floaty, his thoughts quieted, and his body grew weighted on the futon.

River said nothing more, but the quality of the massage changed. He rubbed both hands, warm with fresh oil, up Brent's calves and thighs, then over his hip bones, not touching his erection. With River now positioned between his legs, the direction of the touch felt much more intimate. Just knowing how exposed he was, and that River was *right there*, sent an electric frisson through Brent.

River's hands moved up Brent's ribs and chest, circling over his nipples, cupping his shoulders, then rubbing back down. All the while River breathed in that loud, slow way that was surprisingly sensual. Brent's head spun, and the touch was so good—warm, firm, and tantalizing all at once. It excited the nerves along that pathway and radiated out in waves. His own next loud breath held a bit of a moan.

River did the motion up Brent's body again and again. Then he did it *closer*. River's bare chest and arms—when had he removed his shirt?—made contact as he moved upward, lengthening himself out over Brent's body. As his hands circled up to Brent's shoulders, his chest rubbed against Brent's erection.

Oh God. Brent panted erratically, and he had a hard time not raising his hips. Then River's entire body slid back down, rolling Brent's cock between them until he straightened up again.

Brent moaned louder into his exhale this time. He trembled. He wasn't sure he could stand it.

But River moved back up again, sliding with that delicious friction. His loud breaths reminded Brent to mimic him, to calm down. River's skin was so slick and warm and smooth. Brent didn't feel any chest hair, but he did feel plenty of plump, firm muscle. The sensation on his dick was exquisite.

Oh, Jesus. This was hot. This was... *sex.* He hadn't been with anyone but Kathy in so long.

No, don't think about that. Just feel.

Please. Please, please, please, please, please.

River's sliding body was replaced by his hands. He slid one palm slowly up from Brent's balls, over his cock, open-palmed, pressing it lightly into his stomach in a single upward stroke, first with one hand and then the other. Again, again.

Brent's thighs shook, and he had to deepen his breathing. *Oh God.*

Maybe he should have been freaking out. Or worried. Or trying too hard. But, screw it, he just wanted to *feel.* And goddamn, it felt so good.

Those long, open-palmed strokes were replaced by River circling his cock with one slick fist and stroking up from base to tip with first one hand and then the other, always only doing a single upstroke at a leisurely pace. Then he reversed it, doing a single downstroke from tip to base, with first one hand and then the other.

It felt as good as anything Brent could ever remember feeling in his life, the friction was firm yet not trying to get him anywhere. It truly was a massage. Of his penis.

Oh, man. Whoever invented this was *brilliant.*

The different hand movements went on, each one more of a tease than the last, until Brent couldn't even catalog them anymore. There was one where River polished the head of his cock with his open palm, another where he did a fisted upstroke with a twist, and another where he rubbed Brent's penis between both palms, as if he were trying to start a fire. He ran his thumb up and down the underside vein, making tiny circles, the way he'd rubbed Brent's spine. He massaged the frenulum with a thumb, cupped and smoothed his balls, and pressed with oily fingers around his perineum until he found a spot that made Brent utter a startled cry at the *zing.*

It was all teasing, and fantastic, and so different from the basic up-down, get-r-done stroke he'd used since he was a teenager. But after a while, Brent couldn't stop his hips from lifting up, seeking more. *More, please, more.*

River switched to a fast up-and-down stroke using just one circled finger and thumb, cradling Brent's balls with his other hands as he did it, and, *Oh God,* that was gonna get him there fast. But River only did it for a few seconds at a time, interspersed with other moves. He gradually used the up-down stroke longer and faster, but always stopped when Brent's thighs started to tremble, returning to one of the teasing strokes.

Brent felt like he was harder than he'd ever been in his life, and it seemed like the *lingam* massage had been going on for ages. It was nice that River was in no hurry, but Brent's balls were so tight they ached. He had a goddamn hard-on, and he wanted to come. He wanted to *get there* as a final proof that it was real before it all went *poof* somehow.

He couldn't even remember the last time he'd come. Early in Kathy's illness, probably.

"*River*," he said, his voice a croak. He'd meant to say *please* or *keep going* or something less personal, because the name sounded like a lover's moan coming from his lips.

But it did the trick.

"You want to ejaculate?" River asked, his voice a little thick too.

"Yeah." Eyes still closed, Brent nodded for good measure. *Yes, please. Please, please, please.*

River resumed his hypnotic breathing, but his touch changed. He rubbed Brent's thighs and balls again, then fisted Brent's cock and began a delicious up-and-down stroke, pumping fast.

Brent moaned loudly. Jesus, that felt so... *oh.*

Before he could even think *I'm there, I'm going to come,* he was and he did.

It hit him with the suddenness and power of a bolt of lightning. His body bowed up and clenched as waves of delight ripped through him. It was nearly painful in its intensity, his dick pulsing four, five times as River stroked him through it.

When the waves finally receded, Brent fell back, exhausted and blissed out. Between the incense and the breathing and the massage and the orgasm... *damn.*

He was barely aware of River wiping down his stomach and putting the towel over him again. There were the sounds of River moving around. Some part of Brent's brain knew he probably looked dorky, just lying there, eyes closed and grinning like a virgin after his first blowjob, but he didn't care.

Finally River put a soothing palm on his forehead. "Would you like me to help you to your bedroom?"

Oh. Of course. River needed the futon. He probably wanted to go. Session over. Brent felt a niggle of disappointment.

Hell, what did he expect? A cuddle?

Brent opened his eyes. River was squatting by the mat, looking at him. "Everything all right?"

"Yeah. Fantastic." Brent pushed himself to sitting, and River helped him to his feet.

The towel fell off, and there was an awkward moment where River got Brent into his robe.

"Sorry. Man. I'm out of it."

"That happens." River smiled. "Want me to help you down the hall?"

"No, I can walk."

"Cool. You go lie down. I'll let myself out."

Brent went to the doorway and turned. "Um. River? Thank you. That was...."

River winked at him. "You're welcome. And congratulations."

Brent smiled all the way down the hall.

Chapter 5

Brent

"Holy shit! How much does this guy charge? And will you give me his number?"

A wave of annoyance flared in Brent. He put his salad fork down and took a sip of his beer. "He's a licensed therapist, Sean. Not a call girl."

"Spoilsport." Sean grinned at him and took a big bite of his hamburger.

Like Brent, Sean had married his high school sweetheart. In fact, Sean and Sharon had gone to high school with Brent and Kathy at Center, and they'd been friends ever since. Sean didn't cheat on his wife, so he was probably joking about wanting River's number. Still. The idea of Sean getting a *lingam* massage from River was just... weird.

"So can we set you up with Annette now?" Sean asked. "Now that the engine is running again? Va-room, buddy! And you haven't thanked me, by the way, for finding that sex clinic for you."

"Endless gratitude," Brent said dryly, though he was actually grateful. "As for dating, I'm not gonna rush into it."

"Because...?"

"Because I'm not a jack rabbit. Geez. Give me some time to process."

The dry look Sean gave him indicated he thought Brent had taken plenty of time already. "You should seriously live a little before you settle down again. Play the field while you've got the chance. Hell, you're still young! And not bad looking. Or so I hear. Not that I think about your looks." Sean made an exaggerated gagging sound.

Brent rolled his eyes. "You're literally ten years old. You know that, right?"

"That's two years older than Sharon pegs me for. I feel so mature suddenly. So are you gonna see this, uh, tantric guy again?"

Brent licked his lips. "My therapist says I should go as long as I want. Until I'm comfortable that I've worked through everything."

"Uh-huh. Make sure you've reaaaaally worked things through. Might take, oh, ten, twelve more sessions." Sean made a jerk-off gesture.

"Shut up, Sean."

"Hey, I'm all for it!" Sean proclaimed before taking another huge bite.

As Brent ate his salad, he couldn't help but muse that he was all for it too. He'd woken up feeling fantastic and rather smug. He'd jogged three miles that morning.

It was curious. He'd been resigned to losing his sex drive. With his depression and Kathy's death, it just hadn't seemed all that important in the grand scheme of things. Now it was obvious how much he'd missed it, how much it had dragged down his sense of self-worth to lose his sexuality.

Feeling desire. Feeling pleasure. Being touched. Hell, just getting a huge ol' mondo stiffy. It was so life affirming.

He wanted to live again. He was ready.

"God, look at you smile." Sean snorted. "So are you gonna give me the gory details? Are there, like, toys involved?"

Brent wiped his mouth. "Google it. '*Lingam* massage.'"

He wasn't quite sure what devil made him say that, but Sean's eyes went wide, and he grabbed his phone off the table. He typed it in.

"Not here, Einstein!" Brent protested with a laugh. He glanced around the diner, which was packed, like most places in Seattle.

"I'm just typing it into my notes for later! Give me some credit, bro. Do they have classes? Maybe I can get Sharon interested."

"Probably. Seattle has classes for everything." Though Brent seriously doubted taking a class could make anyone as good as River. It was real with him. Spiritual.

"So... it doesn't bother you at all? That this tantric masseur is a guy?" Sean asked curiously, putting down his phone. "I'm not judging! Just wondering."

"No. Anyway, River is really attractive."

Sean raised an eyebrow. "Wow. Are you… you know… into that? Like, bi or something? I swear I'm not judging!"

Brent snorted. "I'm not bi, Sean." Only once he'd said it, a little gremlin in Brent's head perked up and looked at him doubtfully.

Am I bi?

"So I can keep trying to set you up with Annette? Or would you prefer Sharon's gay cousin, Mario?" Sean smirked. He was a laugh riot.

Brent gave Sean a steely look.

But as Sean changed the subject, chatting about getting tickets to a Seahawks game, Brent's mind churned.

He had questions.

He brought them up at his next session with Dr. Halloran. "How would I know if I'm bisexual?"

Halloran coughed and took a sip of tea. Hell, maybe he swallowed some spit the wrong way. But if he was surprised, his expression masked it well. "Well, primarily, if you're sexually or romantically attracted to a man. You said you'd only been with Kathy since high school. Have you ever felt any interest in men?"

Brent blew out a breath. "I appreciate great clothes or a nice physique or haircut. I've always been a bit more fashion-conscious than some guys."

Halloran nodded encouragingly.

"I know when a man is attractive. Hell, I employ over a hundred people. I have to be aware of the looks of the people I hire. It's aesthetics. But it's normal to be aware when a guy's good-looking, right?"

Halloran smiled. "I'm not real fond of the word *normal*. Has there ever been a specific man that you considered fooling around with, even briefly?"

Brent thought about it. "We had a barista named Lonny. He was stunning. Latino with the best skin I've ever seen on a human being. Really striking eyes. Great body. And he was gay. He made it clear he would be up for something, if I was so inclined." Brent shook his head and smiled fondly at the memory. "I thought about it, thought about what might happen if I let him trap me in the storage room in back. But it never went past the fantasy stage. I was happily married, and getting a blowjob in the back room isn't exactly the way for a responsible boss to behave."

Halloran pursed his lips thoughtfully. "So you fantasized about Lonny giving you a blowjob?"

Brent shrugged, feeling his face heat. "Any red-blooded male might. Don't you think?"

"Possibly. Did you ever fantasize about any other acts with Lonny?"

"No." Brent said, then realized it wasn't precisely true. Some of those fantasies had started out with Lonny slamming him against the storeroom door and kissing him in a filthy way before sliding to his knees. "Well. Kissing."

Halloran just nodded. "Any other instances? What about before you met Kathy, when you were in high school. Or even younger."

"Uh... I had a cousin. He taught me how to masturbate when we were around eleven. We did it together a few times."

That was normal kid stuff though. All boys did things like that.

Halloran rolled his chair back and locked his hands behind his head in a pensive pose. "Today's culture is more open, particularly here in Seattle. I've met quite a few older patients who find themselves interested in exploring options they didn't even consider when they were coming of age. Personally, I think sexuality is a spectrum. Some people are hard-wired to only be attracted to the opposite sex. Others are capable of feeling attraction to a same-sex partner in the right circumstances, or with the right person."

With the right person. That rang true to Brent. River was definitely unique.

It wasn't *just* the massage. Sure, most guys could enjoy a penis massage no matter who was giving it. But the fact was, it had been

River. And Brent had *liked* that it was River. He liked River's hands, the feel of his body as he'd slid against him. Brent's eyes had been closed through most of it. He could have imagined it was someone else touching him, but he hadn't. He *wanted* it to be River. He'd pictured River the whole time.

"What brings the question up?" Halloran asked. "Is this related to your surrogacy sessions?"

Brent licked his lips. "Somewhat. River is a very attractive person. Anyone would think so. And I'm sure there's bound to be a connection with the first person I... to someone who helped me past my mental block. Hell, he's the only person I've been intimate with besides Kathy since I was eighteen years old."

Halloran nodded in understanding. "I'm glad you like River, and that the surrogacy has helped. Just bear in mind that River is a professional therapist. If you think there's any risk of becoming attached, I'll move you to another surrogate."

Brent felt a stab of panic. Move him? But they were making progress! "Oh, no. I'm not getting hung up on him. I just mean, a person should be attracted to their surrogate, right? Physically, I mean. It's perfectly normal."

Halloran raised one eyebrow and took a sip of his tea.

Chapter 6

Brent

Brent sat facing River on the futon, legs crossed, knees touching, his hands holding River's. They stared into one another's eyes.

River's irises looked a little grayer today, maybe because there was cloud cover outside and the light filtering in from the window was duller. A candle flame reflected in one of those blue-gray eyes.

Brent took a deep breath, exhaled.

He was having a hard time concentrating. It should be easier since this was their fourth session, but it was the opposite. Maybe because he knew River better, it was more personal, intimate, looking into his eyes.

Or maybe it was what River had done last time, the *lingam* massage. Holy hell.

No, Brent shouldn't think about that right now. This moment was not supposed to be about sex. This was supposed to be connecting. Spiritual.

Brent focused on his breath, exhaled.

What did he see in River's eyes? Gentleness. Openness. Calm. Like nothing could disturb him.

Was River really like that at all? Maybe Brent was projecting. How much could you tell from a person's eyes, realistically?

River lightly squeezed Brent's hands. "Bring your mind back to your breath."

Brent blinked and refocused. Yeah, his mind was wandering.

River's eyes.

They seemed to look at him warmly. What did River see when he looked at Brent? A thirty-nine-year-old man who'd lost too much weight, who'd retreated from the world? A boring business guy living alone in a too-big McMansion?

A lot of people found Brent attractive. Did River?

What would he do if Brent leaned forward and kissed him?

The thought caused a wave of warmth through his body. The reaction surprised Brent. He wanted to *kiss* River?

Yes. Yes, he did.

Well, why wouldn't he? River had sexy lips. They were full and soft and the beard around them was nicely trimmed and silky. He would probably be a good kisser, given the way he was so sensual with massage.

Probably a *great* kisser.

Heat bloomed in Brent's belly like an opening flower. His dick thickened under his robe. The robe under which he was naked. Not now. Not yet. He looked away from River's eyes and took a deep breath.

River seemed to give up on the eye-staring portion of the session. "Are you ready to lie down?"

He nodded, and as River slipped off the futon, Brent quickly shrugged off his robe and lay down on his stomach.

Staying in the moment wasn't any easier in this position. Now his body knew what to expect from the massage and sparked with anticipation even before River touched him. As soon as River began to rub oil into one of Brent's palms, he shivered, a full-body shake. His dick lengthened against the futon.

He breathed out slowly and tried to calm the electricity racing through him. He appreciated the newfound energy he'd had lately, but he wanted to get back to that relaxed place right now.

River took his time working Brent's arms and shoulders—long, slow, deep strokes and kneading. Brent melted and started to go into his Zen place. But then River carded his fingers up through Brent's hair, fingernails lightly scratching his scalp, and the whoosh of fire was instantaneous. Tingles raced from his scalp down his spine. He couldn't hold back a little moan.

As if taking his cue, River changed the tone of the massage. He moved around on the futon, gently parting Brent's legs until he was kneeling between them, with Brent still on his stomach. He removed the towel. And his own shirt, it sounded like.

Oh. Oh, this was new. And exciting.

River got more warm oil on his hands and stroked up Brent's feet, calves, and thighs, palms pushing over his ass, and up his back, cupping his neck, then sliding up into his hair. His touch was sensual, and Brent loved it. He moaned again. He had to shift on the mat to unstick his erection.

The next time River pushed up Brent's body—slowly, so slowly—he leaned forward, following his hands with his bare chest. His breathing had deepened to that hypnotic sound he'd used during the *lingam* massage.

Oh. Oh fuck yeah.

River's chest slid over the full cheeks of Brent's ass, gliding with the slick oil. He could swear he felt River's nipples. The sensation nearly stopped Brent's heart. He lay stock-still, breathing hard and straining to feel everything. River reversed the motion, sliding down. Up. He rubbed his open palms up Brent's back until he reached his neck, his bare chest sliding over Brent's ass, stopping just at River's ribs. Then he slid back down again.

Again. Again.

The feel of River's skin was fantastic, the pull and push against the cheeks of Brent's ass was maybe the most erotic thing he'd ever felt. Why did it feel so good? He'd never cared very much about his ass. But God, it drove him crazy. Maybe because it felt taboo.

As River continued to do it, Brent wanted more. He wanted River to keep going. He wanted River to slide his chest farther up until he was lying fully over him. He wanted to feel....

Was River hard? Brent had an urge to feel River's groin against his ass, to feel his hard penis rub through the oil there.

Oh, Jesus. Why? Why did he even want that?

Confusion flared inside him, and Brent forgot to breathe. But as River continued to slide up and back, up and back, soothingly, hypnotically, Brent's brain restarted.

He was fine. It was all fine. It wasn't so weird to want that.

Genitalia was erotic. That was all. And of course he wanted to know River felt something, too, if he had a hard-on. That would show this wasn't just a mechanical job to him. It was natural to want your partner to be into it, too, male or female.

Wasn't it?

River isn't your partner. He's a professional, and you're a client.

The thought should have cooled Brent off. But with River sliding up and down his body in that incredibly erotic way, it didn't. On the next pass, Brent couldn't help but push his ass up as River's chest slid over him, demanding more.

"River." The word came out on a moan.

River paused for longer than usual at the apex of his motion, his hands on Brent's shoulders, ribs and tender upper belly on Brent's ass. His loud breathing ghosted along Brent's skin and Brent swore he could feel River's heartbeat trip fast against his skin.

Then he slid back down and off. He removed his hands.

For a moment, there was nothing. Brent wanted to open his eyes and look over his shoulder to see what River was doing. But River spoke.

"Would you like to turn over now?" He sounded utterly calm.

Brent sighed. Yes, he did want to. He began to move, and River shifted back to let him. Brent didn't know where the towel was and didn't care. He felt no shame when he settled onto his back and looked down his body at his rock-hard erection, so hard he was purple at the head and glistening with pre-come. In fact, hey, roll out the parade! He was damned pleased with himself.

Since their last session, when Brent had had his breakthrough, he'd jerked off three times, always to memories of the *lingam* massage, and his dick had worked just fine, thank you very much. As long as he didn't think about... about the cancer.

He pushed it from his mind now.

His gaze moved past his own groin to River, who was settling back into place on his heels. His expression was serene as always. His chest and legs were bare, but he still had his shorts on. Brent looked, but in the candlelight, and with the dark color of the shorts, he couldn't tell if River was aroused or not.

River placed the pillows under Brent's knees, opening him up.

"Close your eyes, Brent, and breathe. Relax," River instructed.

So Brent did.

The *lingam* massage began the same way, with River rubbing his palms up Brent's calves and thighs and hips, leaning over him so his chest ran over Brent's cock, rubbing it between their bodies, and then back down.

His groin still never made contact, but Brent forgot to care. With his eyes closed and his deep breathing mirroring River's, and the intense pleasure of the friction on his dick, he finally managed to bliss out.

Then came River's hands, stroking first one palm, then the other, up Brent's shaft, thumbs massaging his frenulum, the vein in his cock, the hand movement that twisted in a corkscrew as it stroked him upward, the one where River's palm polished the head of his cock, the one where River's two thumbs rubbed up and down his shaft in opposing strokes, like a cross-country skier, the gentle massage of his balls and perineum.

Brent breathed, and he floated. Every nerve ending in his body felt concentrated in his groin. And oh, it was great. So, so good. Ugh. This had to be the laziest form of sex ever, just lying there, and he shouldn't like it as much as he did. But, damn.

His right hand found his own thigh and then River's knee, wanting that contact. River left it there for a while as he worked, but at some point, he gently moved it back down to River's side. And Brent thought nothing of it—at the time.

He could have gone on floating on the plateau of pleasure forever, not in a hurry to get anywhere, and feeling pretty solidly *in the now*. But River switched to the up-down stroke, his fist loose at first and not too fast. Still, Brent's balls knew that move, that rhythm as old as time, and they responded immediately, tightening up so high it felt like they were trying to crawl back up into his body so they could explode out through his dick.

Brent couldn't stop his hips from arcing up, or his moan.

River's next loud exhale held a sigh of satisfaction. He alternated the fist-pump with a few of the teasing strokes, but the fist-pump got faster and longer, faster and longer, until Brent clutched at the futon and raised his hips off the mat beseechingly.

Fuck. He was gonna—

River kept pumping, his fist flying, and Brent came, pulsing all over his stomach, body jerking with waves of pleasure.

Brent rested while River cleaned him up and put things away. He happily floated until River tapped his leg, indicating it was time to get off the futon.

Brent sat up and shook his head to rejoin the land of the living.

River smiled at him. "Feeling good?"

"Fantastic."

"Seems like you had no difficulty getting aroused this time."

"God, no. I was into it right away."

"That's wonderful news," River said with a smile. "You've really had a breakthrough. I think the energy work at your *Svadhishthana* chakra made all the difference. You did so well releasing the blockage there. You're so open to tantra and reiki. And maybe you were ready, huh?"

Brent blinked at him. It sounded a little... clinical? But that had been the point of these sessions, hadn't it? To regain his sex drive. And clearly, he had.

Suddenly conscious of his naked state, Brent put on his robe and left the room to go get dressed. When he was safely tucked into a T-shirt and jeans, he walked River to the door and they had an awkward goodbye. At least, it felt awkward on Brent's part. River seemed as cheerful and unfazed as ever.

And damn, he was so appealing. Brent watched him walk to his car in the driveway—an older black BMW. He couldn't help but check River out. He was wearing shorts and the smooth curve of his calves covered in golden hair was attractive. A really nice ass. Broad shoulders. He'd let down his hair at some point, and the messy blond locks gleamed in the sun.

Nice kid. No, not kid. That was patronizing. Nice person. One hell of a nice person.

River got into the car and drove away.

Brent went into the kitchen and poured himself a glass of wine, even though it wasn't quite five o'clock. He felt... something. Maybe a little upset. He went out and sat on the deck, watched the lake, and tried to get a handle on why.

The session had been great but....

But he'd wanted to kiss River.

He'd wanted to feel River naked against his back—wanted to feel his *hard penis.*

Seriously?

Seriously.

He'd touched River's knee. And River had moved his hand away.

The memory caused a pang of guilt. Jesus, was he that guy? Some creepy handsy guy making overtures to a masseur? Granted, River wasn't just a masseur. Still. he saw what they did as therapy. He probably didn't appreciate being groped.

He probably hadn't been into it at all. Not *that way.* Not aroused.

Brent's brain had tried to turn it into a mutual thing. Which, fair enough. That was how sex had been his whole life. He thought he'd been a generous lover with Kathy, always taking care of her pleasure first. So it was *perfectly normal* that his instinct would be to make the sexual encounter with River mutual.

Only it wasn't. It wasn't mutual. River was a professional providing a service. Brent was a client. End of.

And as Brent finished his wine and poured a second glass, he realized two things.

First, he wasn't the kind of guy who wanted to get off with a professional. He too highly valued reciprocity. He needed to know the other person *wanted* to be there. Wanted him. Maybe he wasn't callous enough for casual.

Kathy was gone. There was no denying that. It wasn't fair, and it had been god-awful, but it was time for his life to go on. When he eventually did get involved with someone else, he needed it to be... fair? Genuine? *Mutual.* And someone suitable. Someone who actually made sense.

Someone like Kathy.

The second thing he realized was that he wouldn't see River again. His mental block or chakra block or internalized grief or whatever it was was better now. There was no medical reason to keep seeing River. And to use him just to get off felt... cheap. And, contrarily, damned expensive at four hundred dollars an hour.

Besides, the desire to get closer to River would only grow. River wasn't interested. Hell, for all Brent knew, he had a girlfriend or boyfriend at home. Someone his own age. A world traveler like him. Someone into chakras and organic bean sprouts.

Expanded Horizons had helped Brent a lot. But now it was time to take off the training wheels, get out there, and pop a wheelie or two. Actually date. Like a regular person.

He should be happy, he told himself. And he was. Or he would be. Once the memory of River had faded enough for him to put things into the proper perspective.

Once he'd forgotten what it felt like to stare into those kind gray-blue eyes, bask in the positivity of that serene smile, and feel the magic touch of River's hands.

PART II: THE DISCIPLE

"In the end only three things matter: How much you loved, how gently you lived, and how gracefully you let go of things not meant for you." – Buddha

Chapter 7

April, 2019

River

River sat on the deck and watched a squat tugboat go by on Lake Union. He idly stroked Lily's head. Lily, an Irish setter, was highly energetic. She jumped up on everyone she met and was terribly spoiled, but she was a sweet dog, and River enjoyed her company. Beauchamp, a grizzled old bulldog, lay in his bed in the shade. River was currently mother and father both to the canines, which meant he had to stay close to the house. He wasn't supposed to leave for more than eight hours at a time.

But these invisible chains were temporary ones. Someone else's house. Someone else's pets. Someone else's life. River was house-sitting. In another five months, he would slip away from this life—the life that included a swanky houseboat on Lake Union, Lily and Beauchamp, a kitchen with white marble countertops, a king bed with expensive white bedding where you could lie and watch the Seattle skyline, and endless photos of a privileged white couple in their forties.

Which meant none of the responsibility for this lifestyle was his. And that was how he liked it.

This place had been a blessing. Last summer, River wanted badly to leave the Sacred Triangle Ashram. Sacred Triangle had been amazing—until it wasn't. One day, it had all come tumbling down, the day the police arrived to arrest Shri Agontha, their guru. Many of the students and devotees at the ashram refused to believe the charges, but River knew they were true.

He knew because it had happened to him.

Come by my rooms tonight, beloved. Prepare yourself.

It still made his cheeks burn with humiliation to think of his foolishness, but River had *meditated* in preparation and dressed in a fresh sari, feeling blessed to have private time with the master. Once alone, Shri Agontha had bent River over a table and tried to penetrate him, scolding him for not being *prepared.*

River struggled to breathe through it and allow it, to find the sacredness in the moment. But it had hurt, and the master had not even tried to connect with him. It did not feel tantric at all. So he'd said *no* and pulled away. Shri Agontha had been annoyed. He told River he was not ready for true tantric union and shooed him away like a misbehaving child.

It had been confusing. It was *still* confusing. River tried to view it all objectively, with detachment, without emotion.

No human being is perfect, not even one supposedly as elevated as Shri Agontha. And one guru's imperfections did not invalidate an entire ancient teaching, or River's own transformative experiences with it. He could separate one from the other.

He'd fallen in love with tantra, with the promise of truly connecting with other human beings in physical-spiritual union. He was still dedicated to that path.

After Shri Agontha's arrest, the ashram became toxic. The doubt there was heavy and dragged him down, the endless bickering and factions, the blind denial. So he'd searched the exclusive house-sitting service he used to frequent and found this place.

Yup. A blessing.

The couple who owned the place, the Reynolds, were off to the UK. *He*, the husband, had been offered a prestigious teaching sabbatical in London for a year. And *she*, the wife, had put her executive job at Microsoft on hold to follow. The two of them had handed River the reins of their life, jabbering instructions right up until the moment they'd entered the taxi.

It wasn't a life River would choose for himself. But squatting in it for year? Did not at all suck.

He watched the tugboat make its way under the Ship Canal Bridge.

Seattle was surprisingly great. He hated the traffic but loved how green it was—having grown up in California, the green was like a miracle. He loved all the water, parks, islands, and marinas. He loved the hip neighborhood eateries and the local university. He especially loved the Expanded Horizons clinic.

The people at the clinic were an inspiration. Dr. Jack Halloran had been an Army surgeon until he was wounded. Poor guy could no longer operate due to the shake in his right hand, so he'd ended up training as a sex therapist. Michael Lamont was another surrogate with a sweet, light-filled spirit. River knew he worked with really tough cases and was also a nurse who cared for the elderly. He was married to a famous sci-fi author, apparently, though River had never met James. Loretta, the receptionist, was unintentionally funny. And Dr. Trudy Kaplan, who ran the place, was so dedicated to healing and so knowledgeable about sexuality.

River loved that the clinic was focused on helping clients with real sexual problems. Working through the clinic, he could operate as a true tantric healer and not deal with people who just wanted kinky sex. He'd had some interesting clients so far.

An image came into River's mind of Brent McKay. Warm energy bloomed from River's sacrum chakra and swirled in his belly.

"*River.*"

The need in Brent's voice. The way he had stared into River's eyes.

River breathed out, allowing himself to feel it, to remember Brent fondly and then let it go.

He'd never been attracted to a client before. Yes, Brent was handsome, with chestnut-brown hair worn longer than was fashionable in a shaggy style, eyes the dark mossy green of a mountain lake, and a trim body. In fact, he was a bit on the skinny side, probably due to prolonged depression, but nicely shaped, with strong shoulders and fine hands and feet.

Still, River was not one to swoon over good looks. On the surface, Brent McKay should not appeal to him at all. He was a wealthy Seattle business man with a multi-million dollar house. River was not into materialistic people. Yet Brent was nothing like he'd expected. He was curious about tantra and asked questions, not dismissing it with a smirk like some Americans, or only interested in the sexual aspect, like pretty much all Americans. And he'd been a fascinating case.

Brent had really low energy when they met, filled up with grief, holding the suffering of his late wife deep in his body. River had never felt a chakra blockage so clearly before. But then, Brent was very open, not guarded like most people, and that allowed River to tune in to his body.

On Brent's higher chakras, there'd been an electric flow between them, a tingling heat dancing from River's hands to Brent's body and back again. It was amazingly strong given that Brent had no previous experience channeling his energy whatsoever. Then, at his sacrum chakra, there had been a dull nothing, as if River's hands touched a brick wall instead of a living body.

It was so amazing that he could feel that!

Better still, they'd been able to break through it, release that bound-up tension, until the energy was flowing again, and Brent was able to access his sexuality. It'd been crazy satisfying. Those were the experiences that told River he was on the right path, that he was meant to be a healer, and that reiki and tantra were the right medium.

Just beautiful.

The *cause* of Brent's blockage was another way in which he was not a stereotypical rich business guy. He'd married his wife young and nursed her through a long illness, had felt her suffering so deeply he'd internalized it. Not many men were that sensitive to someone else's pain or would be that devoted to a partner. It was hard for River to imagine it. Relationships drifted in and out of his life.

Like dandelion puffs.

Like houseboats.

As he sat there on the deck, idly thinking about Brent McKay, another memory snuck in—the way Brent had pushed his ass up as River slid his chest over it, as if begging for penetration, his female *yin* energy rising up and calling to River's male *yang* energy.

Sexual fire awakened in River, just as it had at the time. He took a deep breath and let the hot energy flow through him, warm his belly and thighs, before pushing it up toward his heart and feeling the expansion there.

Wow. Even the memory of that moment was powerful.

He hadn't felt a polarity that strong with anyone, had never gotten physically hard with a client before. But perhaps the sexual energy had flowed in and through both of them so intensely because it had been knotted up in Brent for so long, and it had burst free in a tide. So awesome.

Lily barked, and River rubbed her ears.

After that, Brent hadn't booked another session. Maybe he'd been uncomfortable with the way the practice drew out his female energy. Some men would be. Or maybe he felt he'd made enough progress. Whatever the reason, it was for the best. All for the best.

Someone else's life.

Someone else's Brent McKay.

The door opened on the neighboring houseboat, and Mrs. Smythe came out onto her deck. She wore bedazzled velour sweats in a turquoise color and a matching headband. She filled up her watering can at the faucet and watered the array of containers that lined her deck.

"Good morning, Mrs. Smythe," River called out.

She gave a little startle, as if she hadn't seen him there, but River was pretty sure she had. She always showed up sooner or later when he sat on the deck.

"Well, hello, River. How are your oats today?"

He chuckled. "Just fine."

"I didn't see you doing yoga on the deck this morning. I hope you're not under the weather."

"No, it was just a little chilly, so I did it inside."

"Oh." She sounded disappointed. "It did get cold last night. I was worried for my impatiens." She peered over a container of flowers. Small pink and white flowers were arrayed all around her deck. Now River knew what they were called.

"I've met plenty of impatient humans but never an impatient flower," River mused.

She giggled. "Oh, you! You're a card."

"I'm going to go to the dog park soon. Want me to take Precious?"

"She would love that! Yes, please."

"No problem. And I'll probably hit the market later today if you need anything."

Lily had heard him say "dog park," and she raced around the deck like a demented boomerang, barking ecstatically. Even Beauchamp roused himself from his bed and stood at the sliding glass doors, looking at River expectantly and shimmying his butt with its tight, corkscrew tail. River laughed. Guess they were going *now* instead of *soon*.

River stood and stretched. He got Lily and Beauchamp into their harnesses and leashes, grabbed his wallet and keys, and locked up. He put them in the back of the BMW and went next door. Mrs. Smythe opened her front door and handed him Precious. She was a white poodle who'd seen younger days, but she still had a lot of nervous energy. She shook like a leaf with excitement.

"Thank you so much, dear. And about the store, if you could get me a gallon of 1%, I'd be grateful."

"Sure. Nothing else?"

"Oh, I don't want to trouble you."

River tried to avoid Precious's tongue getting in his mouth as she licked his face. "I'm going anyway. It's not a problem."

"Oh, well, if you're sure." Mrs. Smythe slyly produced a list with about ten items from her pocket along with three twenty-dollar bills.

River bit back a smile and tucked them in his jeans' pocket.

"You're such a nice young man." She patted his arm. "You know, the Reynolds have lived next to me for eight years and never once have they said more than 'hello,' much less offered to do something for me."

River wasn't terribly surprised, but it was sad. "I'm sorry to hear that. It's their loss."

"They've got busy lives, gone at work all the time. You're much better company. Mind your manners, Precious! Thanks again for taking her."

"It's a pleasure. She's a doll."

That was a bit of a white lie. Precious was yappy, but Mrs. Smythe loved her, and it didn't cost him anything to be generous with praise.

River put Precious in the back of the car with the other two dogs. The older black BMW belonged to the wife, Mrs. Reynolds, and was the "dog car." Brent had full access to it during his stay, which was great, since he'd sold his old clunker back in 2017 before going to India, and he'd just as soon not be encumbered with another one.

They drove up the hill to the dog area in Volunteer Park.

Capitol Hill was a terrific neighborhood, filled with big trees and large old houses. But it was sooooo out of his price range, even if he decided to stay in Puget Sound a while longer. Part of him wanted to stay. Expanded Horizons would be happy to let him continue to work there. Perhaps he could build up enough of a clientele over time that he could live off his therapy work. But, for now, it would never pay the bills if he weren't house-sitting. Besides which, the idea of signing a lease, settling down into a normal life...? It didn't suit him.

Why should he pay to live in a tiny, static apartment, when he could live in million-dollar homes all over the world for free?

Someone else's life.

Lily raced around the dog area with a boxer named Jerry, and Beauchamp ambled around sniffing out other dogs' pee. River chatted with a couple of dog moms for a bit. When they left, he took out his phone and checked the house-sitting site for other Puget Sound listings. There were several, but they started before this placement ended in September, so that wouldn't work.

It didn't matter. He could go anywhere. Maybe back to California for a while. Something on the beach. Or London. Tokyo. Rio.

He got the dogs in the car, made a quick stop at the market, and drove back to the houseboat. He dropped off Precious and Mrs. Smythe's groceries, brushed Lily's long red fur so she wouldn't get mud on the rugs inside, and got everything put away. Then he fed the dogs and fixed himself a rice, beans, and veg bowl.

As he sat on the deck watching the sun set, the phone in his pocket itched. It called to him until he took it out and searched the local job listings.

He was just curious. He wasn't staying. Still. A little extra money for a month or two wouldn't hurt.

Chapter 8

"My boy, look at you! You are an Adonis."

Harrison Emmanuel greeted River at the door of his luxury apartment as if they'd known each other for years. He kissed River on both cheeks. He smelled of Vicks and red wine, and his lips were papery thin.

"It's a pleasure to meet you, Mr. Emmanuel." River set his black vinyl case with the portable futon and his duffel bag with oils, incense, and other tools of his trade just inside the door.

"Please, call me Harrison. After all, we won't be strangers for long, hmm?" Harrison looked at River coyly.

"I hope not. What a beautiful apartment."

That was the truth. The luxury apartment on 4th Avenue overlooked the Seattle waterfront. All the walls were painted white and huge windows looked out over Pier 70 and the Puget Sound. A green-and-white ferry went by in the distance. Inside, round cement columns and an open floor plan with a white-and-stainless-steel kitchen gave the place an ultra-modern vibe. The furniture was all white and gray and Scandinavian sleek. Bright abstract paintings on the walls provided the only color.

"Thank you. I've lived in this building for ten years. It's a bit pricey, but, well, it's not like I have anyone to leave my money to." Harrison bustled into the kitchen. "What can I get you to drink? I have an excellent bottle of merlot open, or I have a fumé blanc if you prefer. I also have coffee, tea, water?"

"I don't need anything right now, thank you."

Harrison Emmanuel was eighty, according to his file from Expanded Horizons. He was tall and thin, with narrow shoulders and a head that was too big for his body. Wiry, white hair had been slicked back but was frizzily escaping whatever product Harrison had tamed it with. His long, narrow face with its big nose, thin lips, and small watery blue eyes was elegant. He wore a black silk robe over silky gray pajama bottoms and gray slippers. River didn't know what his profession was or had been, but he obviously wasn't hurting for money.

River looked around, trying to figure out where he'd set up his futon. Normally, he preferred low lighting and candles to create a relaxing atmosphere, but there were no shades or blinds on the huge windows, and it was only three in the afternoon. Even the overcast day outside filled the room with light. Oh well. He had a black eye mask in his bag of tricks.

"If I move the coffee table, I can set up in here." River waved to the living room. "Or did you have another place you'd prefer?"

"Oh, darling. I appreciate your work ethic, but perhaps we can get to know each other first, hmm? I'm not that kind of boy. Have a seat, and I'll bring out drinks."

River considered saying that a tantric session always began with building a connection first, not just rushing into things, but he decided to follow the client's lead. He left his bags by the door and took a seat on the gray linen couch.

Harrison brought a glass of water with ice for River and red wine for himself. He sat close on the sofa, putting their drinks on the coffee table, a beautifully polished all-wood affair that probably cost more than River's last car.

"There now." Harrison crossed his long legs. "Let me look at you. At my age, just looking is a thrill."

River gave him an indulgent smile.

Harrison looked him all over, his gaze avid in a way that made River want to squirm. He didn't.

"What a beauty. I bet you have a magnificent jaw under that beard. Still, the beard does add a certain masculine *je ne sais quoi.*" He sipped his wine. "Such broad shoulders. And utterly exquisite hands." He reached out to turn River's hand over and run a thumb along his palm. "An artist's hands. No, stronger than an artist's. Your palms have muscles. I can tell you're a masseur."

Harrison was charming, but his interest made River feel uncomfortable. He preferred to be the one in charge, to keep the sessions focused on healing, not to feel like a slab of prime rib. He changed the subject. "How long have you been seeing Dr. Halloran?"

"Oh, not long. Let's see, we've had three appointments so far? He recommended a nutritionist. It's a blood-flow issue, you know. Heart disease. Stents. So of course, they want me to give up anything remotely edible. Thank God red wine is allowed. I told Dr. Halloran, I'm eighty years old. My veins will never be what they once were. Give me those little blue pills and a patient, lovely expert such as yourself, and maybe the Lone Ranger will ride again, hmm?"

That made River laugh. "Reiki can help with blood flow. And through reiki and tantric techniques, we can raise your energy levels and awaken the body. I also like to work on appreciating touch and sensuality whether or not there's an erection or ejaculation. The goal is just to relax, enjoy the moment, and get back in touch with your body and your sexual energy."

Harrison gave a faux-shocked expression. "My dear, I've been a promiscuous gay man for sixty-eight years. That's the first time anyone ever suggested getting a hard-on wasn't the point."

"Well, it's not the point in tantric practice. But if it's your wish, I completely understand. What goals would you like to work toward in our sessions?"

Harrison sighed. "Oh, just having you here is lovely. And I'm so looking forward to getting a nice massage. If we can ring the old tower bell, then God bless you, my dear. But if that doesn't happen, please don't take it personally. You're a beautiful boy, and just know that the spirit is willing, even if the flesh is far from cooperative these days."

Despite Harrison's playful words, sadness lingered behind his tone, and River felt a gush of compassion. He squeezed Harrison's hand. "You don't need to do anything except relax."

"I know, darling. That's what 'paying for it' means." The words were bitter and a little offensive, but Harrison rushed on before River could respond. "Dr. Halloran simply raves about you, and I'm so grateful you're willing to work with an old goat like me. But before we start, I'd love to know something about you. Are you from Seattle? Or are you a refugee like myself?"

"Mm. Just here temporarily. I grew up in California, but I've traveled a lot."

"Now you *do* look like a poster for California. All that golden skin! I never lived in Los Angeles, if you can believe it! I had the opportunity a half-dozen times. Potential films, some L.A. theater, but it never happened. Believe it or not, New Yorkers can be awfully snobbish about L.A. And Seattle! You'd think it was a backwater for all Broadway knows or cares."

Harrison was clearly in no hurry to get started on the massage. He was lonely, River realized. And perhaps he needed to talk more than anything. He also seemed to like just *looking* at River, touching his hand, knee, or arm.

And, well, River had no other appointments that day. He let the conversation flow. He learned that Harrison was a theater director. He'd been on Broadway for over twenty years before moving to Seattle to work with the local theater companies. He'd never been married, claimed he "enjoyed playing the field too much."

Harrison told funny stories. He also kept refilling his wine glass, got a little drunk, and began to talk a lot too loud. The session was going to be a washout if this went on. So after a while, River set up his futon and plugged in his oil-warming pot.

"How about we start on the couch?" he suggested, deciding it would be hard for Harrison to sit on the floor, even on a futon. "In a tantra session, we begin with establishing intimacy through being present with one another, gazing and breathing."

"That doesn't sound too onerous," Harrison joked. "Breathing is one of the few things I still do well."

River sat facing Harrison on the couch, took both of his hands, and stared into his eyes. He directed Harrison in tantric breathing.

Harrison had a great deal of difficulty meeting River's gaze. He would for a few seconds, but then he'd glance down to River's lips or his shoulder or even out the window. But he followed the breathing instructions, and he seemed to relax. River decided to call it good.

He asked Harrison to remove his clothes and lie down on the futon on his stomach, with just a towel over his behind. River closed his eyes and meditated for a moment to give Harrison privacy. He prayed for compassion and for healing energy and light. Then he started the massage.

Harrison relaxed deeply under his hands, groaning now and then. His skin was thin and fragile, and his muscles limp and soft, so River kept his touch light and used lots of oil. When he worked down the chakras of the spine, the energy there was weak and dull, stagnant as a sink full of dirty water instead of the swiftly moving current it should be. River's palms grew hot as he had Harrison breathe into them at each chakra, and he poured his own energy outward, trying to stir that weak flow. He spent quite a bit of time on it, and the energy did seem to be less sluggish at the end.

River couldn't help comparing the feeling of this session to working with Brent McKay, the way the energy had sparked and built between them. As if he'd needed a reminder of how rare that was.

But he shouldn't think about another client now. It wasn't fair to Harrison.

He had Harrison turn over and he massaged the front of his legs, arms, chest, and soft belly. There was no movement from under the white towel, and River left it in place. He sensed Harrison would just as soon not have attention paid to his lack of an erection. Instead, River made the massage as sensual as he could through other parts of the body, silently calling up the sexual energy in his client, and sending out loving, healing light.

When he finished, he sat back on his heels and looked up to see fat tears rolling down Harrison's face.

"Are you all right?"

Harrison sniffled. "Oh, yes."

"Let me get you a glass of water."

"My wineglass should be on the coffee table," Harrison said shakily. He opened his eyes and wiped at them, tried to sit up.

River helped Harrison up to sitting and into his robe, then to his feet. He seemed very weak from the relaxation and deep breathing, so River kept an arm around his waist and led him to the sofa. Harrison picked up his wineglass and drained it.

He sighed and wiped his eyes again. "Sorry for the waterworks. It's just been so long since I've been touched."

"Energy work often releases a lot of buried emotions. It's healthy."

Harrison gave a quivery laugh. "I've outlived so many friends. Survived the AIDS epidemic in New York in the eighties, you know. Had a friend murdered for being queer. Others have simply passed on a respectable timetable. And then there's me, alone at the end of the world."

"I'm sorry to hear that," River said. Surely, Mr. Emmanuel had some friends left? Family?

"Ah well. Getting old sucks monkey balls, as they say. But the alternative isn't a barrel of laughs either."

"How do you feel after the massage?"

Harrison took a deep breath and appeared to check in with himself. "Marvelous. Ten years younger. You have magic hands, my boy. And I think I see what you mean. It's possible to have, if not a sexual encounter, certainly a sensual one, even without cooperation from Captain Happy."

River laughed. "Captain Happy gets far too much glory. The brain and heart are sensual organs too."

"Right you are. Now let's see. I want to give you a tip." Harrison got up and looked around, as if for his wallet.

River stood too. "No tip. You paid for our session through the clinic."

"Are you sure?"

"Absolutely." River folded up his futon. "If you'd like to book another session, you can talk to Dr. Halloran or Loretta, the receptionist."

"My dear, nothing would make me happier in this world. I hope it's not too awful, having to touch an old wreck like me?"

River stopped fussing with his bags, stood, and looked Harrison in the eyes. "I don't know what your beliefs are, but I believe life is a cycle. Where you are now, I will be one day. And where I am now, you have been before and will be again, in another life. There's no good or bad about where you are in the cycle. It just is."

Harrison blinked at him. "I wasn't nearly so generous at your age when it came to the elderly. I guess that's what they call 'karma.' Now I'm the dirty old man I used to mock."

He walked River to the door. After opening it, Harrison took River's hand and kissed it. "Thank you. You've made me very happy."

"You're welcome, Harrison. Have a great week." River forced a smile despite a lingering sadness for the old man.

As he took the elevator to the ground floor, he had the fanciful idea that Harrison Emmanuel was like Rapunzel, alone in a tower. Only it was unlikely there would be a prince who'd come and save him.

And what about me? I don't have a prince. I don't even have a tower.

But he did have a job interview. And who knew where that would lead?

Chapter 9

April, 2019
First Hill, Seattle
River

"Double chai macchiato!"

"Venti Winter Wonderland!"

River made drinks and smiled at customers. He moved fluidly around the other barista, Maddy, a twenty-something girl with jet-black hair and three piercings in her face. After just two weeks working at Adrenaline Junkie Coffee, they were as synchronized as dancers. Maddy always took the easier orders like the lattes. River liked the complicated ones. He only wished they'd let him make his recipe for chai instead of using that gross prepackaged stuff.

He made the chai as ordered, though, and passed it to the customer with a warm smile. It was an older woman, and he made eye contact, being sure to really see her. She gave him a cheeky smile. "I must say, the scenery has improved in this place just recently."

He laughed and shook his head. "Have a wonderful day, ma'am."

There was a lull, so River turned his attention to cleaning off the steam nozzles. He overheard Justin say, "Oh, hey, Mr. McKay!"

The name caught on River's mind like a hook. He glanced toward Justin at the register.

Brent McKay stood there. Just as River realized it really was his ex-client, recognition dawned in Brent's eyes too. For a brief second, Brent smiled, his expression glowing with surprise and pleasure. Then the situation seemed to hit him in the face. The smile vanished, and he turned beet red.

Justin was oblivious. "Oh, Mr. McKay, I don't think you've met River, our gorgeous new barista. River, this is the big daddy. I mean the owner, Mr. McKay!"

Justin thought he was being funny, but Brent just stammered. "Oh. I. Uh—" He looked like a man about to be shoved off a very high cliff.

To put him out of his misery, River slipped out from behind the counter and walked over to him. He held out his hand. "Hi, Mr. McKay. I'm River Larsen. It's a pleasure to meet you."

Brent blinked and shook River's hand. "Nice to, um, meet you too."

River gave Brent an amused quirk of his eyebrow. What did he think? That River would say, *Oh, I know Mr. McKay! I massaged his penis.*

As if he knew exactly what River was thinking, Brent rolled his eyes at himself a little and gave a chagrined smile. His alarming color faded.

The handshake had gone on too long, so River gave a gentle tug to disengage.

"River has the most amazing ideas for new drinks," Justin gushed. "I told him maybe he'd get a chance to talk to the owner. You should let him bend your ear someday, Mr. McKay."

A woman with a baby strapped to her chest walked up to stand behind Brent at the register. Brent gave her a smile and stepped aside. He glanced at River and jerked his head. *Follow me.*

"Did you want a coffee, Mr. McKay?" Justin called out after him.

"Not right now, thanks." He led River to an open area near a window, out of earshot of Justin, before turning to face him. "You're a barista?" he asked, his voice low.

River rubbed his hands on his apron, feeling self-conscious. He'd done many jobs over the years, and he wasn't ashamed of any of them. He didn't believe in classism. "I worked as a barista in L.A. It's been a few years, but it's not something you forget."

"Oh. I thought you were a full-time, um, therapist. The tantric thing. You know. Surrogate. That." Brent's cheeks flushed again.

"I don't have enough clients right now for it to be full time."

"Oh."

Brent's nervous awkwardness might have been amusing or even endearing under different circumstances. But River felt a spark of hurt. So he was good enough to give Brent McKay a massage, but not good enough to work in one of his coffee shops? Maybe River had been entirely wrong about the guy.

"If this is uncomfortable for you, I'll quit." River reached back to untie the apron.

Brent grabbed River's arm. "No! God, no. No, I—" He took a deep breath and got a determined expression. "I'm sorry. I've really bungled this. That's not what I meant at all."

River just studied him, unsure. Maybe he *should* go. It was a bit weird to be working in a coffee shop owned by a previous client. And then it hit him. *What are the odds?*

"I didn't know you owned a coffee shop."

"I own eight, among other things. But yeah, coffee shops were what built our portfolio. Kathy and I." He visibly swallowed as a glimmer of pain flashed in his eyes. "We bought our first one in 2002. We were lucky. With the population boom and everything."

Brent gave him a real smile then. Those mossy green eyes softened. "I'm actually really glad to see you, River. I was just shocked, that's all. Sort of a two-worlds-collide kind of moment." He chuckled self-consciously. "But please. Please don't quit on my account. You must be great if Justin hired you. He's got a lot of attitude, but he's one of my best managers."

The hand on River's forearm was still there. As if a switch flipped, energy flowed between them. A warm surge washed through River, coming from Brent's hand—and his eyes.

And River thought again, *what are the odds?*

So Brent owned eight coffee shops. That sounded like a lot. But in the entire Seattle metro area? Eight was a drop in the bucket. And then too, River had applied at a dozen places. Yet here he was, standing in a shop with Brent McKay, *working* for him.

River didn't rule out the idea of coincidences, but this felt like a very deliberate tap on the shoulder from the universe. Maybe he wasn't through with Brent McKay just yet.

"All right." He let go of his apron tie. As River's arm moved to his side, Brent withdrew his hand, almost reluctantly.

"Good. Welcome to McKay Enterprises." Brent gave a modest little tilt of his head.

"Thanks. If it does get weird for you though–"

"It won't. I'm not here that often. Like I said, Justin is a good manager. But he mentioned something about you having ideas for drinks? Would you like to sit down?"

Brent looked around for a free table, but River had been facing the doorway as they talked, and he'd noticed more people coming in. The line at the register was now six deep and Justin was shooting him confused glances.

"It's kinda busy. I should help Maddy."

Brent looked around, surprised. "Oh, yeah. Okay. We'll, uh, we'll talk another time. Later. No rush."

He was still nervous. Now it was kind of cute. "Sure. Nice seeing you, Mr. McKay."

Brent made a face. "That sounds strange. You can still call me Brent."

River just blinked. If all the other employees called him Mr. McKay, then he would too. But he didn't bother correcting the man who was now his boss.

Chapter 10

River

Every day that week, Brent McKay came into the shop. River worked seven to noon, Thursday through Sunday. Brent showed up around ten a.m. He'd get a coffee and something to eat, nod hello at River, sit down, and work on his laptop for about an hour. Then he'd pack up his stuff, say goodbye to the staff, nod to River again, and leave.

It was almost always busy, so River just kept working. And Brent never indicated that he wanted to talk. But sometimes River would look over and find Brent watching him. Brent always went right back to his work, as if it hadn't happened.

On Sunday, Justin commented on it when they had a momentary lull. "I hope my ass isn't on the line."

"What?"

Justin nodded his chin toward Brent. "Boss man has been coming in every day. It makes me nervous. Like, does he not trust me right now? Did a customer complain? Did someone find a short and curly in the egg salad?"

River polished a steam nozzle. "He doesn't usually come in every day?"

"Uh, no," Justin said in a *duh* tone. "Usually, I can hardly get ahold of him when I need to. I mean, I'd leave a message and it might be a day or two before he got back to me. *Weeks* have gone by without him so much as darkening the door. Now here he is. A Regular Reggie."

River hummed thoughtfully. He'd wondered. He hadn't seen Brent at the shop in the first two weeks we'd worked there, and now, suddenly, he came in every day. But it seemed arrogant to imagine it was on his account.

"Have you heard the whole story about Mr. McKay? It's, oh my

God, it's so tragic!" Justin adopted a gossipy tone and lowered his voice, as if to be sure Brent couldn't hear him. He was a cute guy, late twenties, slightly built with red hair and a hyper, over-the-top attitude. "His wife died of cancer a few years ago, and the man was *crushed.* An absolute wreck. I felt so bad for him. And I'm like, 'Oh, sweetie! Of course you don't have to call me back just because our milk distributor went out of business, and I'm buying half-and-half at Walmart! I don't mind *at all.*'"

Justin put a hand to his chest and feigned an overly sympathetic expression. Then he rolled his eyes at himself. "I'm such a pushover. But yeah, he's been through a lot, so we McKay Enterprises managers have just had to deal."

"That's a shame."

"Totally. His wife was so young too. Well, *obviously.* He's not exactly ancient himself."

River shouldn't gossip with Justin, but he couldn't help himself. "What was she like? Mrs. McKay?"

Justin tilted his chin and considered it. "Petite. Blonde. I'd say on a Doris Day to Rita Hayworth scale, she was way more Doris Day. Wholesome. Perky. But really sharp, business-wise. She did all the payroll and ordering." He gave River a dirty look. "Yes, I like TCM. Don't judge. Those forties glamor queens will never be matched, in the humble opinion of moi."

The description of Kathy McKay made River's gut ache and a sad and anxious throb in his heart, as if her being "wholesome" and "perky" made her early death even worse. Or perhaps hearing about her from Justin just made her more real. *More perfect.*

"Someday Mr. McKay will walk in here with a new trophy wife on his arm. He's such a catch—gorgeous, rich, nice.... Why don't they make them like that in *my* flavor?" Justin shook his head and looked River up and down. "The good ones are always straight."

A guy came up to the counter seeking a refill on his Americano, and Justin went back to work.

River didn't bother to correct Justin's assumption that he was straight. The guy flirted enough as it was. But his words gave River a pang. *Someday, Mr. McKay will walk in here with a new trophy wife.*

Yeah, probably true, especially since River had helped Brent past his sexual blockage. He was probably dating someone right now. He'd get married again. He was the loyal type. Lucky woman.

Someone else's Brent McKay.

River acknowledged the pang of jealousy he felt and released it. What a useless emotion that was. You couldn't own another person. And even if some couples chose monogamy, *River* and *Brent* would never be that couple—or any couple at all.

The following Friday morning, Brent came in at ten. It was the first Friday in May, but you'd never know it. The pouring rain and chill outside meant business was slow. After Justin had greeted him with "Hey, Mr. McKay!" and took his order, Brent looked right at River, who was at the coffee station.

"Um, River, grab yourself something to drink and join me. I'd like to hear about your drink ideas." Brent's tone brooked no argument. He sounded like the boss. But River could tell from his eyes he was nervous.

River nodded and made a quick cup of herbal tea, ignoring Justin's raised eyebrows. When he came out from behind the counter, Brent was seated at a small table by a side window, as far from the register as you could get. River sat down opposite him, feeling a flutter of anticipation.

They stared at one another. Brent looked good. There was still some tiredness around his eyes, but his color was warm, and he seemed less drawn in the face, a bit more filled out. "How have you been feeling?"

"Good. Really good. Lots more energy. I've been running again." Brent smiled, but he still sounded uncomfortable.

"That's great."

Brent broke eye contact first. "How about you? I mean, how do you like working here? At our First Hill branch?"

Maddy brought over Brent's coffee and put it on the table. She turned so Brent couldn't see her and made a funny face at River, sticking out her tongue and crossing her eyes, before walking away. River gave her a grin and waited until she was out of earshot before replying.

"I like it. Nice location. Good people. Maddy and Justin are fun to work with." He rotated his mug on the tabletop. "But I'm probably not here for long."

"Mmm," Brent acknowledged, looking down at his cup. "Are you planning on leaving the area or just Adrenaline Junkie Coffee?"

"The area. I'm house-sitting a place on Lake Union until September. When that's up... well. We'll see."

"That's too bad." Brent looked up into River's eyes. "I bet..." He glanced sideways as if to make sure no one was listening. "I bet Expanded Horizons would miss you if you go."

River felt a little tug of melancholy, but he shrugged. "Nothing lasts forever. But I haven't decided yet."

Brent chewed on his bottom lip and stared at River. It was a small table, and they were only three feet or so apart. It felt like their tantric session, staring into each other's eyes—so much so that River's breathing deepened and got a little louder. And he noticed Brent doing the same.

He was perfectly aware that they were doing it, but he didn't mind. It didn't feel wrong to connect with Brent in a deeper way, even here. And staring into those green eyes was no hardship. But Brent's eyes went a little glazed, his cheeks flushed, and he shifted uncomfortably in his seat. Again, he was the one to break eye contact, looking down at his cup.

"So, uh, Justin said something about drink ideas? We don't have to talk about that if you don't want to. It's just that he mentioned it. So I thought... Though we do have enough drinks. Here. Always open to new ideas though. God, I'm sorry, I'm babbling."

River bit back a smile. Brent McKay was a man of contradictions. He was a successful business man, and at least ten years older than River, but he nevertheless had an awkward, boyish side.

River liked that side.

"It's the chai," River said.

"The... what?"

"The chai. You use a commercial premix."

Brent nodded. "Oh. Yes. We've used that brand for years. Customers seem to like it."

River gave a tiny shrug. "It's your place. But it's nothing like real Indian chai. The recipe I have is a hundred times better."

"Yeah? Where'd you get the recipe?"

"I lived on an ashram in Jaipur last year, and we made it the traditional Ayurvedic way. We made big batches in the kitchen every morning. It's fantastic, and very nourishing to the body and spirit."

Brent frowned. "How is it different from the premix?"

"In every way. Chai is meant to balance the three doshas. The ginger, cardamom, and cinnamon warm the *vata* dosha, and milk, honey and fennel cool the *pitta* dosha, and the cloves, peppercorn and tea energize the *kapha* dosha. But the balance is critical. When it's made correctly, it's way better than coffee for making you feel fresh and energized for hours."

Brent's eyes sparked with interest. "Well, I like the sound of that. Can you get the ingredients to make that recipe here in the States?"

"Sure."

Brent looked River up and down curiously. "Would you be interested in making a sample batch for me to try? I mean, I'm not trying to steal your recipe or your ideas. If we decide to use it, I'll pay you a finder's fee, of course."

River huffed a laugh. "I don't want money for it, Mr. McKay. I'll make you some. And if you decide to use it, I'm happy to give you the recipe."

"I'd want to pay you something."

"Not everything is about money. Besides, I don't own the recipe. It's ancient."

Brent left off insisting. He took another sip of his coffee. "Also, you can call me Brent. What else?"

"What else is in the chai recipe? Cloves—"

Brent grinned. "No, Justin said you had ideas for *drinks*, as in plural."

"Oh." River leaned back in his chair, scooting down a bit. Under the table, his knee brushed Brent's accidentally. Brent jerked like he'd been shocked and moved his away.

Wow, he was still nervy. Was it because River had given him a *lingam* massage? Was it because River was a *man* who'd touched him that way? People could be so uptight about the natural functions of the body. It was disappointing to see that Brent was so uneasy about their past intimacy. But River decided to ignore it.

"Homemade kombuchas are amazing. Citrus-ginger, berry, turmeric, hibiscus—"

"Like the bottled kombuchas?" Brent glanced toward the cold case near the register where they sold a few bottles of the stuff.

"Yes, but way better." River rotated his glass on the tabletop again. "It's like the difference between a bottled juice and a juice made fresh in the shop." *Or regular hookup sex and tantric sex*, River wanted to add. But he refrained, given where they were.

"I see. So you make kombucha to order?" Brent leaned forward with interest, elbows on the table.

"Not exactly. Kombucha needs time to ferment, sort of like beer. But you could have a fermented base you add fresh ingredients to on order, like fresh squeezed lemon juice or ginger slices. Or you could have a few fermented flavors already made up, only you make them in house instead of selling the bottled stuff."

Brent's eyes grew wide. "Oh shit. You could have homemade kombucha flavors on tap, like craft beer!"

River nodded enthusiastically. "Absolutely. I'm not sure if you want to go that far, but there's a fantastic place in Mumbai that has kombucha on tap. They had a ton of flavors, and it was the best kombucha I've ever tasted. The place was super popular."

Brent gazed into the distance, as if imagining it. His face lit up as his brain worked it over, like a kid thinking about what he wanted for Christmas.

"That could be... wow. I'm gonna have to do some research, see if anyone's doing that in this area, and what the health department regulations are on kombucha." Brent took out his phone and typed into a notepad app. He muttered to himself, "Brilliant, brilliant, brilliant."

Done typing, he looked up. "What about the food? Any thoughts?"

River chuckled. "Well, your vegan options suck."

Brent blinked. "You don't like the veggie wrap?"

"Not vegan. It has aioli in it, which is made with mayo. And it would be nice to have more choices."

"Oh." Brent's face fell, like he was embarrassed. "Yeah, actually one of my managers, Dani, has brought that up a few times. Guess I should have paid more attention."

River shrugged. It was Brent's business. But he had asked.

"Was there anything else besides the chai and kombucha and vegan offerings?"

River chuckled and took a sip of tea.

Brent grimaced. "Sorry. I sound so greedy. I don't mean it like that. Like I said, I'd be happy to pay you. I'm not trying to suck you dry."

"No? Too bad." River gave a flirty little grin.

It was the sort of banter he might have done with a friend. But Brent McKay was not a friend, and it sounded way too much like a come on. Especially when Brent went red, choked on saliva, and splashed a bit of coffee on his shirt when he picked up his cup in too much of a hurry. He gulped his drink.

"Sorry," River said. "I was just kidding. But that was crude."

Brent put down his cup with a clatter and waved a hand. "No. It was... funny. God, you haven't met 'crude' until you've met my friend Sean. I just didn't, um, expect that. You don't strike me as...." He hesitated.

"As having a sense of humor?" River shrugged. "Joy is a tantric aspect, too, you know."

"Well, I can attest to that." Brent laughed.

They looked at each other, smiling, and their gazes held again. And again, there was that slide into the way they'd stared into each other's eyes in their sessions. Warm energy flowed into River and sparked down his spine, *ping, ping, ping,* all the way down to his *Svadhishthana* chakra where the warmth spread through his groin.

Objectively, as Justin had pointed out, Brent McKay truly was "a hot daddy." But more than that, there was a softer sensitivity to him that appealed to something deep inside River, dragged at him like a tractor beam. Not just in their tantric session. Even here. Even now.

River could acknowledge the attraction now that Brent wasn't a client. But their new situation wasn't any less complicated.

This time, it was River who looked away first. "Well, I should probably get back to work. When would you like me to bring in the chai?"

Brent cleared his throat. "Tomorrow? No, you'll need to get ingredients and maybe you're, um, busy. We can do next week, if that's better."

"Tomorrow it is, Mr. McKay."

Chapter 11

River

When River got a call on a Tuesday morning, and saw the name "Brent McKay" on the caller ID, it took him by surprise. He'd forgotten that Brent had his cell phone number. But of course he did–they'd had each other's numbers when they coordinated their tantric sessions. Still, Brent hadn't used it since then, and it seemed strange that the big boss was calling him directly.

"This is River," he answered.

"Hey. It's Brent McKay."

"How are you, Mr. McKay?"

"Uh, fine. I'm good. Hey, listen, I know you're not scheduled to work today, but if you have time, I'd like to show you something. Work related. On the clock, of course. If you're busy, we could do it tomorrow during your regular work hours. I can call Justin about getting in a replacement."

River was at the dog park. He watched Lily bound around with a German shepherd and considered it. He'd planned to do grocery and laundry later today. But his chores could wait. And he didn't have a surrogacy session.

"I can work today."

"Great. I'll text you the address. What time is best for you?"

The address? So it wasn't at his usual store. That was curious.

They finalized a time and ended the call. A moment later, an address came through via text. It was downtown, several blocks from Pike Place Market. Was it another one of Brent's coffee shops? Was River filling in for someone out sick?

It had been over a week since River made the chai and took it in to the First Hill shop. Justin and Maddy had raved about it, and so had Brent. He'd seemed sincere, anyway, but he hadn't committed one way or the other about switching to it. Which was certainly his call.

River had let it go. *Someone else's shop. Someone else's business decisions.* He had to admit, the idea that Brent valued his opinions had been nice. But ultimately, what did it matter in the big scheme of things? It was never good to let someone else make you happy or unhappy.

That was easier thought than done. Since "chai day," Brent had stopped coming into the First Hill AJC. He hadn't shown up for a week, and it had been hard not to wonder why, hard not to look at the door every time the little bell at the top chimed.

Now, getting ready to go meet Brent, River told himself he was chill about it. But there was a flutter in his stomach as he showered and towel dried his long hair. He wrapped it around his fingers and stuck a rubber band around it, refusing to fuss any more than usual. He put on some cargo shorts and a red mehndi-print T-shirt, made sure Lily and Beauchamp had water, and locked up the houseboat. His flip-flops made a flapping noise on the wooden deck. He'd been there long enough that the noise was starting to sound like home.

When he arrived at the address he'd been given, he found an empty storefront between a Seattle souvenir shop and a pizza place. The plate-glass windows were covered with brown paper, and it looked deserted. River thought he must have the wrong place, but he tugged on the front door and it opened.

Inside was a large room with a glossy cement floor. Holes in the cement gave the impression there'd once been booths or tables here, and in the back was a long counter.

Brent was at the counter looking over a collection of sketches. He smiled big when he saw River and came over. "Hey! Thanks for coming. I marked you down for four hours of work today. I appreciate you making the time."

"No worries."

Brent offered his hand and River shook it. Brent's skin was warm. He was wearing well-worn jeans and a lightweight green summer sweater that brought out his eyes. He looked good, his face bright and lively. Where was the haunted man River had first met? It was nice to see him looking so well. The shiver of attraction that went through River was less welcome, but hell, he was only human.

"I realize this place is a mess, but my real estate agent suggested it. I'm not sure it's quite right for what we need, but the location is ideal. Anyway, I have some sketches. Come on."

Brent led the way over to the counter and River followed, confused. *What we need" for what? Sketches for what?*

Brent pointed out a colored pencil sketch of a line of taps, like beer taps, only the flat handles had names like "Happiness" and "Vitality" and "Soother" in an artsy font, each handle a different color. River felt a catch of excitement in his chest.

"Is this...?"

"A kombucha bar." Brent's eyes sparkled. "I know the brew names might seem a bit much, but people love funky names. The same drink you call *lemon-ginger kombucha* will sell half as well as something called *Happiness*. But obviously, we'll want to come up with names that actually match the properties of the brews."

River blinked.

"Sorry." Brent gave him a half smile, half frown. "I'm getting ahead of myself. Let me back up." Brent took a deep breath as if trying to calm down his nervous excitement. "Your idea of homebrewed kombucha on tap—"

"It was your idea to have it on tap. I just thought it would be nice to serve a homebrew."

Brent waved a hand, as if it didn't matter. "Anyway, it got me thinking. Craft beer has been big for years. Seattle is full of microbrew beer pubs. But *kombucha*, that's new. I looked at the grocery store sales data, and demand for the bottled product has been growing like crazy. It's probiotic, it's got a little kick but isn't really alcoholic, and anything fermented is big in the health food market right now. Plus, it's easy to make in house. I mean, there will be health inspections, and we'll have to regularly test to make sure our fermentation bacteria isn't growing anything nasty, but that's not a big deal."

Brent talked a mile a minute, his face was more animated than

River had ever seen it. He dragged over another sketch, this one of a row of large glass mugs with different colored contents, each with a foamy head. "It won't be *just* a kombucha bar. We'll feature chai, of course. Real chai, the one you made me. And the menu will be healthy but hearty and delicious. Lots of vegan and veg options. And fermented foods. That goes with the kombucha idea."

"Fermented foods?"

Brent bit his lip. "Yeah. After we talked, I did some research. You're right. AJC is so behind the times. Some of the hottest trends in metro restaurants right now are vegan-friendly places. Like, you can make a wrap or a pasta or salad and get your choice of local, grass-fed meat, or tofu scramble, or soy curls, and with vegan cheese or sour cream options. I was just thinking that adding fermented health foods like sauerkraut and kimchi—made in house like the kombucha—could be a nice differentiator."

Brent talked on about his ideas. River was honestly shocked. But looking over the sketches, he could see Brent had put a lot of thought into this already. There were a dozen concept sketches, some of small elements, like a flower in a vase, but there were steaming bowls of soup with hunks of old-fashioned bread, cups of what looked like chai with cookies on the saucer, and mugs of the kombucha next to plates of thick sandwiches. There was even a sketch for a logo. It featured the profile of a backpacker with a circle behind him, sort of like a full moon, with the words "Good Earth Café."

"What's this?" River asked, pointing to the sketch.

"Just playing around with logo ideas. But we need a name first. That's just a stand-in for now. Unfortunately, 'Good Earth Café' is already taken."

"Hmmm. And the backpacker?" River prompted.

Brent's cheeks went a little pink. "Just a doodle. I was trying to come up with ideas for the theme. I mean, it can't just be *healthy* or *vegan-friendly*. It has to be a deeper concept that touches a chord, you know? One idea was to have a global travel theme, foods from around the world. But that might be too complicated. The kombucha bar needs to be the primary focus."

River thought about it. "No, I like that. You could have Indian curry, Thai coconut soup, hummus and falafel from the Middle East.... Yeah. Could be cool."

The more the idea settled on River, the more he liked it.

"I know this probably seems too fast, even impulsive." Brent looked chagrined, making River wonder if his friends or advisors had called it that. "But this feels good. It feels really, really good. It's been a long time since I've been inspired. Way too long. And I have a feeling for this sort of thing. I know what Seattle likes. This could be a monster hit, I know it." Brent's eyes burned with conviction.

River smiled, bemused. "And here I thought you were just considering whether or not to change out the chai at Adrenaline Junkie."

"No. I mean, I thought about that at first. To be honest, Adrenaline Junkie could use a makeover too." Brent shook his head with a grimace. "Every other corner has a coffee place that's knocked us off."

He played with the edge of a drawing that showed a blackboard menu with a vine-and-leaf border. "But I soon realized, this idea is its own thing. It's too big to be stuck on AJC. It needs to be ground-up—name, decor, menu, advertising, the works. We test-drive with one shop. And if it takes off, we can start more."

River wasn't sure what to say. This felt big, and a little overwhelming.

He looked at the sketches again. "Did you draw these?"

Brent looked sheepish. "Yeah. When I think, I sketch. It helps me visualize."

"They're really good."

And they were. Not just technically good, but they captured a vision. There was something conveyed in Brent's sketches, a vibe that the whole of planet Earth *was* good, that every culture had a unique way of presenting that bounty in beloved, handcrafted foods. It definitely struck a chord in River.

It should be cozy, he thought. The kind of place where a community could gather. Maybe even a community of travelers. They could have a bulletin board where they posted notices for local hostels or rooms for rent, spiritual classes, meditation groups.

Reiki and tantric massage.

Stop. You won't be here long enough for that.

No. But a community place like that would benefit others. For the first time, River saw the Brent McKay who had built a successful coffee chain in Seattle.

"It sounds amazing," River said honestly.

Brent let out a breath, as if he'd been unsure of his reception. Then he frowned. "I hope you don't think I'm ripping off your ideas."

"Nope. This is all you, Br— Uh, Mr. McKay."

"You inspired this. I never would have thought of it in a million years." Brent had been meeting his eyes only briefly today, but now he locked gazes with River, his eyes soft. "I want you to know I appreciate that. And what you did for me before too. You know." He bit his lip. "I think I'd given up. And it's like you woke me up again." He chuckled self-consciously, but his eyes held real gratitude.

Hot energy flowed into River from Brent's gaze and from his words. He took a deep breath and basked in it for a moment, enjoying the feeling of connection, the fullness of his heart. "You're welcome. But I was just doing my job. Both times. You're the one who took the spark and made it into a fire. Both times."

Brent looked away, blinked. "Maybe. But, um, anyway. I was gonna ask.... I'd like for you to be involved with this. The thing is, you just saw, organically, what AJC needed to innovate. And I don't know anything about vegan food. I can google, but that only goes so far."

River's gaze drifted down to the logo with the backpacker again. Brent's cheeks were pinker now, and River wasn't sure what to make of it all. "That's flattering, Mr. McKay. But I'm not a food expert. Not even a vegan expert. I mean, I mostly eat vegetarian, and vegan when I can, but I'm not a hundred percent strict about it."

Brent shrugged. "You know a hell of a lot more than I do. I think you're perfect."

And it was too flattering suddenly, the sense that River mattered, that he mattered *to Brent*. That couldn't be real, and River couldn't get attached to the idea.

He took a step away and looked around the room. "But, um, if you're going to do it here, it'll take a while, right? So I guess I'll just keep working at the First Hill AJC for now."

"No. Sorry. Geez. Sometimes ideas are so real in my head, I forget other people can't read my mind." Brent took a deep breath. "I was wondering if you'd be interested in consulting on the project starting right away. Helping me figure out the menu, the kombucha flavors, the décor. All of it, really. We even need a name." He smiled. "Eventually we'll get a chef involved, of course. But first we need a clear concept. And I've been living on boxed foods and takeout for a while now, so healthier choices aren't exactly second nature to me."

River snorted. "I've lived on my share of ramen."

"But you know better."

"I do know better. I even know how. I've made kimchi and sauerkraut from scratch."

"See? It's like I read your mind. You're perfect."

They smiled at one another. River had to take a few deep breaths to keep from jumping up and down or otherwise displaying his excitement. "How many hours a week would this new thing entail?"

"Whatever you can give me. I know you've got, uh, other things going on. So if you want, you could work the same hours you have now. Only instead of being a barista at AJC, you'd work with me on this project. I'll double your hourly wage. We can start there and see what makes sense as we get closer to opening. How does that sound?"

River turned away so Brent wouldn't see the stupid grin he felt on his face. He strolled around the room looking the place over, as if he was thinking about it.

How did it sound? Working on a new store concept instead of making drinks all day. Same hours, so he could keep working with surrogacy clients and Expanded Horizons. Double the money. And working with Brent one-on-one. It sounded too good to be true.

It also seemed like a signpost. Brent had been a client who'd never quite been *just* a client. Then River picked up a random barista job only to learn Brent was the store's owner. Now the hands of fate beckoned again, wanting to draw him even closer to the guy.

Wow. Sometimes life was frustratingly subtle about doling out direction. And sometimes it just bitch-slapped you right upside the head.

For a moment, River flashed back to a vision Brent, naked, under his hands, the way it felt to glide along his smooth skin. And of Brent sobbing in his arms in that first session when they'd found the grief he'd buried. Or Brent, his ass rising up in invitation, *yin* to River's *yang*. It was surreal that somehow they'd gone from that to this.

He snuck a look over his shoulder at Brent, who was leaning back against the counter, arms crossed, waiting. A doubt crept in. Was this smart? Wasn't this just asking for trouble?

Brent could have any woman he wanted. He wasn't interested in River like that. And River already felt more than he should for his boss.

But no, River wasn't going to be brought down by fear and negative projection. He wasn't going to run from such a clear opportunity. If Brent could forget their past relationship and work together as professionals, so could he.

There was, however, one problem. "Would we open by September? Because I'm not sure I'll be in Seattle past then."

Brent blinked, a frown appearing between his brows. "Um, yeah. I'd like to be up and running by then."

"Great." River crossed the space between them. He offered his hand and a smile. "I guess I'm in, Mr. McKay."

Brent took his hand. "It's a deal. But only if you call me Brent."

Chapter 12

River spent the rest of the week working at the AJC on First Hill, giving them time to find a replacement. On Friday, Justin cornered River when he took a load of dirty dishes into the small kitchen in back. He stood in the doorway, crossed his arms, and tapped his foot.

"So Mr. McKay said he needed you elsewhere in McKay Enterprises. Are you going to be working at another branch or what? Is he making you a manager?"

"You'll have to ask Mr. McKay if you want more details. I'm not sure what I'm supposed to say or not say."

"But…. You are moving to another AJC?" Justin bit his lip. "It's just that I know most of the managers. We have a retreat once a year, which is pretty cool. So if one of them is being replaced…."

River gave him a serene smile and wiped his hands on a towel.

"Is he opening up a new store?" Justin asked.

"You'll have to ask Mr. McKay." River walked around Justin and went back to the coffee station.

For the rest of the weekend, Justin kept watching him with annoyed confusion, like, *how do you rate?* River let it slide off his back.

He had Monday and Tuesday off. He went into Expanded Horizons for the weekly staff meeting on Tuesday and had a tantric session with Harrison Emmanuel. As usual, they spent more time talking about Harrison's years in the theater than they did on massage. And River had to discourage him from getting too handsy several times, despite the older gentleman's lack of response from "Captain Happy."

On Wednesday morning, River drove to Brent's house on Lake Washington. It was strange to be back there, pulling into the driveway in the black BMW—*someone else's car*—of the two-story, cottage-style, multi-million-dollar home. He wasn't Brent McKay's surrogate today, and he carried in a laptop, not a massage futon. There was a moment of disconnect.

If it felt strange to Brent, he didn't show it. He led River into the back of the main floor where the family room and dining room boasted huge windows and impressive views of the lake. Brent had his computer set up at the dining room table. French doors opened onto a deck but were closed now in deference to the May chill.

River got out his laptop while Brent went to get them tea. There was a large sketchpad and various colored pencils at the ready.

He brought a copper teapot and two cups to the table, then sat down and pulled the sketchpad closer. "Okay. So… have you had any ideas for a name yet?"

River smirked. "Oh, was that my homework assignment? Sorry, teach."

Brent laughed. "It wasn't. Just wondered if inspiration struck."

"Nope. But I did look up some recipes."

"Perfect. Just stick the name thing in your subconscious to ferment. Like kombucha. So tell me about the recipes."

River leaned back in his chair. "Well, something I learned at the ashram is that the most healthful meals have a balance of elements. We don't really need to get into the reasons for that, but—"

"No, get into it," Brent said with interest. "I'm curious."

River pursed his lips doubtfully. *Really?* But Brent's intent expression didn't change, so River went on.

"OK, so Ayurveda is an ancient system of health and medicine in India. And a lot of people there still eat according to Ayurvedic principles. They teach that the *doshas* are types of energy or mind-body states. Sort of similar to personality types, I guess. All of us have all three *doshas*, but generally one is dominant. For example, a person who is *vata* dominant tends to be antsy, anxious, and have a very active mind. Someone who is *pitta* dominant is more fiery, hot-tempered, impatient, and sharp-witted. Whereas a *kapha* personality is more laidback and calm, very methodical in thoughts and actions."

Brent leaned his elbows on the table, his face intent. "So it's sort of like Myers-Briggs."

"Sort of. Only Ayurveda is five-thousand years old."

Brent picked up a red pencil and jotted down the three states, asking River to spell them. "I think I have to cop to being more *vata* than anything. And you're *kapha*, maybe?"

River watched him doodle around the names, amused. "You really find this interesting."

Brent looked up in surprise. "Yeah, I do. I have to admit, since meeting you, I've had my horizons expanded in a number of ways."

River raised his eyebrows.

Brent blushed. "I didn't mean that. Well... sort of." He hesitated, looking like he was trying to make up his mind about something. "Hang on."

Brent got up and disappeared into another part of the house. River looked at the pad and added the air, fire, water, and earth symbols for each of the *doshas* above Brent's doodles.

Brent came back and put a book on the table. It was a large, softbound book. *Tantric Sacred Practice*. On the cover were a man and woman, scantily clad, sitting facing each other, holding hands, and gazing into each other's eyes.

Brent chuckled but his cheeks were pink. "A little light bedtime reading. I wanted to learn more about it after working with you."

The phrase, *working with you*, and the book cover, had the effect of dissolving time. The memory of sitting with Brent like that, of holding his hands and gazing into his eyes, was intense and momentarily disorienting, like déjà vu. River blinked and looked out at the bright day to ground himself in the here and now.

He cleared his throat. "How is it? The book?"

"Um... good. I've just read the first five chapters, which are about the philosophy of tantra practice. But I did have one question."

"What's that?"

Brent looked uncomfortable. "Well. The foundation of tantra is the idea of male and female polarities working off each other to create a higher, uh, a higher energy, I guess. But how does it work when its two guys? It seemed to work with us." His cheeks turned redder.

Hell, yeah, it did, River wanted to say. But he refrained.

"That's a great question. I had that same question when I first got involved with tantra."

"Oh. So you are..." Brent hesitated. "Are you gay? Or do you just work with any type of client?" It was obviously fishing, and Brent looked abashed. "Never mind. That's inappropriate. It's not really any of my business."

River gave Brent a gentle smile. "It's fine. Yes, I'm gay."

"Oh." Brent swallowed.

"About your question—you're right, tantra is about using the polarity of feminine, or *yin*, energy meeting male, or *yang*, energy to build up a powerful sexual charge that expands consciousness. But remember how I said that even though we all have a dominant *dosha*, we still contain all three doshas within us?"

Brent nodded, looking like he was listening intently.

"Well, it's the same with feminine and masculine aspects. Even though most people have a physical gender, everyone carries both *yin* and *yang* energy. When two guys are together in tantra, one can express their feminine side and one the masculine, in order to build that polarity. They can even switch what aspects of themselves they express from session to session, or even within the same session. When I'm with a client, I try to read what type of energy they're putting out and respond by bringing the opposite qualities of myself into the practice."

"Oh. Wow. That's fascinating." Brent studied River's face. "I can see that about you. You look really masculine. I mean. You're a man, obviously. And you're strong, in a calm, grounded sort of way. Like nothing bothers you. But you have a gentleness too. A nurturing side."

To River, that was a high compliment, and he felt flattered. "You're the same. You have both energies very clearly." He had an urge to reach up and stroke Brent's cheek. Or to talk about the beautiful *yin* energy Brent had expressed during their tantric sessions.

Of course he didn't do either of those things. Even if Brent weren't now his boss, most straight men wouldn't appreciate being told how strong their feminine side was.

Brent blinked and stood up. He took the tantra book and placed it on a nearby hutch. "Sorry for the detour. You were telling me about the *doshas* and the recipes?"

River took a deep breath. Exhaled. "Yeah. Getting back to the *doshas*. Even though we are all born with a dominant *dosha*, the idea is to balance the three. So, for example, if you naturally have too much of *kapha's* lazy energy, you want food that will stimulate the other *doshas* and wake you up. But if you're already bouncing off the walls with *vata* energy, you want food that will calm you down."

"Makes sense." Brent sat back down and jotted notes on the pad.

"But the best bet for a restaurant would be food and drinks that are inherently balanced, like the chai, so they're good for everyone."

"So what food would calm down my nervous *vata* energy?" Brent smiled.

"Heavy, sweeter, soothing foods like cream soups and vegetable stews. For people who have lazy *kapha* energy you'd want spicy dishes like curry that heat the body. And for hot-headed *pitta* you want more astringent, colder foods like salads to cool it down."

Brent made more notes. "Wow. I've been in food service my entire career, and I've never heard this. Does it work? Have you ever tried it?"

River shrugged. "Can't say I've made a study of it. But I did love the food at the ashram, and it was super healthy. The traditional meals we ate there were balanced overall—a spicy stew served with milk and a vinegar-dressed salad, for example. And a lot of traditional restaurants in India will balance meals this way, even international restaurants."

Brent looked surprised. "Are there are a lot of international cuisines in India? I mean, like Chinese or Mexican restaurants?"

"Sure. I spent a few weeks in Mumbai. I love that city! They have every kind of food imaginable there. In fact, that's where I found that kombucha pub I told you about."

Brent didn't comment, just chewed his lip thoughtfully.

"Anyway. It was just a suggestion, and maybe it's a dumb idea, but we could balance the meals at the cafe. For example, if there was a spicy Mexican dish, serve it with a side of homemade sauerkraut and bread with thick butter or cheese or vegan cheese. It's just another way to look at the whole 'healthful food' concept."

"I love it," Brent said earnestly. "Even if we don't advertise that we're doing that, it's a way to put a kind of secret sauce of thought and care into what we serve."

They smiled at one another.

"I'm not sure if I should be impressed or worried about how quickly you assimilate this stuff," River joked.

"It all fascinates me. I can't really explain why, but it does."

River had an urge to reach out and touch Brent's arm. The admission was so openhearted and almost vulnerable. But he just smiled instead.

"You don't need to explain it. Instinct, attraction to things... we feel that when the thing in question harmonizes just right with something inside of us. It can't be explained logically."

Their gazes locked and held. River couldn't help noticing that Brent's eyes were the same mossy green as the lake outside today. And just as unfathomable.

Brent looked away. "So... you mentioned curry. I definitely want to have at least one curry dish on the menu. There are various kinds, right? And a number of countries have curry dishes. What do you like?"

They discussed the menu for hours. River showed off photos and recipes he'd found online, and described some of his favorite dishes he'd found in his travels. They looked things up online and discussed what could easily be heated up or kept in a cold case.

The lake outside shimmered and got tiny white caps. The water was alternatively bright and somber as the clouds rolled in and away.

And the tantric book stayed on the hutch, forgotten.

Chapter 13

River

"The sky is so blue today. And the sun seems to think we're in the south of France. Could I entice you to take a little stroll along the waterfront, hmm?"

River had barely put down his portable futon and duffel bag before Harrison was suggesting an outing. He walked over to the large windows in his apartment as if to demonstrate the beautiful day outside.

"We should focus on our session," River said.

Focusing on their sessions was getting more and more difficult with Harrison. He wanted to talk. He wanted to go out to eat or for a walk. He was so charming, it was hard to remember why they shouldn't.

"Right you are." Harrison clapped his hands together. "How about we have our session, and afterward we can walk down to Ivar's. I'd love to buy you lunch, and we can soak in this rare gorgeous day."

It was Tuesday, and River didn't have anything else pressing. But he did want to work on some ideas for the cafe before he met with Brent tomorrow. And, of course, he had Lily and Beauchamp duty. "Sorry. I have to work this afternoon."

"Posh! It's only eleven. Let's do the session now, and that will still give us time to walk down there, have lunch, and be back by two. You'll have the rest of the afternoon for your work." Harrison's expression turned sad. "It's just that, at my age, I worry about walking by myself. And I do so miss going out for lunch."

Well, damn. River gave an internal sigh. "All right. But let's get started on our session. Okay?"

"Brilliant!" Harrison smiled.

River set up his futon, oil-warming pot, and pile of small towels. He removed his T-shirt. They began on the couch as usual, with tantric breath and eye-gazing. Harrison had never gotten any better at this and had a hard time meeting River's gaze. Instead, he looked at River's chest or out the window. But he clung to River's hands and relaxed under the heavy breathing.

They started the massage with Harrison on his stomach on the futon. In the five weeks they'd been working together, Harrison had never gotten an erection. He'd mentioned Viagra, but River suspected Harrison loved his wine more than he wanted to use Viagra, the two of which did not mix. Though he knew Viagra didn't cure all cases of erectile dysfunction either.

Harrison didn't seem worried about it. *My boy, just having your hands on me is a thrill.* He said he felt better than he had in years. It did seem like the reiki work was helping the old man's chakra energy flow. And his loneliness too.

When River finished his healing work on the chakras along Harrison's spine, he had him turn over so he could massage his front side. The towel, as usual, was not tented. River positioned himself at the side of the futon and, breathing deeply, stroked up Harrison's legs, focusing on sending out healing energy.

Harrison watched him, eyes narrowly open. "Will you remove your shorts?"

River paused for a moment, then continued the massage. "No. I never take off my shorts with clients."

Harrison pouted. "But it might help me if I could see your cock. Visual stimulation. Hmm? Please?" He put a hand on River's thigh. "I'd be happy to pay extra."

"No." River removed Harrison's hand from his thigh and put it at his side. "Do you want me to stop? We can be done for the day."

Harrison's nostrils flared. "No. No. Please continue. It was just a suggestion." He closed his eyes, took a deep breath, and relaxed on the futon.

River continued. He was a little amused—Harrison was persistent—and a touch annoyed too. He'd made his boundaries clear. But there was no point in holding on to anger or resentment.

He felt compassion for the old man, and that was what he should focus on.

After the massage, Harrison sat right up, more eager than relaxed. River helped him to his feet. "Just give me a moment. I'll get changed for lunch." He rushed off.

River almost said he wouldn't go, but Harrison didn't give him a chance. Plus he'd already said he would do it. He packed up his things, washed his hands, and put on his T-shirt.

Having lunch with a client was crossing the line. But hell, they'd already spent as much time talking as in their tantric sessions. Harrison was very good at blurring lines. And it wouldn't hurt River to help an old man make an excursion out for once. He should be honored.

Harrison came out wearing all black—black trousers and a black silk shirt. He added a flamboyant floral silk scarf around his neck and a long black coat.

Outside, it truly was a lovely afternoon in late May—sunny, around 65 degrees, with a slight breeze. Boats of all kinds were out on the water, and the sidewalk was crowded with tourists and locals. They walked past the aquarium, which looked packed.

Harrison was unsteady on his feet. River held his hand securely, and they moved at a leisurely pace.

"You said your current house-sitting position is up September tenth?"

"Yup." That reminded River that he needed to check the house-sitting website again. He'd been ignoring the problem lately, with all the excitement around the new cafe.

But by September, he would have been here an entire year. Seattle was great, and he would miss it. But plenty of other places were great too. The new cafe would be open by then, Brent said. It would be perfect timing to move on. Find a new situation. New horizons.

Someone else's life.

Then why did the idea make him sad?

"I'm waiting for inspiration to strike," River said. "It'll happen. The path will appear."

Harrison looked delighted. "Well, call me Mr. Inspiration, because I have the perfect solution for you. What would you think of house-sitting at an adorable little apartment near Saint Peter's and Piazza Navona in Rome, hmm? Rome, after all, is the Eternal City. And if you haven't been there, you haven't lived, my boy!"

Harrison was so exuberant, it made River smile. "Sounds intriguing. How did you hear about this place?"

"Let's just say I know the owner." Harrison's eyes twinkled.

"Hmm. How long would it be for?"

"Up to a year if you like. If one goes in September, one really must stay through the fall. And the holidays! You've never had a Christmas until you've seen the Vatican in all its seasonal glory. And then, if you're there after the New Year, it's imperative to remain through spring. Spring in Rome is incomparable. Simply incomparable!"

They reached Ivar's seafood restaurant and the conversation was dropped until they were seated. There was nothing on the patio, which was probably for the best. Harrison would get chilled, despite the nice day. They got a table near the window.

Harrison immediately ordered a glass of wine. As long as he stuck to just one, he probably would be fine to walk back. River hoped.

"So how do you know about this apartment in Rome that needs a house sitter?" River asked again, after the waiter had taken their order.

Harrison leaned forward and smiled. "Because, dear boy, I own it."

"You own an apartment in Rome?"

"I do! I bought it in 2008 when the Italian market crashed. Rescued a dear friend of mine who was positively drowning. It only has one bedroom, but it's on the Via Ezio. A gold mine on Airbnb, trust me. I used to spend a month there every year, but I haven't been since 2016 because the trip has gotten to be too much for me." He spoke with great pathos, his eyes damp. "With your help, darling boy, I could visit my beloved Roma one more time before I leave this mortal coil. Christmas in Rome. Imagine it!"

"That sounds wonderful. But... what would the financial arrangement be?"

Harrison's eyelids fluttered. "I wouldn't charge you a thing. You'll be helping me out by being my companion. As I said, the trip is too much for me to do on my own. Say yes. Hmm? This is your path, my boy. Embrace it."

River took a sip of iced tea and watched a ferry make its way toward Bainbridge Island.

Was this the open door he'd been waiting for? Maybe it was. He could look into what he could do while in Rome. Maybe he'd find something like Expanded Horizons or an upscale massage house he could work at. An alternative medicine practice. Hell, even being a barista or waiter in Rome for a few months sounded amazing.

It was the kind of life experience his mother would adore. *Be a dandelion puff, floating wherever the wind takes you.*

Harrison was offering a significant gust of wind.

But if he accepted, what would the old man expect in return? *Companion?* River had no qualms with helping Harrison travel, being his friend. He didn't want to be more than that. Moving into his Rome apartment would definitely smash the surrogate-client relationship to smithereens.

"You say it has one bedroom. How would that work?" he asked neutrally.

A flicker of something like annoyance crossed Harrison's face, but he hid it behind a genial look. "There's a large bed. These old bones don't take up much room. But the couch also makes into a bed, if one positively must have one's own space. The place is advertised for four people, so I'm sure we could limp along."

His slightly chiding tone made River feel like an ingrate. "It's sweet of you to offer. Sounds amazing. I need to give it some thought, check into a few things. Can I get back to you about it?"

"Of course! I'd hardly expect anything less. But do let me know soon, hmm? The place will start booking up for the fall and I hate to cancel too many reservations. If we're going to stay there, I should take it off the market."

"I'll let you know in the next few weeks."

"Perfect, dear boy. Perfect." Harrison's smile was brighter than the day outside.

Chapter 14

June, 2019

River

They spent two weeks working at Brent's house. They outlined the first eight kombucha brews—complete with funky names. Brent talked to a health inspector and looked at the logistics of producing large quantities of kombucha. River researched vegan restaurants around the world and checked out popular foodie blogs. He spent a half day on sauerkraut recipes alone. You could easily have as many types of sauerkraut as kombucha, but he picked two of the most appealing to try. He found a TV series about a guy who went around the world finding the best street food, and he and Brent binge-watched it on a Saturday afternoon.

On the second Sunday, they worked for only an hour at the dining room table before Brent pushed back his chair.

"Hey, want to take a drive? I've been starting to think about the décor ideas, I need some inspiration. There's an Indonesian place on Mercer Street and a World Market on the waterfront."

"Are we ready for that?" River asked, surprised.

Brent shrugged. "I'm a very visual thinker. I like to shop for ideas."

"Okay. Sure."

They took Brent's car, which was an old olive-green Range Rover, funky and sporty.

"I pictured you in something like this year's Lexus," River commented after buckling his seat belt.

Brent mocked horror and put a hand to his heart. "You wound me."

River laughed. "Sorry. Guess that was judgmental."

"I love this beast. Had it for ten years and wouldn't part with it. Certainly not for a Lexus."

Loyal, River thought again. Brent stuck with things. It was something River admired, even if it was far from his personal experience—or temperament.

"Kathy and I were never big spenders," Brent continued as he drove, his voice a little strained. "We put everything we made back into buying more stores or fixing up houses. She used to joke that we were playing real-life Monopoly. The house I live in now was one we bought to flip. But after we fixed it up, Kathy got sick, and I just haven't dealt with selling it."

River wasn't sure he hundred-percent bought that. The furnishings were pretty damn nice. But then, if you bought a house to fix it up and flip it, maybe having decent furniture was part of the investment for when you had to show it. Anyway, it wasn't any of River's business.

It was interesting, though, that Brent made excuses for his wealth. Most rich people bragged about their money, didn't they?

The Indonesian furniture store was a bust. They had lots of imported teak dining tables and chairs, very stuffy and formal. It reminded River of what the Kardashians would own if they lived in India. Not his style at all and not right for the cafe. It was also outrageously expensive.

After giving up on that place, they parked near the Space Needle and walked six blocks to the World Market store. It had goods from all over. Some items River really liked. But they were budget home goods, not things that would hold up to heavy restaurant traffic. Brent and River looked at some ceramic plates and glasses and colorful linens, but neither of them were inspired by the selection.

"We usually buy furniture for the shops from restaurant wholesalers," Brent commented, spreading out a woven placemat that looked like it wouldn't last a month. "But I'm not sure what I'm looking for. I like the global theme, but I'm having a hard time visualizing it."

"Afraid I'm gonna be zero help to you there," River grimaced. "Decorating is not my thing, and I honestly don't pay attention to furniture and interior design and such. When I travel, I'm more focused on the landscape, nature, the exterior of buildings, the people…" He smiled. "I love temples and churches, so I pay attention to those interiors, but I don't think that's the look you're going for."

"Yeah, probably not."

They left the World Market and strolled along the waterfront. The June day was cool and overcast, but it was still beautiful. Beyond the waters of Puget Sound, to the south, the white cap of Mount Rainier floated like a mirage.

"The trouble," Brent mused as they walked, "is that I've hardly ever left the country. I went to Germany once, and that's it. So I just don't have the juice in my subconscious to feed my creative mind. Not about the décor anyway. It's like I try to pull up ideas and I'm just… I've got nothin'."

"Hmm. Maybe you should remedy that. Go on an inspiration pilgrimage," River suggested lightly.

Brent stopped walking and stared at him, eyes wide.

River laughed. "What? You have that 'I just had an epiphany' look."

"You know my looks?" Brent asked in surprise.

River felt his cheeks heat, as if he'd been caught out. "I just mean you looked like you had an idea."

"It's, um… nothing." Brent started walking again. "I just thought of something I should look into. But I need to, uh, look into it. First. Hey, there's a great Thai place a few blocks down. I'm starving. Want to grab lunch?"

"I could eat."

"Then maybe we could hit Elliot Bay Books on the way back over the hill. See if we can find some design books."

"Sure."

There was no doubt who was the *yang* on this project. Brent's energy was all forward-drive. And, for now, River was content being his *yin*.

PART III: THE SOURCE

"Thousands of candles can be lit from a single candle, and the life of the candle will not be shortened. Happiness never decreases by being shared."– Buddha

Chapter 15

Brent

"You're what?" Sean stuck a finger in his ear and wiggled it. "'Squeeze me?"

Brent rolled his eyes and picked up his glass of IPA from the bar, took a sip. "You heard me."

"You're taking a trip to India. With your tantra guy. The guy who did the *lingam*–"

Brent stuck his free hand over Sean's mouth. The bartender gave them a knowing smirk. "Shut up, Sean. Ever heard of the word *discretion*?"

Sean waggled his eyebrows as Brent removed his hand. "Discretion, got it. I won't say anything about the guy who did that thing, that kinda kinky thing, involving a beloved part of your anatomy, and how you've got him working for you now, and how you're going to India with him, just the two of you. And this is, for sure, just a business deal. Got it. So when can Sharon and I meet him?"

Brent had to laugh. He shook his head and ate a french fry.

They were at Hopvine Pub on Capitol Hill on a Friday evening, and Brent was in too good a mood to be pissy with Sean. Even though Sean deserved it.

"It *is* just business. I'm opening up a travel-themed kombucha bar and café, and I've hardly been anywhere. It's absurd. Plus, there's a kombucha bar in Mumbai I need to check out. And loads of great vegan and vegetarian options. It's legitimate research. And it's tax deductible."

"Hmmm." Sean's expression wouldn't have been amiss on an FBI agent questioning a lying suspect. "Still. Taking this guy with you?"

"For fuck's sake, Sean, his name is not *this guy* or *that guy* or *the tantric guy*. It's River. And yes, I'm taking him with me. He knows

Mumbai. He knows where to go and how to get around. Plus, he's part of the project. The whole thing was his idea. More or less."

They focused on their salmon burgers for a while. Sean looked thoughtful. "Seriously, dude. I know I ride your ass, but I'm..." Sean blew out a breath. "I'm happy for ya. And intrigued. And confused? Yeah, a bit confused. But hey, it's all good."

"Sean—"

"So what's this River guy look like? I was serious when I said Sharon and I want to meet him. I'm having a hard time picturing it. Him. You and him. Doing that."

Brent shook his head. Sean was relentless. "I told you, I'm not romantically involved with him. There's no reason for you to meet anyone. Or picture us doing that."

Sean stared at him and stuck out his lower lip. Puppy-dog eyes were employed. "What's his last name? Can I at least google him? Since you won't describe him to me, your best friend in the entire world."

Brent knew he was making a mistake, but he couldn't help himself. He kinda wanted to see what Sean thought of River. So he picked his phone off the bar and scrolled to a photo.

He'd taken it on the waterfront the day they'd looked at furniture. River had just turned and smiled at the camera. Wisps of blond hair floated around his face, and his eyes were warm and alive. The photo was from the waist up, and his strong shoulders and arms were evident in his T-shirt. His face had that beautiful, positive light that Brent loved. He was such a pleasure to be around. He somehow made Brent feel more positive too. After years of depression, the feeling was addictive.

Brent had looked at this photo far too many times.

He handed the phone to Sean with a nervous flutter. Sean's eyes went wide. "Holy shit. Wow. Kinda hunky, I guess? So this does it for ya, huh?"

Brent huffed and went to take back the phone, but Sean held it out of his reach. "I mean, he's good-looking, but he looks like he should be dating my daughter."

"You don't have a daughter, Sean."

"I might. Someday."

Brent scowled. "River is twenty-six. You'd have to have been a father at thirteen to have a daughter his age."

Sean grinned. "You already figured that out, huh?"

Yes, Brent had figured it out, wondering how big the age gap was between them. But just because he'd thought about it didn't mean anything was ever going to happen between them.

He grabbed for the phone again, but Sean held it away. His expression softened though. "Just... give me a minute. Chill out, man. Seriously."

Brent relented and Sean looked at the photo some more. Then he set the phone on the bar. "He looks nice. Like a nice person. I'm really happy for ya."

"I told you, it's not like that."

Sean studied him for a minute. "Look, Sharon and I—we've been real worried about you. You just... you weren't really there. Ya know? Just going through the motions. And you expect that at first. Losing Kathy and all. But as time went on, we got worried."

Brent swallowed a hot lump in his throat. "Sorry I worried you."

Sean shook his head. "Seeing you come to life again the past few months... it's been more than I even hoped for."

It had been great. Brent felt very fortunate. "Expanded Horizons helped. And I've got a new cafe project I'm excited about. I feel like I've got my mojo back."

"Kombucha on tap is a great idea. You'll make a mint, you rich fuck."

Sean attacked the rest of his burger while Brent smiled and sipped his beer.

As much as he doth-protest-too-much with Sean, Brent couldn't deny that his interest in River was... complicated. In fact, he'd had moments where he wondered how much of his fascination with this new cafe concept was really a fascination with River.

If some random barista had mentioned authentic chai, homebrewed kombucha, and vegan food to him, would he have been as open to the idea? So immediately entranced? In a word: no. But that didn't mean it wasn't a great opportunity. He'd done due diligence. Worked out the figures. Got feedback from friends and colleagues he respected. He wasn't a complete fool.

Still, it was River who made the concept approachable. Appealing. Just as Brent had been fascinated by tantra since meeting him, so too, the cafe idea had hooked into him because River made it seem cool. Before he'd met River, Brent thought of vegan food as obsessively healthy and bland, about as natural as a one-legged dog. Now it seemed delicious and intriguing. Not that he was going vegan personally, but the more he'd looked into current restaurant trends and some of the vegan recipes and food pics, he realized how wrong he'd been.

And then there was the *theme* of the new café. Brent had such a gut feeling about what he wanted—something hip, glowing with health and vitality, American, yet suffused with a global spirit of travel and adventure, something honest, grounded, and real.

A lot like River himself.

Only could Brent really pin that down? Or was he trying to capture the light of the moon in a jar?

Yeah. A lot like River.

The theme was so obviously based on River, it was kind of embarrassing, actually. But maybe no one would notice?

Hey, inspiration struck where it struck. Brent was lucky he had a muse. He wasn't going to apologize. Or mention it to anyone.

So he was infatuated with the café concept. *Was he infatuated with River too? That way?*

That day three weeks ago when he'd walked into their First Hill branch and saw River, it had been a total shock. He knew he'd acted like an idiot, but the thought of what River had done to his naked body being exposed there, in his place of business, had been alarming. Of course, that was stupid, because River would never tell anyone.

After the shock wore off, it sank in that *River Larsen worked for him.* The tantric surrogate he'd been so drawn to, that he'd thought was gone from his life, was back with a vengeance. Suddenly Brent knew where River was to be found. It was all right there on the company employee database. Even his home address.

Not that Brent would ever invade River's privacy at home. But there was no reason why he shouldn't go into his own damn coffee shop for breakfast in the mornings. He hadn't been able to resist the urge to hang out there. Just being in River's presence was... not soothing. The opposite of soothing. Energizing. River made him *feel*.

"If I *was* attracted to him, do you think that would be weird?" Brent asked Sean, before he thought better of it.

Sean choked on his beer and wiped his mouth. He shot Brent a look. "Weird? Being attracted to sheep would be weird. Wanting to wear a black ball gag to work would be weird. Liking a guy is just... unexpected."

Brent caught the bartender looking at them again and he lowered his voice. "Dr. Halloran says sometimes you figure things out later in life. I got married so young. And I loved Kathy. I never thought seriously about anyone else."

"Of course you loved her. Everyone knows that."

But Brent felt a stab of guilt. Yes, he'd loved Kathy. But at the end, it had been so bad. He felt guilty that he hadn't loved her enough at the end, that there'd been nothing he could do for her. That he'd been relieved when it was finally over.

It still hurt.

Sean clasped his shoulder. "Dude, don't go there. Okay? Look, this is a new chapter. A new chapter in the book of Brent McKay."

Brent nodded. "Right. You're right."

"And this chapter has dicks, apparently."

That made Brent laugh. "I haven't had any dicks yet. Not even sure I want to." Okay, that was a lie. He'd wanted one at least, during that last tantric massage. "Anyway, it doesn't matter. Nothing's going to happen. River is my employee. He's practically a partner on this new cafe. And he's too young for me, as you pointed out."

"Hey, I was teasing! What's thirteen years between friends? Men marry younger women all the time."

"No, it's true. We have nothing in common. He's a young world traveler on a spiritual journey, and I own coffee shops and have barely left Seattle. And even if, by some miracle, he actually liked me back, he probably won't even stick around this area for long." Brent forced a smile. "It's just that I really connect with him. You know me. I don't get that close to many people. River is... special."

Sean watched Brent, his expression growing worried. "Geez. You're really twisted up in knots over this guy."

"Not *knots*."

"Dude, you're practically macramé. Just be careful. You need some happiness in your life, not more hurt and stress."

"I have been happy. *Happier* anyway."

Sean's frown deepened. "So maybe it's not such a great idea to do this India trip, you and River."

"I told you, it's business. We'll only be gone ten days."

Sean put a hand on Brent's shoulder. "Look, why don't you let me set up a dinner with you, me, Sharon, and her friend Annette. Huh? I think you'd really like her. Maybe it'll help you get some clarity, you know? See there are options out there. And, hey, if you still decide you really like this River g—I mean *River*—then that'll be good info too. Amiright?"

Brent had to admit, that made sense. "Fine. I'll meet Annette. After I get back from India, okay?"

Brent couldn't hide a secret, and very unlikely, hope that after India, it would be too late.

Chapter 16

June 2019
Mumbai, India
River

"We're next to each other," Brent said, handing River a keycard. "Rooms 201 and 203."

"Sounds good. Thanks." River inwardly laughed at himself for feeling a touch of disappointment they weren't sharing a room. As if Brent would have done that. He'd kept their relationship strictly professional. Or maybe on the "friends" side of professional. And this trip was strictly business.

They were in the lobby of the Novotel Mumbai, a gleaming, modern space that could have been anywhere in the world. It wasn't what River would have chosen, but it was certainly nice and, for River, free.

"My travel agent picked this place," Brent said, looking slightly abashed. "It's on the beach and close to the markets. And she got a nice discount."

"It's great."

"So, uh, what do you want to do?" Brent checked his watch. "It's noon here. If I stay in, I'll sleep. Want to drop off our things and go out for a bit? If you're too tired, I can walk around on my own."

"Nope. Definitely need to go out. We should stay up until at least eight tonight. We can grab some coffee to help with that."

Brent smiled. "My first Mumbai coffee. You know how to motivate me."

River smiled back. "Absolutely, Coffee Man." He held back a wink that desperately wanted to come out, but the flirting tone was bad enough. He was tired from their thirteen-hour flight, and his normal filters were askew.

They went up in the elevator together, went into their side-by-side rooms, and ten minutes later were back out on the street.

They grabbed kaapi from a cart on the harbor. The Indian brew was made from pouring hot water through a fine coffee-bean powder in a filter, then adding boiled milk. The result was thick and strong. Brent watched the vendor make it with studious interest, then sipped it the way a wine connoisseur might test a new wine.

"Robusta beans," he declared. "The milk tastes different."

"Yeah. I think it's the breed of cow. It's mostly Sindhi and Sahiwal cattle. Do you like it?"

Brent nodded. "Very much. I can get robusta beans for our place. Maybe we could offer a traditional kaapi. But I doubt we can reproduce the flavor of the milk. Of course, most customers won't know."

Our place. That made River's heart thump double time, even if it was really just Brent's place—legally and in every other way. "The good news is, kaapi will definitely keep us awake."

Brent stretched, coffee in hand, his face tilted to the sun. "The sunlight doesn't hurt. It feels wonderful."

River had to admit, after almost nine months of living in Seattle, the hot Indian sun beating down on his hair and shoulders felt like a blessing from heaven.

Just being back in India was a blessing. He hadn't expected to return so soon, but it had been impossible to turn down a free trip. And how could he refuse the chance to take Brent McKay around Mumbai? He was excited—and a little confused—about yet more opportunity to spent time with him.

Maddy had been equally confused when he recruited her to house-sit for the Reynolds while he was gone. "So what's up between you and Mr. McKay? First he steals you from us to work on some secret project, and now you're both going to India at the same time. Hmm." She'd tapped her chin in mock thought. "I detect shenanigans. Sexy shenanigans."

"Not at all. He's working on an idea for a new cafe, and I'm helping him. That's all." River had managed to sound calm and matter-of-fact.

She'd shaken her head, still frowning. "Lucky you. I guess."

She'd probably gossiped about it with Justin. Hell, Justin would probably have a litter of kittens over it.

Expectations, man. Truly the source of all pain.

River didn't care what they thought, but he did value self-awareness. Maddy's reaction had reminded him to pause and check in with himself before he called Brent to confirm that he could go.

Was there something going on? Did this trip have hidden motives? For Brent? For him?

River was an intuitive person. He didn't have difficulty reading most people. But he had trouble reading this situation. In the four weeks they'd been working together at Brent's house, he would sometimes find Brent watching him, as he had that week he'd come in to AJC. Or mid-conversation Brent would look at his mouth—or his hands—and stare too long. But he always went back to discussing the café as if those looks meant nothing. Plus, they'd spent hours alone together at Brent's home. If he was going to make a move, he didn't need to take River all the way to Mumbai to do it.

That logic didn't do anything to clear up River's confusion. Or put a damper on his own growing feelings.

He liked Brent. He could like him a lot more. But the dozens of photos of Brent and Kathy around his house were a constant reminder that Brent had a different path. Of course, lots of straight men were happy to receive a *lingam* massage—and probably a blowjob too. What if Brent asked for that? A freebie repeat just to get off? He'd been nothing but respectful so far, but River knew well enough that people didn't always live up to their higher natures.

And if he does ask? What then?

It would be seriously tempting. River was no monk, and he was attracted to Brent. But if he was going to be intimate with someone, it couldn't be one-sided. He wasn't a sex toy. It had to start with respect, mutual give and take, a true connection.

It's not going to happen. You've got great chemistry for a productive working relationship. That's all and that's enough.

Maybe this trip would finally help him accept that and let go of any other ideas.

They walked the promenade at the Mumbai harbor, alongside the currently placid waters of the Arabian Sea. The huge arch called the Gateway of India was crowded with tourists, but Brent and River admired it from a distance. The iconic Taj Hotel, with its white facade and round red domes, was shabbier than River remembered, but still a crown jewel of Mumbai. There were dozens of colorful boats in the water, including two-story tourist boats. India was nothing if not visually and culturally rich.

By the time they reached the end of the promenade, River was lightheaded. At first he thought it was the heat, but then he realized he hadn't eaten a decent meal since they left Seattle. "I could use some food. You?"

"Starving," Brent agreed. "Our first meal in India. What do you recommend?"

"Follow me."

Restaurants were ubiquitous in Mumbai, especially near the harbor, so it didn't take long for River to find the sort of place he was looking for—a tiny family-run restaurant with a traditional Gujarat menu. River ordered thali, a large platter for two with a mix of vegetarian dishes and sauces in small silver bowls. It came with a heap of methi thepla, a flatbread, for scooping and dipping.

It tasted incredible, sparking memories of joyful meals shared at the ashram. They both ate too much. Brent commented on the flavors of each dish and took photographs, wondering aloud about how they might or might not work for the cafe. He was enthusiastic, curious, and adventurous, trying even the most sour chutney. He especially loved the vegetable curry dish.

"Have you traveled much?" River asked him as they ate.

"Not a whole lot. Kathy and I were always too busy with the shops. When we did take time off, we'd go up to Canada or to Montana." He wiped his hands on a napkin. "We went to Hawaii for our twentieth anniversary. And we did a river cruise up the Rhine shortly after she was diagnosed." He blinked, looking down at his plate. "That trip was something else. Germany is so beautiful."

Pity washed over River. Kathy was diagnosed with cancer, so they'd finally taken time off work to travel. So many people put off living until mortality made itself undeniable.

Not him. That would never be him. Just the idea made his feet itchy.

"I suppose you could travel more now, if you wanted," River said.

Brent looked up at him and smiled wryly. "And here I am." He raised his teacup.

"And here you are."

Without thinking, River put his hand over Brent's. The connection was immediate and strong. There was so much in Brent's eyes—entreaty, sadness, hope, gratitude... affection? Energy tingled in River's body, a rising tide called to the full moon. Then Brent yawned, laughed, and apologized, and River removed his hand. The moment passed and they finished their meal.

After lunch, they meandered toward the heart of the city, taking in the tall buildings, international banks, and mix of Western chains and local businesses. They didn't talk much, but Brent's eyes were huge as he took everything in.

Mumbai was a vast city filled with skyscrapers and traffic. It was insanely busy, even overwhelming. River had only spent a week there once, but he was at least familiar with traveling in India, able to slide into the culture like a car merging onto a crowded freeway. He knew basic words and signs, enough to get around. He knew what to order, how to ask for a bathroom, and how to use the local transportation. Compared to Brent, he felt like an expert guide. It gave him a warm satisfaction to lead the way, to play the part of the sophisticated adept, even if he was aware of the fact, and able to chuckle at his own vanity.

When they'd had enough walking, River pointed out a bus that would take them back to the area near the hotel, and they ran to catch it. River stepped up into the open doorway and grabbed

Brent's hand to pull him aboard. Perhaps Brent enjoyed the sense of security in the gesture, being a fish out of water, because he kept hold of River's hand for several long minutes as they chatted about how crowded the bus was and the public transportation system. Brent held River's hand until it became too obvious that it was unusual, and he finally let go, seemingly reluctant to do so.

It was that vulnerable side of Brent, that yielding side, his *yin* energy, that drew River like a magnet, called up his protective, dominant, *yang* nature, made it impossible to resist or ignore. He looked out the window wordlessly for a moment to let that pull ease, until the urge to take Brent's hand again or to put an arm around his shoulders and pull him tight subsided.

At the hotel, they took the elevator up and said good night at the doors to their respective rooms with tired smiles.

Chapter 17

Brent

The kombucha bar was located not far from the University of Mumbai, on a street with a mix of convenience stores, services, and budget eateries aimed at students. The front was nothing exciting. It was a narrow storefront right next to a restaurant that appeared to offer low-priced local vegetarian food. The sign painted on the window had the shop's name in Marathi, the official language of the state of Maharashtra, and in English. The English name read "Elixir of Health Bar." Brent figured it was probably more poetic in Marathi.

Inside, the place was surprisingly reminiscent of a classic British pub. A long bar in a polished mahogany loomed to the left. There was a mirror behind the bar with a long row of huge glass jars of kombucha in front of it. The jewel tones of the kombucha were bright and appealing, lit from above by recessed lights, and reflecting colored beams into the mirror behind. They looked like magic potions. The colors ranged from raspberry to deep red, from gold to green to a dark brown that looked like iced tea. It was a beautiful display. Heavy barstools lined the bar, and to the right was a brick wall with small round wooden tables along it. There was only a single narrow aisle.

In the restaurant business, atmosphere was everything, and Brent liked the vibe of the place very much. It was sort of old and funky and sort of hip at the same time, casual, warm, and cozy. It seemed like the kind of place college students and young professionals would hang out, though it was deserted at this early hour of 10:00 a.m. local time. They'd only just opened.

Brent had emailed the owner, a man named Falan Acharya, and Falan had readily set up an appointment. But Brent wasn't sure what to expect now that he was here. Falan came out to greet them with enthusiasm, wiping his hands on a white apron. His black jeans and red stripped button-down shirt were informal, and his thick black hair was long and floppy. He looked close to Brent's age, maybe a few years younger. His nose and broad grin were both slightly crooked, but his expression was unambiguously friendly.

"Hello! Mr. Brent McKay! All the way from Seattle!" Falan gave Brent a hearty handshake, pumping his hand. "And who is this?" He looked at River.

"My name is River Larsen. I'm a work associate of Mr. McKay's. It's an honor to meet you." River placed his hands together and gave a slight bow.

Falan did the same. "The honor is mine, Mr. Larsen. I am so pleased you are both here! It is not every day I get to meet with fellow restaurateurs from so far away. Come, come. Let's sit down and have something to drink. It's going to be hot today!"

They sat at the bar, Falan between River and Brent. There was a young man working behind the bar, and he came right over.

"You want to try the booch, yes?" Falan asked.

"Absolutely!" Brent eyed the glass jars with interest. "Do you have a sampler?"

"A sampler? What do you mean?"

Brent explained the common practice in microbreweries, where you could order a beer taste sampler. Usually it was served in a wooden tray with six or more small glasses.

"We don't offer such a thing currently," Falan said, "but I like the idea very much. I may have to use it. Ahmed, would you please put a little bit of several brews—" Falan held his fingers up a few inches apart. "—in glasses. Let's see... Let's start with lemonade, health tonic, turmeric, and raspberry mint please."

They sat at the bar and tasted kombuchas for a good hour. They learned that Falan had been born in Mumbai and studied at Oxford. His parents had wanted him to go to medical school, but his grandmother had been all about using food and herbs as natural remedies, and Falan became fascinated with the subject himself.

"Kombucha has so many beneficial properties," he told them with the fervor of a true devotee. "The enzymes help your body absorb the vitamins and minerals in other foods, you know. So it is good to have kombucha with every meal. It's loaded with healthy probiotics that keep your gut running optimally. And it improves your immune system. Me? I am never sick! And if you ever are sick, in the stomach…" He rubbed his hand over his belly. "…kombucha can help restore balance and cure nausea. It's very good for those with stomach problems."

Brent couldn't contain his smile. Falan was just so enthusiastic. "Is it popular here in Mumbai?"

"Very popular! Besides this bar, we also sell the brews to many restaurants and hotels in Mumbai. We cannot even keep up with business. Kombucha is not as popular in the United States, I think?"

"It's still considered a specialty product, but it sells quite well in groceries stores," Brent said. "I think Seattle is ready for a kombucha bar. This is delicious, by the way." He sipped the one Falan called lemonade. It tasted like a fizzy, deeply steeped Arnold Palmer, part iced tea, part lemonade, with a ginger kick. It was fantastic.

"You can try them all if you like," Falan waved his hands at the glass jars. "When we first began, our kombucha master tried many recipes from books. I can recommend some to you." He rattled off the names of a half-dozen kombucha books available online. "As time went by, we perfected our own recipes. Big trade secret." He winked. "I'm sure the same will be the case for you. But even simple recipes will taste good. You really cannot make a bad booch. Have you ever made it yourself?"

Brent looked at River.

"I have," River said, sipping the raspberry brew. "Where I grew up, we made it. It was even a project in school."

"Really?" Brent asked, surprised. He realized he didn't know anything about River's childhood.

River nodded. "Yup. Kefir and yogurt too. I grew up thinking everyone did that."

Brent wanted to ask River more questions but decided he should save that discussion for later. "Do serve food here?" he asked Falan instead, looking around for a menu.

"Not us, no. The place next door is owned by my cousin. We encourage patrons to bring his food to our tables and vice versa. As I said, we also make kombucha for many other businesses, so we have our hands quite full."

Falan took them on a tour. The kombucha was made in the basement, which was a large room, much larger than the storefront upstairs. It resembled a mad scientist's laboratory with wooden racks filled with glass jars of kombucha and yeast cultures, baskets of fresh fruit and herbs, things growing in pots under lights, big commercial sinks, and a row of enormous wooden tables where the prep work took place. There was a yeasty, earthy smell, and it was quite warm.

Falan introduced them to a pretty, petite Indian woman in a long gray tunic, slim white trousers, and flats. "This is our kombucha master, Mrs. Anya Acharya. Who also happens to be my wife."

River greeted the woman with a slight bow, so Brent did the same. Anya appeared shy and unsure of what to say. She quickly excused herself to return to cutting up oranges.

Something about Anya's petite build, and the fact that Falan and Anya worked together, reminded Brent of Kathy. A gut-churning wave of sadness washed through him. He wondered what she would think of this new café project or even of this Mumbai bar. He fought an urge to say something to Falan—something about appreciating the time they had together while they had it. Healthy young people didn't like being reminded of such things, and he was not close enough to Falan for such advice anyway.

When he turned away, he found River watching him, his eyes knowing.

"What is this?" River asked Falan, pointing to a glass jar of kombucha in a gorgeous rose color. It seemed like he was trying to give Brent some space.

"Ah, that is a very special kombucha we make only this time of year," Falan said proudly. "It is made with local cherries that are in season for a short while. We can never make enough of this one to please our customers. Every year there is a mad clamor for the stuff. I would let you taste it, but it's not ready yet. Isn't that right, Anya?"

She nodded. "No tasting for another week. It must sit."

"I bet it's delicious. I love cherries. And what a beautiful color," River commented.

Brent nodded. "Seasonal drinks are super popular at my coffee shops in Seattle too. For example, there's a drink we only do for two weeks around St. Patrick's Day. It is amazing how customers go crazy for that. They count down the days, come in every day to get some while they can." He smiled. "Absence makes the heart grow fonder, I guess."

"It's human nature. You always want something more when it's hard to get," River agreed.

He gave Brent a meaningful look, like he meant something deeper by that. And Brent felt it down to his toes. But what could he mean? Brent was certainly not hard to get. River was the one who qualified for that description. Or maybe Brent was reading way too much into it.

"Mrs. Acharya, could I ask you some questions about your mother cultures?" River asked.

Anya's eyes lit up and she readily agreed. She led River over to jars that contained big, gooey, pancake-like things, which Brent recognized from his kombucha research as SCOBYs, aka Symbiotic Cultures Of Bacteria and Yeast, sometimes called "the mother." Like beer yeast, it was the SCOBYs that fermented sweet tea and turned it into kombucha.

Brent would have liked to listen in on their conversation, but Falan asked questions about Brent's shops in Seattle, and soon they were deep into a conversation about coffee.

When the talk wound down, Brent suggested they take a photo with the four of them in front of a rack of fermenting jars. Falan called down Ahmed from the bar to take the picture so they could all be in it.

"This will be the first photo in the new café," Brent said, checking his phone to make sure it turned out.

"We are honored," Falan said. "And please to email me a copy, so I can put one up here as well. It will link us kombucha purveyors across the ocean. I trust you will stay in touch and let us know of your progress. You must be a huge success. The more kombucha in the world, the better! Maybe then, people would be nicer to one another."

"Good gut bacteria makes you a pleasant person?" River asked with a teasing smile.

"Well, the opposite is certainly true!" Falan laughed.

By the time they left, it was noon, and both the bar and the restaurant next door had filled up with young people having lunch and drinking tall glasses of "booch." Brent took that as a good sign. Not only the volume of patrons but the age. Appealing to young people was always a good sign you were on trend.

Outside on the sidewalk, the sun was hot and nearly blinding after the darker basement. Brent took in a deep lungful of air and sighed happily.

"So what did you think?" River asked, raising his eyebrows. "Was it what you expected?"

Brent clapped his hand on River's shoulder. "That was worth the trip to Mumbai all by itself. I love this place. Adore it."

River's smile was relieved. "Yeah. It's even better than I remembered. And it was such a privilege to see behind the scenes. The Acharyas are good people."

Brent nodded in agreement. "They sure are."

"So you still want to continue with the kombucha bar concept?"

Brent laughed. "Are you kidding? I've never been more excited about something, or more sure of it, in my life."

"Good."

As if on impulse, River slipped his own arm around Brent's shoulder and gave him a brief squeeze. It was unexpected. They'd just spent the past two hours being very much "Mr. McKay and Mr. Larsen, his employee." But the gesture was welcome. Very welcome.

River's expression was alight with such positivity and joy that it nearly stopped Brent's heart. Here on this Mumbai street, River was in his element, and he'd never been so beautiful or, simultaneously, elusive. As if he could blend right into the crowds here and vanish in a heartbeat.

You always want something more when it's hard to get.

Brent had a feeling he was going to learn the truth of that in a very real way—and very soon.

Chapter 18

River grabbed Brent's elbow and pulled him back as a moped roared through the narrow street, just missing him and an old lady in a sari, who vigorously yelled after the motorcyclist, shaking her fist.

Brent grimaced at River. "You take your life in your hands in this place."

"The rights of the road are sacred here." The twinkle in River's eyes confirmed he was joking.

"Maybe we'd be safer if we got around on a cow," Brent quipped.

River squeezed his arm. "Fear not, baby bird. I will protect you."

River steered them across the street—himself, Brent, and Brent's glowing heart, which warmed in idiotic fashion to River's teasing words, and to how close River was, brushing against him as they wove and jogged. Of course, River had to be close. The crush in the markets was like Coachella during the headliner act.

They found a smaller side street that was less crowded and dodged into it like racecar drivers pulling into a pit stop.

River grinned. "So a leisurely day shopping. It'll thin out in a bit. Early mornings are the busiest, I think."

"Good to know. I think I'll sleep in tomorrow."

"Easier said than done with the jet lag. I was up at five."

"Me too."

Brent imagined River in the hotel room next to his, lying awake at 5:00 a.m., rumpled and warm in bed, long hair spilling over the pillow, maybe reading on his phone. Brent had been doing the same.

Imagine how much more fun it would have been to be together.

"Were you looking for anything specific?" River asked.

"No. Just want to take it all in."

River pointed down a row of promising-looking market stalls, and they headed that way.

The Chor Bazaar district ran for blocks. There were larger streets, like the swamped PB Marg they'd just navigated, side streets, back lanes, and nooks and crannies. Some streets had long buildings with bays very much like small garage bays, only they held individual shops, their names printed at the top, their contents spilling out into the street. It was a flea-market cornucopia. Old dial telephones, plates, antique watches, brass teapots, rugs, electronics, cheap framed prints, and clothing were displayed on tables, crates, or carpets set on the brick and asphalt streets.

The local population wore a mix of Western wear and traditional Indian clothing—lots of long white coats over white pants on men and saris on women, especially the shopkeepers. The younger Indians were inevitably in jeans, T-shirts, and sneakers and drove mopeds like they were auditioning for *Mad Max*. He saw a Hard Rock Cafe Seattle T-shirt on a gorgeous young woman with long black hair. Soccer club logos were ubiquitous.

As with any US flea market, most of the items for sale didn't interest Brent. But his inner artist enjoyed the hunt for the rare golden find among the dross. They wandered for hours, Brent leading the way and River following along patiently. Brent bought a few small items he thought would be nice for the café, and some mementos for home. But mostly he soaked it in, not just the items but the people, the crowds, the *landscape*, as River would put it.

By noon, the sun was baking down on them as if they were two eggs sharing a frying pan. The streets had emptied out—the natives were not idiots with limited time and less sense, unlike Brent. Even imperturbable River had wilted. His long hair was twisted back into a loose knot, the wisps hanging limply, and his white T-shirt had a dark V at his neck and spots on his back.

They reached an intersection, where Brent started looking at some wooden chairs at the corner shop, but River stepped in front of him, arms folded across his chest.

"We should take a break to eat. This sun can make you sick if you get too much of it. We need to get out of it for awhile."

"Sorry. Yeah, let's get some food. I suppose a restaurant with AC is out of the question?"

"Such a Westerner," River tsked, shaking his head. But he did it with a smile.

River took the reins and led them through the crowds until he found a restaurant to his liking. Like the amazing one they'd eaten in the day before, this was a local family-run place. River led them inside. There was no AC, alas, but the interior was cooler and had large ceiling fans that created a light breeze.

Brent's feet ached when he sat down, reminding him that they had been standing or walking for hours. River ordered varan bhaat, a spiced lentil dish over rice, and helped Brent decide on baida roti, which River explained was something like a meat pie, with chicken and veg wrapped in a pastry envelope. There was an iced-tea drink served with heavy cream, rather like a Thai iced tea, that Brent drank greedily. The caffeine would help.

After the waiter took their order, Brent slumped back in his chair. Jet lag and the effects of the heat hit him like a truck. A sleepy-time truck. The breeze from the fans tickled his sweat-slick skin.

"So we're done with Chor Market?" River asked. His tone was hopeful, and Brent sniggered.

"You're not a big shopper, are you?"

River made a noncommittal sound. "I don't have the patience to wade through it all, not like you do. I can admire your immersion in the experience though. And you have a good eye."

"My, that's diplomatic. What can I say? I know what I like when I see it." River blinked at him, and Brent realized that sounded kind of flirty. "I mean, I recognize uniqueness and quality, that's all." Brent realized that *also* sounded flirty. But he didn't want to take it back. Not when it was true—about shopping and about River.

The waiter arrived with their food. Brent wasn't all that hungry. The sun had made him feel a little lightheaded, but he tasted his baida roti. It was good. It made a good finger food. Might be something to consider for the cafe. He took a photo of it.

"Do you do any painting or sculpture?" River asked. "You seem particularly drawn to art prints and carvings. And your sketches are really good."

Warmth spread in Brent's chest at the compliment. "Uh... I did watercolors when I was younger, but I haven't for years. The stores were my creative outlet. And the houses we owned. We flipped five of them. I like interior design, but I'd never want to do it for anyone else. I'm too selfish. When I have a vision for something, I don't want to have to stray from it to please anyone else."

God, that made him sound like an ass. Brent rephrased. "What I mean is, if I'm working with a partner, and we share a vision, that's different. That's not like compromising. That's like...." He struggled to find the right word.

"Harmonizing," River supplied.

Brent smiled. "That's it. Harmonizing. I like working with someone like that. But I wouldn't want to work for a client, having to implement *their* vision. God. Never mind. I sound like an asshole. I'm not trying to say my vision is superior."

"Brent." River's tone was serious. "People assume because I take my spiritual path seriously that I'm Gandhi or something. Believe me, I'm not. I have negative thoughts and do stupid things, just like everyone else. I'm not going to judge you."

Brent swallowed. "You just seem so ..."

River cocked an eyebrow. "Oh, do go on."

Brent laughed. "So together, I guess. Like you never get angry or frustrated, you'd never say something cruel because you're tired or impatient. You're not selfish."

River seemed to consider this as he drank some of his iced tea. "I get angry and frustrated. Get my feelings hurt. Feel too much pride. Impatience. Want things that I shouldn't. I try to recognize my emotions from the outside rather than dwelling *in* them. But sometimes that's easier said than done. Meditation helps."

He put an arm over the back of his chair, turning to face Brent a little more. "As for not being selfish, some might say following a spiritual path is the most selfish thing you can do. I go where I feel I need to go, when I need to go there. I do whatever I need to do whether that's taking a new class or joining an ashram or... or working as a tantric healer. It can be lonely, you know? Because chances are, no one else is on the exact same journey as you."

Yes. That did sound sad to Brent. Did River ever let anyone close? For how long?

Brent wiped his mouth with a napkin. "That reminds me of an interview I read once. This guy was the first person ever to walk both the Appalachian Trail and the Pacific Crest Trail in the same year. Crazy, right? That's almost five thousand miles. Do you know what he said was the hardest part? Not the sore muscles. Not roughing it. Not bad weather. He said the hardest thing was the loneliness. He couldn't walk with anyone else, because no one could keep up with his pace.

"It made me wonder. So he set this record, which was great. But maybe, in that year of his life, which will never come again, he might have been happier forgetting about the record and just walking with someone he loved."

River gave him a funny look. "You're an enigma, Brent McKay."

Brent huffed. "I'm really not. I'm pretty basic."

"You project that on the outside. But you're not actually basic at all."

Brent met River's gaze and held. He stared into those beautiful stormy blue eyes long enough to recall their tantric sessions, long enough for his appetite to vanish completely and his pulse to flutter.

Jesus. This feeling, this connection between them.... It couldn't only be there on his side, surely.

The waiter came to refill their iced tea.

"What you said about harmonizing. I like that. Our kombucha cafe is sort of a harmony. A combination. Global food but grounded in Seattle. Healthy but also comfort food." Brent hesitated. "You and me."

River tilted his head. "Harmony. Harmony Cafe."

Delight sparked in Brent. "I love it. Might be too common though." He picked up his phone and googled. "Yeah. There are quite a few 'Harmony Cafes.'"

River looked disappointed. "Harmony... something. Harmony Moon?"

Brent's eyes flickered to a mural of a tree painted on the restaurant's wall. It was an amateur effort, with clunky green leaves and stick-figure birds. But he could imagine such a mural done in a modern, elegant style. "Harmony Tree. Harmony Tree Cafe."

River's face lit up. "Brent, that's perfect! The tree is a symbol of spirituality, with all its roots and branches, the way it offers shelter and provides a home for so many creatures. It even produces oxygen, the breath of life."

Brent felt a surge of rightness so strong it was almost too big to contain. "Christ. That's it. And what you just said... you just wrote our About page too."

They smiled at each other until it got a bit creepy. Brent picked up his phone again and fired off an email to his lawyer asking him to do a legal search on the name and file paperwork if it was available

River sat up straighter. "So we're done shopping, right? We could go to the harbor and find a spot in the shade."

Brent laughed. "Wow, you're *really* not a fan of shopping. Kathy wasn't either. When I went antiquing in Snohomish, she'd hang out in a little bookstore and read."

It felt good to mention her, as if Brent was showing himself, and her, that he hadn't forgotten. But it also hurt, to think about how he'd once taken for granted that Kathy was just down the street, waiting for him at a coffee shop. As if she'd always be there.

Now he was losing his mind over a beautiful young man. Christ.

River reached across the table and squeezed Brent's arm. "You're right about me and shopping. I would absolutely have been hanging out in that bookstore with Kathy."

"Yeah," Brent said, his voice rough. "You would have been."

He could picture it. Kathy and River sitting in adjacent overstuffed chairs in that little bookshop in Snohomish, reading. In this vision, rain pelted against the bookshop window—as it often did in Snohomish, but the two of them were cozy inside. The scene was oddly comforting.

"Yup. And we would have been gossiping about you, of course."

"I'm sure. Allllll my deep dark secrets."

"I would love to hear those," River said, his eyes warm. "They'd give me some leverage."

"You already have leverage," Brent pointed out—referring, of course, to their tantric sessions.

River raised one eyebrow. "I guess I do. Too bad I'd never use it. Anyway. We're sort of flying through our agenda. We've a list of restaurants to hit, but we've got plenty of time left. I can dig it."

"Good. That means we'll have lots of time to sightsee."

River licked his lips. "You wouldn't want to go home early?"

"Hell no! I plan to make the most of this trip. See everything. Do everything. I won't get this chance again."

And weirdly, that felt like flirting too. But if River caught that vibe, he didn't show it. He simply signaled for the check.

Chapter 19

River

On their fourth day in Mumbai, they took a break from restaurant hopping and toured the local temples. The Sri Sri Radha Gopinath Temple had fantastic paintings of the Krishna and Radha saga as well as a garden on the grounds and numerous animals that were protected within its walls. The Swaminarayan Temple, dedicated to Lord Krishna, had impressive architecture with a many-domed roof. The Mumba Devi temple, the oldest in the city, had a thick vibe of sacredness about it. It was dedicated to the goddess Mumba, with her black hair and orange face.

Although it was a sightseeing excursion, River spent some time in prayer and meditation at the Mumba Devi temple, while Brent walked around at a leisurely pace, taking everything in. After a while, Brent knelt next to River at the railing.

"Is there a specific deity you believe in?" Brent asked. "I mean, that statue—"

"Goddess Mumba."

"Right. I never heard of her before. Is that who you worshipped at the ashram?"

Brent was being very careful, his tone respectful. But the idea that he might think River worshipped an ancient goddess statue with an orange face made River smile. "No, Brent. I don't worship any specific deity. I believe in a divine force, but it's more an all-encompassing energy."

Brent looked thoughtful. "Cool. I guess that's more or less my idea of God too."

"You have an idea of God?" River feigned innocent surprise.

Brent narrowed his eyes. "Are you calling me a heathen?"

"Sorry. Just teasing you."

The more comfortable River got with Brent, the more his acerbic sense of humor made itself known. Fortunately, Brent didn't seem to mind.

He nudged River with his arm. "You wound me. Seriously, though, Hinduism does worship specific gods, right? Even Buddhism."

"Well, some Buddhist sects do worship Buddha as a god. But others see him as an enlightened teacher."

They got up and started strolling out of the temple. River went on. "I think most people need to have something specific they can visualize and pray to, to give God a face and a name. But usually a specific deity just represents one aspect or interpretation of the universal God."

"Like the blind men and the elephant," Brent said.

They stepped out into the bright Indian sun. River looked at Brent quizzically.

"Dr. Halloran reminded me of that old parable. You know, the one where a group of blind men try to figure out what an elephant is by touching it, but since one feels the ear, one the trunk, one the side, and so on, they all reach different opinions about what an elephant is."

River nodded. "That's a great analogy. Sometimes I think a deity says more about the worshipper than God. For example, there's a whole tradition in Hinduism that worships Bala Krishna, basically Krishna when he was a baby. In that tradition, the worshipper is like the mother, and they see God as an infant they love and protect. So you could say those worshippers are most able to access their spiritual side through their mothering instincts."

"Even for men?"

"Sure. We all have *yin* and *yang* aspects inside us."

The temple was in the middle of the city, and the streets were busy. They took a seat to the side of the temple steps to stay out of the fray. There was no rush to get anywhere and that was lovely in itself.

"So who do you pray to when you pray? Or meditate." Brent grimaced. "You must get sick of me hammering you with questions."

"Not at all. Your curiosity is beautiful." River had an urge to kiss Brent's cheek, so he did.

Brent's cheeks went a mottled pink. "Um. T-thanks. It's just— I was raised agnostic, so all of this is new to me and really fascinating. You *make* it fascinating." He looked out over the scenery. "There have been times where I believed in God, in some kind of higher power, and I thought of it like you said, as more of an energy or grand design or something."

River nodded.

"I guess I lost even that much faith after Kathy got sick. It's hard to believe there's a purpose to things. To suffering." He hesitated. "I wish I could believe we don't just disappear. At the end."

His expression grew tense and haunted. Brent had never shared any details about his wife's illness, but River had the impression it had been terrible.

"I absolutely believe there's a part of us, our soul, that survives death."

Brent looked at him sharply, gazing into River's eyes with a slight frown, as if wanting to see if River meant it. "But how do you know? It's hard to believe without proof, and that's impossible."

River smiled.

"What?" Brent asked.

"I just figured out where we're going after lunch."

The University of Mumbai was a beautiful place to walk. It was particularly lush, with palm trees and vast green lawns. The magnificent stone buildings had traditional Western elements, like archways and the rose window on the chapel, that made you feel you were at an Ivy League school—someplace like Harvard or Princeton. But then you'd encounter a twisted tower or dome that was very much Indian.

River led Brent into the Jehangier building and down several flights of stairs from the ground level. He'd visited this place when he'd previously been in Mumbai, and he hoped it was still there.

It was. One or more passionate professors had set up a small museum of reincarnation. It was currently empty except for a young woman, obviously a student, who sat at a small desk inside the door.

She greeted them in English, had them sign a guest ledger, and invited them to look around.

The entire museum was housed in just one large basement room, but there were at least a hundred displays, each one a case study. Most had a text plaque in several languages, photographs, signed affidavits, even some with physical mementos.

Brent looked at River with both eyebrows raised. "Really?"

River gave him a *well you asked* smile. "You have questions. Maybe this room has answers. Maybe not. That's for you to decide."

The most famous and well-documented cases of reincarnation in India were examined here. Hindu scholars had taken the concept seriously for thousands of years and had applied as much scientific method to the topic as they could. There were incidents of young children who remembered the names of their previous families or villages, and researchers had tracked them down, testing if the child recognized relatives or had memories that those in their past life could verify. There were cases of unusual birthmarks that coincided with wounds from previous lifetimes, the ability to speak dialects the children had never been taught, or irrational phobias that could be traced back to previous lives or traumatic deaths.

One case, that of Shanti Devi, had even been investigated by Mahatma Gandhi himself and proclaimed to be genuine.

River knew there were cases in the US as well, but because reincarnation wasn't a mainstream belief there, they typically weren't investigated as rigorously.

Brent went from display to display. The room seemed to beg for silence, like a library or a shrine, so they didn't talk until they left an hour or so later.

They walked across campus under the shade of palm trees, enjoying a light breeze. Finally, Brent spoke. "Thank you for showing me that. I had no idea reincarnation was such a well-documented phenomena."

"It's a big part of the culture here. The idea of karma, for instance, that what we do in this life will be rewarded or punished in our future lives."

"Do you believe it?" Brent stopped at a short stone wall in the shade and sat down.

River sat next to him. "I do, yeah. What do you think? Reincarnation…?" He held his thumb up, then down, making an exaggerated questioning expression.

Brent smiled. He tilted his head and looked up at the palm fronds. "The evidence in there was pretty convincing. I want to believe."

"Well you're in luck, because belief is a choice. That's why they call it a leap of faith."

Brent turned his head sharply to look at River with surprise. At first, River thought he was going to ask why River didn't think faith was an absolute. But then Brent chuckled. "Huh. I never thought of it that way. It sounds a lot like marriage."

"Does it? I wouldn't know."

"Mmm. If reincarnation is real, I have a feeling I lived in India once. I feel… I dunno. It feels familiar to me here. Like part of me is home. And I'm so interested in tantra and chakras and doshas and all of that. But maybe that's just because you make it interesting."

"Me?"

Brent visibly swallowed. "You explain things in a way that I just get. And you kind of… radiate a confidence and goodness that I envy. It's like that line from *When Harry Met Sally*—I'll have what you're having."

Heat bloomed in River's heart chakra. "That's the nicest thing anyone has ever said to me. Thanks, Brent."

Brent smiled shyly and looked away.

They sat there for a while. Students moved around the campus, mostly young Indians in jeans and T-shirts and hoodies. A guy rode by on a bike wearing neon green Nikes.

East meets West. Like him. Maybe like Brent too. It was curious that Brent said he might have had a past life here. Shri Agontha at the ashram had said much the same to River when they met, that he was Western now, but his soul was Indian.

Perhaps he and Brent had known each other then. Brent had come into his life for a reason, River was certain of that. Maybe he owed Brent some karmic debt. Maybe they'd even been lovers once.

They'd had an unusual connection from the start. And now that they were here, in India, it felt deeper, truer, than any connection River had felt in a long time. Maybe ever. He had no idea what to do with that. Except try to enjoy it for what it was and not ask for more.

Chapter 20

Brent

Sanjay Gandhi National Park was on the northern outskirts of Mumbai. They spent their fifth day there, wanting a respite from the crowds.

They visited the Gandhi memorial and took the big-cat tram tour where they saw lions, leopards, jaguars, and monkeys. After lunch at the park cafe, they set out to hike the Upper Kanheri Trail.

The path wandered uphill through a lush green forest. There'd been rain that morning while they were on the tram, and the damp green of the woods was practically effervescent. Brent enjoyed the chance to stretch his legs on the trail, and he and River kept up a fast pace.

River wore a navy hooded rain jacket that had probably been around the world and back again. His hair was up in a careless knot in that completely unselfconscious way of his that only someone as good-looking as River could get away with. His eyes shone with the joy of being here–in India, in this gorgeous park–as if it made him come alive to the next level. His smile was constant.

And Brent was really, most certainly, in trouble.

The trail opened onto a broad plateau where a stone cliff held the Kanheri caves. They were impressive–one large temple-like structure with columns, and dozens of other cave rooms along the cliff wall, from vast to teeny-tiny.

"These were Buddhist caves," River explained, as they explored the small rooms along one long ledge. "They were built starting in the first century BC. This place was occupied for a thousand years. These little rooms were monks' cells, and the bigger ones were used for cooking, worship, or study."

"Not exactly cozy," Brent commented, peeking in a small rock cave that he'd have to stoop to walk into. He could only sleep in there sitting up.

River's eyes twinkled. "Asceticism was a thing. Also, not sure very many places were comfortable back then. Unless you were a king."

"True."

Brent tried to imagine that life as they explored the caves. Dozens of men living together in these stone surroundings, dedicating their lives to philosophy and worship. It seemed sad to him; kind of a waste. Not that contemplating higher things wasn't important, but what could we truly know, in the end?

Of course, he hadn't always lived his own life to the fullest, but at least he'd....

Enjoyed it?

Yeah, not always. But he was determined to enjoy it now. Just being here, on this day, seeing a place so unique and beautiful, in the company of the beautiful and gentle River Larsen, was a hell of a good start.

He wanted more days like this. A lot more. The thought was a stone on his chest.

They found a viewpoint a short distance from the caves, out of the other visitors' way. They sat on a rock and unpacked the snacks they'd bought. River had had the foresight to pick up some bottled water and munchies from vendors at the train station.

They chatted about the park and about other hikes River had done in India. By the time they were putting their trash in the backpack, Brent was relaxed and warm and felt an itch to get more personal. To at least try.

"How did you get involved in tantra? And how'd you end up living on an ashram in India?"

River sat back on his elbows on the rock and crossed his long legs in front of him at the ankles. Brent tried, and failed, not to find that pose incredibly attractive. River's T-shirt stretched tight across the shoulders and outlined his pecs. Even his nipples were visible.

"Hum. Do you want the short version or the long one?" River asked.

"I'm not in any hurry."

"I grew up in that life. My mom is a total free spirit. I was raised on a Buddhist commune in Southern California."

"Oh. Interesting. Is that where you made kombucha in school?"

"It was."

"What was that like? Growing up on a commune?"

"It was great. We kids just ran free. If you were tired, you could go into any cabin and lie down. Or if you were hungry or hurt and couldn't find your mother, another adult would get you something to eat or patch up your cut or whatever." River slapped at a fly on his leg.

His tone was fond, but it didn't sound so great to Brent. His mom and dad had been amazing parents, taking he and his younger brother, Seth, on camping trips and hiking in the Olympics, to the science museum, and up to Canada. His mom especially had always been there for him—made his lunch every day, took care of him when he was sick. An image came into his mind of a five-year-old River wailing for his mother in a hot, sunny, dusty common area, his skinned knee bleeding, and eventually some other woman coming over to patch him up.

"But sometimes a kid really wants his mom, no?" Brent asked carefully.

River got a tiny frown between his brows, his gaze distant. "I guess that's part of what you learn growing up on a commune. Not to get too attached to a specific person." He shrugged. "There was always someone around if you needed them."

Brent didn't think that sounded so great either. But what did he know? Maybe he just didn't get it. "And you went to school there, on the commune?"

"Yup. There was a classroom building, but usually we held classes outside. There was a lot of what you might call nontraditional stuff taught. Nature and spirituality. Gardening. Cooking." River hesitated. "My dad, though, he was worried that the commune school wasn't good enough to get me into college. So he convinced me to go live with him for high school. He lived in Pasadena. My mom and dad

separated when I was just a few years old." He laughed. "My dad...
he's a lawyer. Definitely not the commune type."

"Are you an only child?"

River turned his head to look at Brent for a moment, his
expression amused, as if Brent's questions were quaint. "I'm an only
child, yes. My parents were never legally married. My mom... like I
said, free spirit. Free love. She calls herself a perpetual wild child. A
dandelion puff floating on the breeze. She's not one to ever settle
down."

"Oh."

"I'm the only kid for both my parents. Maybe I broke them." He
chuckled, but it sounded a little hollow.

"Well. You would be a tough act to follow," Brent teased. "So you
left the commune and went to live with your dad when you went
into high school? Were you upset about that?"

"Just the opposite. I was really excited about it. I had a
romanticized idea of what *normal* life was like. You know. The white
picket fence, casseroles in the oven, a dog, all of that. Of course, it
wasn't like that at all, in reality."

Brent thought about that for a bit as they watched birds wheeling
in the sky. Apparently, ninth-grade River wasn't as enamored with
commune life as he let on. "Did you not get along with your dad
when you went to live with him?"

River chewed his lip thoughtfully. "When I think about it now, I
realize how strange it must have been for him, taking in a teenager
with long hair and ratty clothes who was used to absolute freedom.
He and my stepmom were both workaholics and weren't used to
having a kid around. I wasn't used to a regular school and a lot of
rules. We all had to adjust. And then I was gay on top of it–just
another way my dad couldn't understand me." He picked up some
pebbles and tossed them from hand to hand. "I lived with him until I
graduated high school, but we were never super close."

"Are you still in contact with him?"

River gave him a funny look. "Of course. He's my father. What
about your family?"

"Me? My parents are great. They live in Bellevue, so we see each other often. My younger brother married a pretty Canuck and moved to Vancouver, but we all get together for holidays." He hesitated. "That must seem boring to you. Living in one place your entire life."

"Depends on what you do there," River said with an eyebrow waggle. "I mean, if you're building a coffee empire...."

Brent laughed. "Oh, yes, that's the height of adventure. Definitely equivalent to living on an ashram in India."

"Eh. Like I said, I grew up in that life, so it wasn't that exotic to me. I'd always wanted to visit India, and I was really interested in learning tantra. So I looked for a place where I could study."

"Why tantra? Sorry, I don't mean to interrogate you. See, this is what you get when you say you like my curiosity. You fed the beast, and now you must pay."

River shifted to lie down on the rock on his side, head propped up on his elbow. His expression was soft and amused. "Ask anything you want. Only be warned that turnabout is fair play."

"Fair enough." Brent lay down on his side, head on his hand, mirroring River's pose. There was maybe two feet between them.

River was such a beautiful man. And yes, Brent was attracted to him, full stop. River had the ability to make Brent stupid, to make his blood run hot then cold, to create emotional shivers, to turn his tongue to wood and make him stutter. He hadn't been attracted to anyone like that in a long time. And River was a guy.

Fair enough.

"I studied Eastern Religions in college," River said. "But what I was really interested in was alternative medicine. After I graduated, I studied reiki and got my license as a reiki practitioner. Then I got a regular massage license so I could offer that. Then I discovered tantra. I loved it—the idea of connecting with others on a deeper level, physical and spiritual. After studying it in the States for a year, just casually, I learned about the ashram and decided to move there to immerse myself in it and get certified as a tantrik."

"You just picked up and moved from Southern California to India. Without knowing anyone there?"

"Sure. Why not? I was mostly house-sitting anyway, so I didn't have a permanent place I had to sell. No stuff I couldn't easily give away."

And no one you couldn't easily say goodbye to, Brent thought. And that made him feel a stab of pity. But again, River's life wasn't his. He was in no place to judge. Look at all the exciting things River had done.

"So you have a degree in Eastern Religions, and you're a licensed reiki energy person—"

"Practitioner. Or healer."

"Right. Plus you're a licensed massage therapist."

"Yup. From a school in San Diego."

"And you're a certified teacher of tantra."

River nodded. "Yup. I like to learn. And I like knowing that, no matter where I end up, I'll have a skill I can use. Plus, the disciplines overlap. Knowing how to manipulate reiki energy helps me be a better massage therapist and tantrik. And vice versa."

Brent shook his head in wonder. "And yet you got a job at AJC as a barista... why?"

River managed to blush and go pale at the same time, his throat and face getting blotchy. Brent must have hit a nerve, and he felt like absolute shit. "Sorry. That was a stupid thing to say. I'm so glad you started at AJC. It doesn't matter why."

"No. It's just that...." River blew out a breath. "It takes time to build up a clientele for massage or reiki—word of mouth, putting out flyers, all of that. When I got to Seattle, I got the job with Expanded Horizons to do tantra work, but I haven't been as busy with that as I'd hoped. And then it was sort of too late to try to build up a private practice when I wasn't going to be there for long. I can pick up a barista or waiter job quick, make some easy money, and disappear when I need to."

Disappear. Is that the way it would be? One day, River would just be gone. The thought upset Brent more than it had any right to. He sat up, forearms on his bent knees and looked back over the view. Down below, endless palm trees floated in a green canopy.

River reached out with his foot and kicked Brent's running shoes with his own worn sneaker. "Turnabout's fair play. What about you? How'd you end up being the coffee king?"

Brent forced a smile. "Coffee king? Can't claim that title when I live in the town where Starbucks was founded. But, uh, my grandfather was a real estate guy. When he passed, he left my brother and I each a hundred grand. To get started in business, he said. Kathy and I were young, but we took it seriously. We bought a little coffee shop in Pioneer Square that had decor and a menu from the fifties and remodeled it. It took off."

"You and Kathy worked together?"

"Oh hell yeah. We were partners in McKay Enterprises. She had the head for business, finances, and I was the creative one. I got the big ideas and she'd crunch the numbers, make sure it was practical, keep my feet on the ground. Everyone always assumed it should be the other way around, but nope."

River sat up too and must have scooted closer, because their elbows nearly touched as he matched Brent's pose. He studied Brent with a thoughtful expression. "Did that bother you? That people thought you and Kathy had the traditional roles reversed?"

"No. It worked. Why should it bother me what people think?"

"It would bother some men. People get hung up on trying to live up to society's expectations. Especially men. When a lot of times, those expectations are nothing but a prison of the mind."

"I don't give a shit about expectations." Brent spoke with conviction, hoping River understood what he was really saying. "I don't care what people *think* I should do or be. When you've seen what I've seen—" He swallowed down a stab of pain. "When you have been around death, you know the value of life. Health. Happiness." He looked out over the view again. "Of a moment like this."

With you, he wanted to add. Only that wasn't exactly a subtle lead-in.

Brent sat there, trying to figure out how to say what he wanted to say. Why not bring it up now? This was as good a time as any. But icy dread flooded his gut. It had been so long since he'd put himself out there, risked rejection. God, he was a complete newbie at this sort of thing.

Dating, that is.

If nothing else, this trip had given him clarity. He'd been drawn to River from the start. But a dozen reasons why it would never work, or was a bad idea—their working relationship, his own insecurities and confusion, even guilt over caring about someone new after Kathy—had pushed that attraction away like an unwanted houseguest.

But being with River here in India, walking with him in the sunshine, seeing the way River moved so easily through the world, being so close to his beauty, his joyous smiles, his easy temperament day upon long day—God, now Brent was practically writing sonnets!—but it was true. River was a dream to travel with. Honestly, Kathy had been an uptight and nervous traveler, and that had made Brent tense. But River made every moment a pleasure. And he was so naturally thoughtful and protective, always looking out for Brent in this place where he was a bit lost, the same way he'd guided Brent through their tantra sessions....

Why was that so deeply appealing? Brent was no child. Hell, he was the older one, the boss. He should be in charge. Yet he couldn't deny how much he liked it when River calmly took the wheel. If he were pushy or dominating, Brent would have been out of there. But having someone steady and strong to lean on? It was nice. Better than nice. It was heaven.

Kathy had been strong too. He'd always called her "his rock." There was nothing wrong with liking a strong partner.

Partner? Getting ahead of yourself a bit?

Okay, yes, he was getting ahead of himself. But the point was, all the *yes's* when it came to his feelings about River had grown louder, more solid, more real, until the *no's* had become unimportant. And Brent was a grown-ass man of thirty-nine. He could do this. He could express an attraction. Millions of people did it every day.

Oh God.

River made a thoughtful noise. "That's a great description of 'being in the now.'"

"What?"

"What you just said, about how you know the value of life, the value of a moment like this. That's 'being in the now.' You're pretty enlightened for a businessman."

River's tone was teasing, but Brent felt pleased nonetheless.

River hopped to his feet and held out a hand. "Let's start down. I feel like walking."

"Uh... okay."

Another moment to say something was gone. But maybe confessing his interest in the middle of a hike wasn't the best idea. There was no place for either of them to escape to if it all went to shit.

He grasped River's hand and let himself be pulled to his feet. River's hand was warm and firm, and it brought up a visceral physical memory of what those hands felt like on his body. Brent shivered, an involuntary spasm that ran through him head to toe.

River frowned. "Are you cold?"

"N-no."

River gave him a confused little smile and headed for the trail.

Chapter 21

On their way back to the hotel, they grabbed another incredible meal at a small Chinese restaurant that was on their list. Brent was quiet over dinner, trying to focus on analyzing the food, but really figuring out what he wanted to say. He had a surge of cold feet about saying anything at all. He should just leave well enough alone—remain River's boss, maybe his friend. Done.

That lasted about five minutes, until River sucked some sauce off his thumb and gave Brent a look while doing it that might have meant nothing—but could also have been flirtatious? It caused Brent's palms to sweat and arousal to flood hot in his veins, combusting his cold feet in a *whoosh*.

Shit. What had Brent just been thinking about, truly living his life and not sitting it out any longer? He had to say something. The chance to be with River was worth it. It was worth anything.

They strolled back to the hotel, still quiet. Then they were on their floor, and Brent's heart lodged in his throat as they stopped at the door to River's room.

"Good night," River said, taking out his key card.

"Wait."

River stopped, card in hand, and looked at Brent, his expression unreadable. *Oh God.*

Brent felt like he was standing on a diving board over the deep end. He was scared. Scared of diving in headfirst. Scared of retreating. But if he was ever going to do this, it had to be here. In Seattle, they were more clearly boss and employee. And his house held memories of being client and surrogate, and of Kathy too. In India, they had stepped outside all of that for a few rare days. Here, they were just Brent and River.

"Brent?" River asked. "What is it? You have your contemplative look."

That made Brent smile. "You know my looks?"

River just gazed at him fondly and raised one eyebrow.

"Okay. So the thing is..." He took a huge breath and dove. "The thing, actually, is that... I like you."

River's expression turned serious. He studied Brent's face and said nothing.

Okay. That was not the reaction Brent had hoped for. But he was over open water now. He had to carry through.

"I mean, I'm attracted to you," Brent clarified, feeling his cheeks grow hot. "I was hoping you might be attracted to me too. That you might want... more."

River continued to simply stare at him. Shit. Oh. Ugh. This was bad. He'd misread this, hadn't he?

River cleared his throat. "Are you telling me you want another massage? Right now?"

His words were very slow and careful, very neutral. Even so, Brent knew what River was asking, and he felt a spark of shame. "No! No. I'm not asking for you to– No." He sighed in frustration. "I want... what I really want is to kiss you. Just... hold you."

Oh, man, that sounded lame. Like they were in elementary school. But Brent didn't know how else to say it. He could go on–*kiss you, hold you, take your hand, look at you over a candlelit dinner, walk with you in fields of flowers.* It sounded ridiculous.

River turned his back and slid the card through the card reader. Brent's throat stung as disappointment crashed through him. He started to apologize. But then the door was open, and River took his hand and led him into the room.

*   *   *

River

River let the door swing shut, then backed Brent up against it. He'd left a bedside lamp on, and the soft light played over Brent's features. His eyes were worried and wanting. He was tense, as if ready to flee. He was *shaking.*

And River just wanted to take care of him.

He cupped Brent's face, thumbs caressing his cheekbones. He gazed into those nervous green eyes. "You want to be with me? As a lover?"

Brent nodded energetically, but he didn't speak. Maybe he couldn't speak. His eyes said *yes* and *please* and held a depth of desire River wasn't sure had ever been directed his way.

That gave him pause. This had potential for heartbreak. They were playing with fire and, very probably, with Brent's heart. Still, the moment felt inevitable, as though their lives were two meteors moving through space, their arcs on a collision course, despite the two of them being from entirely different galaxies.

Hadn't Brent been different from the start? Like visiting a home River was sure he'd lived in before, only he couldn't quite remember when.

And, selfishly, River simply wanted him. He'd been half-aroused all day. The pull he felt toward Brent had grown undeniable. Despite their being so different on the surface, the material things that ultimately didn't matter, and the life trajectories, which mattered very much, their energy simply worked together, the *yin* and *yang* of them.

River had tried to allow himself to feel that attraction, to enjoy Brent's company, without becoming attached to the idea that *they* had to happen, that he needed to make it to happen. But now that the moment was here, a warm joy spread through him, and it felt just that—inescapable. He was already falling from the plane. He couldn't stop it if he tried.

And, God. He didn't want to.

He traced down Brent's cheeks with his thumbs and caressed the corners of his lips. He let that joy pass through his gaze, feeling the energy that was always there between them build and grow hot. Brent relaxed against the wall, his eyes softening, his will melting to River's. His breathing grew deep.

"This isn't about just getting off for me," River told him. "I want to be intimate with you."

"Okay." Brent's voice was raspy. "Yes. Whatever you want. I just want to be with you."

So River kissed him. Slowly he explored, pressing his mouth to Brent's again and again, soft and sensual, learning the texture of Brent's lips under his. He closed his eyes and felt the moment, the moment Brent McKay became his lover.

The stars realigned and the Earth stopped its spinning. At least, in River's universe, they did. Something new was born.

Brent moaned, a simple sound that sent a rush of liquid desire through River, pulsing and pooling low in his belly, expanding his *Svadhishthana* chakra and engorging his penis. Brent's hands came up to hold his waist and then moved up his sides. The touch left tingles in its wake, but the shirt between them was an irritant. River wanted to feel Brent's hands on his skin. He broke the kiss so he could pull his shirt over his head and drop it to the floor.

Brent watched him. A deep flush crawled down his neck and disappeared into his button-down shirt. He was breathing hard, his eyes roaming over River's bare chest and shoulders. Then he blinked, as if realizing he should be doing something. He straightened from the wall and started working on the buttons of his shirt, fingers clumsy and trembling.

River used the moment to center himself. How were they going to do this? He couldn't go back to the way sex had been before tantra, getting naked and a quick suck, fuck, or hand job until they both came. Intimacy meant more to him now. He craved a deeper connection.

At the ashram, tantric sex had been long and ritualized, with both parties practitioners who used desire and touch to build up energy. But Brent had only ever been on the receiving end of that, he wasn't ready for full tantric sex. And now was not the time for lessons, or for any words at all.

River would just have to play it by ear and do what felt right.

His shirt now off, Brent looked up, biting his lower lip. He reached out and traced a finger down the center of River's chest, down to the start of his fuzzy happy trail. "I haven't been with anyone except Kathy since I was eighteen years old. And never with a man. So I apologize in advance if our first time isn't great."

Our first time. The words reassured a last tendril of doubt in River's mind and warmth bloomed in his heart. "How about we strip down to our underwear, get on the bed, and just explore?"

As if the words were a key that unlocked the next step, the uncertainty evaporated and the heat of anticipation returned, sparking from Brent's eyes directly to River's belly. They removed the rest of their clothing unhurriedly, watching each other with soft smiles. Brent's underwear showed the tenting of a full-blown erection, and River's groin ached.

He sat on the bed, cross-legged. Brent joined him, mirroring his pose, their knees touching. If this were a tantric session, they would begin with deep breathing and gazing into one another's eyes to initiate a connection. But it felt like they were already past that, already so aware of each other it hurt.

So River cupped the back of Brent's neck and leaned forward to kiss him.

This time, the kiss was passionate. Lips parted and mouths sucked greedily. Brent's hands settled on River's bare thighs where they sent heat and electricity into his groin. He was already hard, but the waves created a steady pulse of want there. He pushed the sexual energy up his spine and it radiated out through his entire body, giving him a natural high and feeding back into his lover. Brent made sounds deep in his throat, became more and more pliant under River's hands as he went into a deeper state of consciousness.

As before, it was the *yin* energy, the feminine, that rose in Brent, the *pull* force that called out to River to *push*. His dominant side came forward, heady and strong.

He guided Brent down onto his back and lay over him, breaking the hypnotizing kiss. River stayed propped up on his hands, elbows straight, gazing down at Brent. Like this, his hips on top of Brent's,

Brent's erection throbbed against his own through their underwear. River had to stop himself from rutting against it.

He wanted a moment to look into those green eyes. He was already breathing hard and it felt natural to go into tantric breath, letting everything he felt radiate throughout his body. Brent's pupils were huge and his face and chest rosy with desire. He looked drunk with it. He looked ten years younger.

His hands slid up River's sides, then tugged gently in invitation. *Lay on me.* But River stayed where he was, holding that gaze.

Brent swallowed. "I don't even know what this is. What I feel with you," Brent whispered. "It's like... like..."

"Intoxicating," River supplied.

"Yes. Is that you? I mean..." Brent licked his lips. "Do you have this kind of chemistry with everyone? Is it a tantric thing?"

River shook his head slowly. He wanted to say, *It's never been as strong with anyone as it is with you.* But that seemed too much, revealed too much, promised too much. "You and I—we sync together very well."

Brent's smile was blinding, so proud and pleased. But it was only momentary before his expression grew lax with desire again as he moved his hands over River's chest, fingers gliding over his nipples.

River took a deep breath at the surge of pleasure, let it out.

Encouraged, Brent's hands skated down River's belly to where their hips were flush. River's hips were a little higher up than Brent's, and the tip of his cock peeked above his underwear.

Brent gave a low moan when he saw it. His fingers went to it, brushing across the slit lightly, finding stickiness there. Another shaky breath and his hips pushed up, needy. "*Please*, River."

A fresh, hot wave of sexual energy went through River, and he let it take him, lowering onto Brent fully, reclaiming his mouth hungrily, and grinding down his hips. He rode the wave, setting up a rhythm that sent pleasure spiraling tighter and tighter, then stopping when Brent's thighs began to tremble and he got close, or when River himself needed a moment to pause and push the energy up his spine, away from imminent orgasm. The pleasure was intense, hot and sweet and rich. River filled up to the brim with it.

After a long while, he rolled them onto their sides so he wasn't crushing Brent any longer. Brent's face ended up in River's neck. His ragged breathing caused goosebumps to break out.

"Jesus. You really know how to torture a guy."

River smiled and ran soothing hands up and down Brent's back. "You okay?"

"Huh? Yeah, fantastic. I just... I want... Can I touch you?"

"I would love it if you touched me."

As if shy, Brent kept his face in River's neck as one hand crept down. It slipped under his waistband and circled his cock, squeezed.

River let out a long breath, surprised at the swift rush of pleasure that almost made him come. He breathed deeply, eyes closed, as Brent experimented, running his palm down to cup River's balls, then sliding up his shaft. He made a twisting motion up and around, a move River had used on him during the *lingam* massage, rubbed his thumb over the frenulum.

River took another deep breath, let it out. "That feels so good."

"I've never done this." Brent's tone was apologetic. "Well, not to someone else."

"You're a natural. But, just to let you know, I don't want to come."

Brent pumped him lightly. "You... really?"

River sucked in a breath as Brent squeezed his head and chuckled. "In tantra, the goal is not to have an orgasm. It's to build sexual energy and spread it to the higher chakras. When I get close, I prefer to take that explosion that would normally occur *outward* and turn it inward. It's an amazing sensation, a total buzz. And it leaves you feeling energized instead of tired. I can teach you, if you want. But not tonight. Or not at all, if you prefer. It's fine if you want to come."

Brent squeezed him again and then cupped his balls, running a thumb over them as if memorizing the texture.

"It feels so sexy to touch you like this. I wanted to before... during that last session we had. I've never had that urge with a guy. I'm not sure I know myself anymore. But I do know you're the sexiest thing

I can imagine. All of you. Especially this." He laughed a little, even as his hand worked River so sweetly he couldn't help but press into it with his hips.

"Mmm. Just let yourself feel what you feel. Don't try to define it."

Brent raised his head to peer into River's eyes. "I'd like to try to do that... get you to that point where you're close. Should I just use my hand, or–?"

River pulled down a pillow. It was a long one and he moved it under both of their heads. Then, lying facing one another, and staring into each other's eyes, River placed his hand over Brent's and showed him the rhythm that would take him to the point of orgasm.

He let go and moved his hand up to Brent's shoulder as Brent continued to pleasure him. He traced the line of Brent's jaw as the energy coiled tighter in his belly, coaxed up and up and up by Brent's stroking hand. Oh. *Oh yes.* River's breath grew deeper and louder, a machine that he used to move the pleasure up his chakras. His eyes wanted to flicker closed at the intensity of the sensation, but he kept them fixed on Brent's.

Brent's face tightened as he moved his hand faster, up and down, thumb and forefinger circled, the way that drove River crazy, the way that felt so good. Brent's expression grew pained as if it was his own orgasm he was chasing. The energy built and flowed between them. It felt like they'd been lovers for years, as if there were no barriers between them at all.

River's thighs shook and he panted loudly as the crest rose up in front of him. He grabbed Brent's hand, stilling it, as the pleasure peaked. Using his breath and his will, he turned the ecstasy inward and up–up, up his spine, lighting up the chakras, until it expanded in his heart and flowed out the top of his head.

It was so much better than a physical orgasm, the feeling of happiness, the rush of endorphins, the lightness of being. And River stared into Brent's eyes for all of it.

A smile spread across his face as his heart rate slowed down.

And the best part of all? He softened only a little. He could go again. But Brent was not ready for an eight-hour lovemaking session. River was suddenly aware of Brent's erection throbbing against his leg.

"Wow," Brent said. "That was *amazing*."

River let out a laugh of pure joy. He sat up and flipped Brent onto his back. He felt incandescent, buzzing with energy–like he could lift Brent over his head if he wanted to. But he had a better idea.

He moved to kneel between Brent's legs, parting them with a firm touch and pulling down Brent's blue boxer briefs to reveal a very engorged penis. It wasn't the first time he'd seen it, of course. But it was different now. Now it could be an object of desire. Now he and Brent were... well... equal. In this together.

Brent gazed at River and licked his lips. His hips tilted up ever so slightly in supplication.

River bent down and took the tip into his mouth, suckling lightly. Brent gave a choked sound and grabbed the comforter in both fists. "Oh my God. Yes! I didn't... does tantra....?"

River gave the shaft a long lick before answering. "Do oral? *Oh*, yeah."

"Oh my God, I'm dead," Brent whispered.

River proceeded to prove the point, edging Brent until he was begging him not to stop, to let him come. It was so sexy to have a man in his mouth again, stiff and throbbing. River became the receptacle, moving into a softer *yin* energy and encouraging Brent to thrust and take his pleasure. When he cried out and spilled his release, River took it all, his own member stiff and throbbing in sympathy.

Brent slumped afterward, a smile on his face, his eyes sleepy. So River pulled down the comforter and nudged Brent into the bed. He didn't ask if he could stay, and River didn't offer. It was simply going to happen that way. This wasn't only sex. It was connection, and even if they didn't make love all night, River wanted the intimacy.

He wrapped his arms around Brent and lay there floating in a deep well of peace.

Chapter 22

Brent

They slept late, their bodies still on the wrong time zone. When Brent opened his eyes and looked at the bedside clock, it was eleven. He was groggy for about thirty seconds until his brain caught up to the fact that he was naked in bed with River. They'd made love. *They were lovers.*

That woke him up fast.

Before he could turn to face the warm body behind him, River was up. He stood next to the bed and stretched his arms to the ceiling, completely unselfconscious in his nudity. Brent stared. Wow, what a body. River's long hair was down and it flowed to the middle of his back. Broad shoulders, lightly muscled delts, trim waist, long legs that were beautifully shaped, neither skinny nor bulky, and an ass that made Brent want to stick a knuckle in his mouth and bite it, like Austin Powers.

River's ass was more meaty than pert, nicely rounded, with clear indentations on the side where the muscle attached to the hips. It was an extravagant ass, and Brent's stomach warmed just looking at it.

River laughed. Brent glanced up to see River was looking over his shoulder, bemused. "See something you like?"

Brent grinned. "Always been an ass man."

River raised one eyebrow knowingly, and Brent got a strange little thrill in his chest.

Oh shit. Right. Last night he'd had sex for the first time with a man. And yeah, maybe the ass thing should have been a clue.

"You doing all right?" River asked, his voice and expression softer now.

"I'm fucking fantastic. I'd be even better if you got back into this bed."

"Nope. We've just got time to hit the breakfast buffet before it closes. How about we do that; then we can come back up here and lounge?"

Brent's stomach reminded him that there was, in fact, more to life than sex. He hopped up and got dressed.

Over breakfast, Brent tried not to stare at River too much across the table. His mind was a jumble.

He'd had sex with River. Were they a thing now? He wanted to be a thing. He wanted it all. He knew he was getting ahead of himself, but that was just who he was. As much as Sean encouraged him to play the field, insisting this was his opportunity to sow some later-life wild oats, etc., that just didn't appeal to him. Not when he felt such a strong attraction to, and connection with, River. How could some random person at a bar compete with that?

Did it bother him that River was male?

No, it did not. He'd met River in, what, March? Now it was mid-June. He'd gotten used to the idea. He liked River, full stop. So apparently he was bisexual. He had no problem with that. What mattered is that it felt right. Being with River felt incredible.

Honestly, last night he hadn't even thought about the fact that he was interacting with his first not-his-own penis. He'd been so turned on. He'd just wanted to touch River, be with him, in every way possible.

Hell, now that Brent thought about it, he hadn't even given a moment's thought to his previous blockage or performance anxiety either. It had been green lights all the way.

"That smile is a textbook example of cat-who-ate-the-cream," River noted with amusement after polishing off his toast and eggs.

Yeah, Brent could feel the grin on his face. He tried to remove it. It didn't work. "Feeling pretty good this morning."

"Good?" River asked skeptically.

"Smug," Brent admitted.

River chuckled. "Well, I suppose you're entitled to a little smugness. What do you want to do today? We talked about taking the bus to Pune."

"Or we could stay in." Brent hesitated, then decided, what the hell. "You said something about, uh, eight-hour sessions?"

River's smile faded, and his eyes darkened. "It takes training to do that."

"So teach me. I want to learn." Brent looked around, but they were the only guests in the room, and the woman dismantling the buffet was too far away to hear them. "I guess to go that long you need to do that thing you did... where you don't, um..."

"Ejaculate," River supplied, eyes twinkling.

"Right. That. Why do you suppress it? I mean, tell me more about the theory there."

"Well, when you ejaculate, you expel all your sexual energy in a very concrete way along with your seed. That drains you. When you instead internalize the orgasm, you keep all that energy. It feeds and expands your chakras, energizes instead of depletes. It's a kind of high. And it has the added benefit, especially for a male, of allowing multiple orgasms. In my experience, the longer the session goes on, the more times you reach that peak, each one just gets better and better."

"Until you die from exhaustion," Brent quipped. "Like in that movie *Brainstorm* with Natalie Wood."

River laughed. "Well, eventually you do get hungry, or tired, or just ready for the intensity to end. It doesn't usually reach the death-by-sex stage."

"Oh, Good." Brent smiled. "But you don't find it sort of disappointing? Stopping short like that?"

"It doesn't feel like *stopping short* at all. In fact, once you're used to it, ejaculation feels... petty by comparison. Like a sneeze–a momentary peak that's gone too soon. When you internalize the orgasm, it's much more intense, waves of pleasure flood your entire body for minutes. And you can just keep going and going."

Shit, that sounded good. "Will you teach me?"

*   *   *

They sat on the bed nude, legs folded cross-legged, knees touching. River took Brent's hands and gazed into his eyes. The pose was familiar from their surrogacy sessions. But, of course, they hadn't been nude then. Brent was very aware of River's soft, thick cock lying in a nest of blond hair, even if he wasn't looking at it. He shivered in anticipation.

"Breath is very important in tantra," River said. "Loud, deep breathing helps excite and channel your internal energy."

"I remember. It puts you in kind of an altered state."

River nodded. "And you're a natural at it."

"I am?"

"Definitely. The breathing is especially important when you redirect an orgasm. When we get there, I'll guide you."

Brent nodded mutely. He felt his penis trail along his thigh as it filled and rose, excited merely at the words, at the idea of it. Tingles ran through his balls, and they hadn't even started. He took a deep breath.

"Tantra is about connection. Stay aware of your partner. Don't go into your own head. Be present in the moment, in your partner's body and spirit." River took a deep breath and let it out slowly and loudly.

Brent mirrored him. Already his head felt a little light.

River's eyes were so blue today. The hotel room was on too high of a floor to be seen into from the street, so they had the curtains open. Sunlight flooded the space, casting warmth across Brent's back. It didn't feel strange to do this in bright daylight. It felt perfect, as if being with River was all about heat and warmth.

"Let your thoughts go. Just focus on your breath and on me," River instructed.

So Brent tried to stop thinking. It did help to focus on the loud breaths. And on River's eyes. The intimacy was profound and grew more so as the moments passed.

Is this why he'd fallen for River? Because he'd stared into those eyes in their surrogacy sessions? How could you see into someone's soul like this and not love them?

And yet, River worked with many people like this. How could you form such a strong connection and then move on to the next?

But he wasn't supposed to be thinking at all, much less getting anxious. So he just focused on River. River being *with him*. Just about the time the urge to move, to touch River, was getting unbearable, River leaned forward and kissed him.

Brent's eyes slammed shut, and his hands moved to River's hair. He'd put it up for breakfast, and Brent's fingers explored his neck, the skin so downy there, a contrast to the coarseness of his hairline at his nape, and the softness of his beard. He breathed out through his nose with a moan as River's sweet mouth explored his—leisurely, thoroughly. Brent sighed again, wanting nothing so much as to slump down onto his back and pull River on top of him.

How had he managed, after so many years of his sex life being a wasteland, to find himself in an affair as exciting as this? Life could be good after all.

There was no hurry to their lovemaking. None in the world. In fact, *hours* had been mentioned. So he explored kisses with River—deep kisses, his tongue thrusting in River's mouth, River's in his, shallow kisses, sucking on River's lush lower lip, tracing the outline of his mouth with his tongue. Sucking lightly and sweetly while hands explored.

Brent loved the dip at River's waist, the silky flesh there, the sweet vulnerability of that yielding place between River's hard ribs and hips. His fingers rubbed the fuzz of River's happy trail, dipped into his belly button, and traced up to his heart. He could feel its beat, strong and steady, against the pads of his fingers.

River explored, too, tracing Brent's back, arms, and shoulders with a featherlight touch. When he brushed Brent's neck and ears, an electric zap made him arch his back and moan.

River guided him down onto his back. He broke the kiss and gazed into Brent's eyes, starting the tantric breathing as he picked up a bottle from the bedside table. It was massage oil. River squeezed a line of the stuff up Brent's body from dick to neck. Brent hissed as the colder oil hit his heated skin, and River smiled. He put more oil in his hand, smoothed it over his own chest and stomach, and then over his dick.

The sight of River's hand on his own erection sent a wave of urgent lust through Brent, but River didn't linger. He placed both slick palms on Brent's chest and rubbed the oil through his chest hair, over his nipples, onto his neck, squeezing gently, and down his belly.

God. That felt so good. He'd craved River's hands on him again, like this. River glided his hands onto Brent's inner thighs and spread oil to his balls and behind them and then coated his dick, using one hand after the other to twist up and around.

Brent arched his hips and something too akin to a whimper left his throat. He couldn't help it.

"Breathe," River reminded him, as he stretched out and laid his oily body on top of Brent.

Oh God.

It was so much more intense than it had been even in their surrogacy sessions—River sliding his slick body up Brent's, slowly, sensuously, while they both did the tantric breathing and stared into each other's eyes.

Brent's eyes were open this time, for one, the connection between them like a live circuit. And River was naked and hard, for another. This time, River moved all the way up Brent's body until they were eye to eye. The burning rod of his dick rolled between them, sometimes straight up, sometimes to the side, and sometimes alongside his. Brent felt his own hardness as defined against the plump muscles of River's pecs and the soft skin of his belly.

It was the most erotic thing Brent had ever felt in his life. He was wild for it. The skin contact, yes, but especially River's erection. There was just something about feeling how hard River was for him, imagining how that glide, that friction, felt against River's dick, that made the pleasure rolling from his own genitals twice as intense.

And the breathing. And the gazing. He could *see* the pleasure in River's eyes. The way they narrowed just a tiny bit when a wave of ecstasy hit, the way they grew heavy-lidded, the gray-blue irises darkening to steel, the *God yes* in their depth.

It was intense. Brent trembled beneath River, every glide of his body edging the sensation in his dick higher, tightened and tightening the spiral. His brain floated with the deep breathing. His fingers tingled as all his blood pooled in his core.

"Oh my God," he breathed. "I'm really close. Sorry. It's just–"

"Shhh. It feels amazing."

River shifted up to sit on his calves between Brent's thighs. Brent's dick pulsed in protest at the loss of contact.

"Want to try internalizing your orgasm?"

Brent nodded eagerly. Yeah. He wanted to come, but he wanted to try that more. "Not sure if I can hold onto it though."

"Don't worry. Either way, it's all good."

River slid his oil-slick palms up Brent's erection, first one, then the other, pressing it into his belly. He groaned loudly. He was so far gone now, every touch felt like heaven.

River kept stroking him like that as he talked, not enough to get him off, just enough to drive him mad. "Okay. So we're going to take you right to the edge. When you feel like you're about to come, say stop or just tap my arm. I'll take my hands away."

Oh holy hell.

"Deep, loud breaths, okay? You're gonna use those breaths like an engine as you build up to the peak. And then, when I take my hands away, keep breathing through it, deep, as deep as you can. Visualize taking all that pleasure that's in your genitals at that moment and using your breath to push that sensation up your spine, through the *Svadhishthana* chakra, the *manipura* chakra, the *anahata* chakra–" As River named the chakras, he moved his right hand slowly up Brent's belly to his chest, as if demonstrating the path. "From your *anahata* or heart chakra, imagine those waves of pleasure expanding out, flooding through your entire body, through your arms and legs to your fingertips and toes, and up to the top of your head and bursting out, connecting you to the divine energy."

He moved his palm up Brent's neck, lightly over his face, and through his hair to open at the top of his head.

River's left hand was still palm-flat against Brent's erection and it throbbed against that hand, throbbed at River's words, which were oddly arousing. Brent's breathing deepened further, and his head swam. He nodded. "I'll try."

"Okay. Here we go."

Jesus, it didn't take long. River played a little, doing that thing where he twisted his hand around Brent's cock on the upstroke, then followed with a downstroke and twist with his other hand. Brent's gaze was fixed on the sight of River touching him, and his hips refused to stay on the bed, lifting, begging. His loud breaths were a stream of moans, and everything inside him tightened until River's hands on him, rubbing him, was all there was in the world.

River began the up-down stroke, fast but with a light grip, just using the circle of his thumb and finger, right under the head of Brent's cock. Jesus. An intense white light flashed through him. He was going to come.

"Stop!"

Brent thought he was too late, but River's hands vanished and he hung on the precipice, a stone balanced on a ledge.

"Breathe, Brent," River gently reminded him.

And he remembered what he was supposed to do. He took faster, deeper breaths, almost sobs, and slammed his eyes shut, focused on the intense pleasure in his dick and balls. He imagined moving that up, up his spine, sending that pleasure out into the rest of his body.

His thighs shook. Even his belly quivered with his breaths as the pleasure expanded and moved, rolling outward in a wave. Maybe he was half-hypnotized by the breathing or River's power of suggestion, but he *felt* it. It was like having an orgasm in his heart, sending ripples of sexual pleasure washing through all parts of him until he wanted to cry.

He basked in the pleasure for as long as he could until it slowly faded. He stopped shaking and lay on the bed, limp. He opened his eyes.

River was still kneeling between Brent's legs. He grinned. "Well, how was that?"

"Fucking incredible." Brent's voice sounded like a stranger's. His ears rang. His fingers tingled. He laughed. "What the hell did you do to me?"

"You did amazing. It took me weeks to do what you just did."

"Really?" Brent sat up on his elbows. Instead of feeling lethargic, like he normally did after an orgasm, he felt tingly with energy, like he'd plugged in to a light socket.

He felt *incandescent.* "Wow."

"Feel energized?"

"Hell, yes. It really worked!"

River chuckled. "Four thousand years of yogis can't be wrong." His expression grew serious. "Seriously though. It's one thing to learn to hold back an orgasm. But the energy you create—the way you connect with me, with yourself, with the universe—without any training. You blow me away, Brent. You're incredibly intuitive."

It was the most sincere, and rewarding, compliment Brent had ever received. He felt his eyes prickle with heat. "Well. You're a very inspiring teacher."

River rubbed a hand up Brent's arm. "I wonder if that's because you're an artist. You've been tapping into creative energy, using your imagination to bring your visions into reality, your whole life."

Or maybe it's because I got so close to death, Brent thought. *For a while, I felt like I had a foot on the other side.*

But those were dark thoughts, and he didn't want to have them now. He pushed up to sitting, then got on all fours, eying River hungrily. His dick grew heavy as it swung between his legs. Oh, man. He could really get into this go-for-hours thing.

"I think it's your turn to touch the divine," Brent threatened.

"Oh, is it?" River smiled and leaned back on his elbows, placing his bobbing cock very much at Brent's mercy.

In for a penny.... Brent had always loved oral sex. One of his and Kathy's favorite positions had been sixty-nine, with Brent on top so that his genitals hung down. It was going to be interesting being on the other end of that. But he found River's penis fascinating, and he wanted to try it.

So he lay on his back on the bed and managed, with some pulling and guiding, to let River know what he wanted. River swung over Brent on all fours, knees spread by Brent's head, and let Brent play. River deepened his breathing as Brent tested his new toy, licking through the nutty taste of the oil to the salty, musky flavor beneath. One nice thing about tantra was that playing and teasing were great. There was no pressure to get your partner off.

He held the base with one hand so he could trace one throbbing vein and tickle the slit. He suckled the head first, then tried taking more in. The silky skin was velvety against his tongue, and he found he liked having his mouth stuffed full. It was sexy to feel like his lover was filling him up, almost to choking, as if he were helpless. Why that was hot, he didn't know, but it was. Especially when River shifted a bit, lowered his head, and sucked in Brent's again-hard erection.

River licked and teased, worshipping his *lingam* lazily. Which was good, because with River in his mouth, Brent didn't think he'd have the control to internalize another orgasm.

River's shallow thrusts grew erratic, and his thighs trembled. When he called "Stop!" Brent stilled utterly. He slackened his mouth, but he didn't pull off. River could easily withdraw if he wanted. But he didn't. His penis grew even harder and jerked once in Brent's mouth as River's loud breathing filled the room. Brent swore he could sense the energy as River internalized his orgasm. He seemed to expand over Brent in every way. Finally he relaxed and withdrew his penis, which had only softened a little.

Another benefit of tantric sex—no need to swallow come. That was a challenge Brent was just as glad to pass on for now. As for the oral sex itself—it surprisingly didn't feel strange or even all that different. Of course, the mechanics were different, but it was still a huge turn-on giving someone pleasure, teasing, being sensual, using his mouth. If Brent had any lingering worries about being with a man, they were now put to rest.

They didn't make eight hours, but they managed five before they got up and went out in search of a meal. Tantric sex was a win, though Brent wasn't sure he would survive it.

He had five more days in India to try.

PART IV: FIGHTING THE TIDE

"When it hurts, observe. Life is trying to teach you something." – Buddha

Chapter 23

River

Lily and Beauchamp were ecstatic to see River when he got home from Mumbai on a Friday night. Maddy had only left them two hours before, according to the note on the counter, but the dogs acted as though they'd been alone for *days*.

As tired as River was from the long flight, he couldn't help but be buoyed by the irrepressible canine joy. He got on the floor and gave them kisses and pets as they bounced around in delight. Then he took them out for a short walk along the row of houseboats.

Returning to Seattle felt like coming home. Any place could feel like home after you'd been there a few weeks, in River's experience. *Home* was a state of mind. Still, there was something special about driving toward the downtown skyline in Brent's car on the way in from SeaTac airport—a sense of security, a sense of rightness, a sense of settling back into his place in the world.

The long kiss Brent gave River before he exited the car felt right too. It shouldn't have. When River had left Seattle, Brent was his boss. Now he was his lover. Yet it felt as natural as the water lapping along the sides of the houseboat.

The doubts showed up the next morning. When River arrived at Brent's house to work, he felt unusually tense. India had been a step out of time, a retreat from their regular lives. How could they do this now that they were home? Maybe Brent wouldn't even want to try.

That thought bummed River out, even though he told himself it was fine. Whatever happened was fine.

Brent greeted him with a big smile and a long hug, an "I missed you," and a kiss. It seemed things would only be awkward if River made them so. He chose not to. Since they were working together at Brent's house, there was no one there to judge. And the step-out-of-time continued. For now.

The first weekend back, Brent checked in with all the AJC branches and then got absorbed with the decoration of the cafe. He had a bunch of his photos from India printed along with images he'd found online of other places around the world, travel iconography, images of gardens, food, and anything else that inspired him.

By Sunday, his dining room table was covered with photos, drawings, paint chips, and fabric swatches. River was assigned to nail down the menu and kombucha brews.

It was the tail-end of June, and the weather was sunshine sweet, warmer than it had been all spring. River sat on Brent's deck with his laptop, searching out recipes and making lists. He had dozens of dishes to research, including things they'd tried in Mumbai. It was a challenge to figure out how to adapt some of the foods for their cafe system and to find recipes that were authentic without being ridiculously complicated. Of course, he'd be working with a chef to really pin things down, but he wanted to get a list of suggestions organized.

River loved the idea of having a signature dish from each country, with plenty of hearty vegan and veg options. It was easier than he'd assumed. For Germany, he wanted brats on a pretzel-bread roll with sauerkraut. He found a faux-meat company that made vegan brats so they could offer the meal with regular brats or the vegan version. For Italy, it had to be pizza, and pizza was easy to adapt toppings to include meat and cheese or not. Israeli salad, hummus, and falafel wraps were already vegan. The task had the downside of making him constantly hungry.

On Monday, he picked up the kombucha bacteria culture, the SCOBYs, from a local organic store, and created a first fermentation batch with good black tea and sugar. He made eight one-gallon jars and put them in Brent's basement next to the furnace. The bacteria would eat the sugar, turning the jars from sweet tea into kombucha in about a week's time. Then he'd be able to do a second fermentation, adding flavorings and sealing batches in smaller jars to get carbonization.

Even though they were each focused on their own projects, they stayed connected. When River passed Brent on the way to the kitchen, Brent stopped working long enough to give his hand a squeeze or initiate a quick kiss. Or River would be working on his laptop and feel hands on his shoulders and a press of lips to the top of his head as Brent took a short break.

For the first three days, they were in a world of their own. Brent had groceries delivered, so they made lunches out of the fridge and sat on the deck to eat, discussing their progress, or just soaking in the sun. Brent would reach across, and River would take his hand. Faces tilted to the sky, River warmed inside and out, enjoying a few minutes of bliss in-the-now until it was time to get back to work.

On Tuesday morning, River went to the regular staff meeting at Expanded Horizons. It was nice to see everyone again, and they all asked about his trip.

Jack had two new clients for him, both older men. One man in his fifties had trouble achieving and sustaining an erection. The other was a porn addict who couldn't function well in a relationship, and Jack thought the client might benefit from having the sexual brought back into the realm of the spiritual. Plus, River was still working with Harrison too.

Of course, his surrogacy work would pick up just as he entered a personal relationship.

River thought about it all the way back to Brent's in the car. He and Brent hadn't discussed his surrogacy practice, or how Brent felt about it. But then, they'd so recently become lovers. Why would they? Now that it looked like things between them would continue, he supposed being open about it was the best policy.

When he got back to Brent's, he asked if they could talk. They went out to the dock in Brent's backyard and put their feet in the water. River told him about his new clients.

"I'm not sure how this goes," River confessed. "I haven't been in this situation before. How do you feel about it?"

Brent's expression was studiously neutral. "Well, I knew you were still working as a surrogate."

"Yes. I have a calling to be a healer. It's important to me." He didn't say *more important than the cafe*, but it was. Working on Harmony Tree Cafe was fun, but his heart would always be in working with people.

Brent's words were careful. "I know it is. And you're great at it. You helped me tremendously. I have to admit, I don't love thinking about you touching other men's penises. But I also know how professional you are, that you keep a certain distance with your clients. Even when I was one and I hoped you wouldn't." His smile was wry. "I'm not going to tell you that you can't do your work, River."

"Okay. If it becomes a problem for you, you'll talk to me about it?"

Brent nodded. "And if something happens with one of your clients that's more personal...."

"It won't."

"Deal."

Brent gave River a long hug. He seemed vulnerable, and River hugged him back hard, wanting to reassure him. He wondered why he'd even felt the need to discuss this. The word "monogamy" had never been mentioned. And, hell, he wasn't even here permanently. But his gut told him Brent McKay cared for him, and he wanted to honor those feelings.

Every afternoon at five, River drove back to the houseboat to take Lily and Beauchamp out for a walk, give them some attention, and feed them dinner. Then he drove back to Brent's, where they made love for a few hours, before he went home to Lily and Beauchamp for the night.

It wasn't the most convenient routine, but it seemed to serve all masters. Except that Brent looked disappointed when River left for the night.

On Thursday, when he packed up his laptop and went inside, Brent paused mid-sketch and came around the table. He put his arms around River's waist.

"Mmm. You're warm from the sun." His cheek pressed against River's hair.

River smiled at the blossom of pleasure in his heart chakra. He kissed Brent's neck and gave him a squeeze. "I have to go take care of the beasts."

Brent pulled back far enough to look in his eyes but didn't release him. "I was thinking—why don't you bring Lily and Beauchamp over here? That way you don't have to keep running back and forth all the time. They'd have more company, and you could spend the night."

The idea was tempting. Brent's place was so comfortable, and the drive, though not that long, was usually clogged with traffic. At the same time, it made River uneasy. He and Brent already worked together all day. If he brought Lily and Beauchamp over, they'd basically be living together. River couldn't relinquish his independence. Boundaries were important.

"I can't just abandon the houseboat. The owners are expecting me to keep an eye on things, to be living there."

Brent chewed his lip. "I'm not saying you'd never go back."

"Besides, I don't want to stress out the dogs. They're used to their place."

"I bet they'd appreciate being with us all day and not being alone so much. Maybe you could bring them over tomorrow morning, and we can see if they settle in? If they like it here, you'd at least have the option of spending the night a few times a week, or leaving when you feel like it, instead of being a slave to the eight-hour thing."

The eight-hour thing *was* a pain in the ass. River glanced over Brent's shoulder at the family room, which held mostly white furniture. "You sure you want dogs here?"

"I would *adore* it," Brent said firmly. He cupped River's jaw and kissed him, the slide of his tongue sending eddies of sensual energy down to stir in River's groin.

Mmm. Nice.

The energy between them was incredible, and River would miss it when he left. So why not spend time together while they could? Brent's proposal sounded too reasonable to resist, especially the part about only staying overnight a few times a week. Boundaries could still be in place, right? And it truly would be better for the dogs.

River reluctantly broke the kiss. "Okay. I'll bring them over tomorrow. But I think I'll hang out over there tonight. They've been alone too much."

Boundaries.

"Perfect." Brent gave him a final soft kiss and let go. His smile might have been a little self-congratulatory, but River let it slide.

That evening at the houseboat, it felt colder than could be explained by the breeze. Since the night in Mumbai when Brent had confessed that he wanted more, they hadn't gone a day without making love. In India, they'd spent hours absorbed in each other's bodies, nights spent curled in each other's arms.

But they were back to real life now, and River's "real life" included more than Brent McKay. It had to.

So he ignored the urge to go back to Brent's. Instead, he invited Mrs. Smythe over for a glass of wine. They sat and chatted and watched Precious, Lily, and Beauchamp play around on the deck as if they hadn't a care in the world.

Chapter 24

River

"I missed our sessions while you were gone, darling boy." Harrison greeted River at the door with a kiss to both cheeks. "Come in, come in! Set those things down. It makes my back hurt just seeing you carry all that."

River put his portable futon and duffel bag down by the sofa while Harrison went to fix some tea. "How was India? Such an exciting life you lead, River Larsen. India, Seattle, back to India, and, hopefully, soon Rome!"

"Mumbai was wonderful. Very hot. And very productive." River smiled. It had been productive in unexpected ways.

Harrison poured hot water into a cup. "Oh! Look at that folder on the counter. I spoke to a friend of mine in Rome, and he said there's a tantric school there. I thought it might interest you, so I printed out some information. They're sending me an actual brochure, but it could take weeks. Italians aren't known for expediency."

River opened the manila folder on the counter. Inside were printouts about a place called Sacred Tantric Yoga in Rome, Italy.

River turned the pages with interest. The About page said the discipline was established by Yogi Garunda, a master of Kundalini Yoga, in the eighties. It combined aspects of meditation, yoga, and tantra. There were regular classes for practitioners and a series of workshops for those wishing to be certified as teachers.

They had a new certification program starting October first.

River blinked. Oh. Interesting.

A familiar itch awoke in his heart chakra—to learn, to study, to become. To find… what? That elusive meaning of life? Several times he thought he'd found it—when he discovered reiki, when he first went to the Sacred Triangle ashram to study tantra. But ultimately, neither had been everything he'd hoped. He was still seeking. Maybe he always would be.

"Does it seem like something that would appeal to you?" Harrison asked innocently. He handed River his tea.

"Yeah. It does." River eyed the pages again before taking a sip.

"Mmm. I've heard it's exceptional."

"Really? Do you know someone who attends classes there?"

Harrison waved a hand vaguely. "Not specifically. But you'd be surprised how small a community Rome truly is." He blew on his cup. "So... shall I take the apartment off the market then? Starting September eleventh? Hmm? I already have a few reservations I'll have to cancel. Oh! And we should book flights immediately if we've a prayer of getting a decent rate."

River hesitated. He felt torn. Hell, the word *torn* was inadequate. He felt literally of two minds.

The idea of Rome had lingered in his consciousness ever since Harrison had mentioned it, lingered as *the thing he'd most likely do next*. He couldn't overlook the way this had fallen into his lap—a great apartment for free in the heart of Rome. A chance to help out a kindly old man. And now a chance to study a new discipline complete with a certificate to add to his growing resume. He'd played with the idea of studying yoga more seriously. The idea of *tantric* yoga was intriguing. If one believed in signposts, this one was in flashing neon.

But, on the *other mind*, there was Brent and the new cafe. There was the dog park on Capitol Hill, and Dr. Halloran, and the rest of the team at Expanded Horizons clinic. There was the way Seattle had felt like home just a week ago when he'd driven toward the city lights on his way in from the airport.

Then again the clock was ticking on the houseboat. What would he do when time was up? Maybe Brent would offer to let River stay with him. But he couldn't do that. He couldn't just be subsumed into Brent's life. Sure, they had an amazing connection, but they'd only been intimate for... what? Two weeks? It was hard to believe. It felt like much longer, but really, it had just begun.

Reality had yet to intrude, but it would. He and Brent would never work long term.

River was not another Kathy McKay. Not even close. How would he fit into Brent's life? With his family and friends? Business associates? Even if they could get over the idea that Brent was with a man, he was so different in every way.

Plus, River was a surrogate. He had his clients, his work as a healer. Brent claimed to be okay with it, but for how long? River's lifestyle wasn't meant for monogamy.

Somebody else's Brent McKay.

Finally, there was his freedom. River never stayed. There was a whole world out there. Sometimes it was hard to leave places. Leave people. But in the end, nothing was permanent anyway. Life was, to put it titularly, a river. *He* was a river. Things flowed to him and away again. Or, as his mother put it, he was a dandelion puff floating on the breeze. To attempt to cling to things, expect things from people—that only led to disappointment and heartbreak. Better to not expect. Better to let experiences pass through your fingers like sand, neither judging them or trying to hold them fast.

"River, my dear, you look as though you're trying to solve the problems of the universe. It's a year in Rome, not rocket science. Say yes."

"Can I give you an answer by tomorrow?" River asked Harrison.

Harrison scowled. "*Tomorrow*, darling. But no later. I really must get my things in order. Oh! Do yourself a favor and look at photos of Rome on your computer tonight. Piazza Navona, the Pantheon, the Vatican. All the little streets and restaurants. The arts! The shopping. It's simply heaven." Harrison placed a trembling hand on River's arm. "And it would mean so much to me to be able to see it again before I die. I wouldn't be able to go without you, you know. You'd be doing me a tremendous favor."

River forced a smile. "I'll let you know."

Harrison was a perfect gentleman during their tantric massage. He really was a dear old man.

*   *   *

River needed to talk to someone. He had friends, but they were the kind who, after not seeing him for five years, would throw out their arms and hug him with a heartfelt "It's good to see you, brother." They were not the kind who sent birthday cards. They were not the kind you called to talk things out.

His best friend from high school had pretty much dropped River after he'd gotten serious about a girl. His closest friend at the ashram, Davie, was wonderfully wise. River would love to have a heart-to-heart with Davie, but he was now somewhere in Tibet, and he'd repudiated cell phones.

If this were about money or legal issues, he might call his father. When it involved a gay relationship? Never.

Sitting on the deck of the houseboat that night, watching the lights around Lake Union emerge to do battle with the gloom of twilight, he clutched his phone in his hand, just needing.

A man who returns again and again to a well with bitter water is a fool. Or, possibly, someone in whom hope never dies. River called his mother.

He got her voice mail the first two times. He tried once more, knowing she might pick up if she thought it was urgent. He was still surprised when she answered.

"River! How are you? Is everything okay?"

"It's fine, Mom. Where are you?"

Where are you was always the first question with Verona Nilson.

"Marseilles, lambchop. At least for now. The coast is so pretty."

"Oh? Are you staying with someone?"

"Francois. I told you about Francois, didn't I?"

River rubbed his forehead and tried to recall. "Hmmm. Is he the one who was mayor of a small town?"

"Yes, that's Francois. Wonderful man, but so serious!"

Her tone was chiding, which meant Francois was probably on his way out. He likely was wanting to get *serious* about her.

"I'm glad things are going well, Mom. I was wondering—do you have time to talk?" River heard the skepticism in his own voice and swallowed it down.

"Sure, lambchop. I'm just sitting here watching the sun come up, all cozy on the couch. So what is it?"

He leaned forward, elbows on his knees, and rubbed at a heavy ache in his chest. "I have a chance to go to Rome in September. Stay there for free with a friend. Maybe get certified in a tantra yoga discipline. There's a school there."

"It sounds wonderful! What's not to love? Oh, and Rome isn't that far from Marseilles! I could come see you. Wouldn't that be fun? You and me in Rome."

River's heart gave a meaty thump. "Really?"

"Of course! It seems like forever since I've seen you. It's been, what, a year?"

River clutched the phone tighter. "Three. Last time was in California just before you left for Peru. You came to my graduation ceremony at the massage school."

River remembered it well. It was the first graduation of his that his mother had ever attended. She'd just happened to be in San Diego to get on a cruise ship. She wore a flowery sleeveless dress, her long blond hair thick and wavy as ever, her face and body still beautiful. His stepmother, Michelle, had loathed her on first sight. And his dad had stared at his plate all night at the restaurant.

Yeah. That had been an interesting family dynamic.

"Oh Lord, River. It hasn't been that long!"

"It's been that long, Mom."

"Ta! Then we *have* to meet up in Rome. Let's make that happen, okay, lambchop?"

"Are you even going to still be in Marseilles by September?"

There was a hesitation on the other end of the line. "If you're coming to Rome, I'll make sure of it."

River sighed. She sounded so confident. He really wanted to believe her. He suddenly wanted to see her with a deep, hollow ache in his chest. It was like a broken bone that had never been set right and flared up in the winter cold. But he knew it was just as likely she'd be on the other side of the world come September.

You can't control her actions. But you can control your lack of generosity in refusing to believe her, forgive her.

River closed his eyes. "I'd love that, Mom, seeing you in Rome. The thing is, I'm not sure I'm going. That's what I wanted to talk to you about. See, there's a man."

"There's *always* a man, lambchop. But go ahead. Tell me about it."

So he did. He told her everything. Sometimes it helped to just say things out loud, brought clarity. But there was no such relief this time. When he was done, he felt more twisted up about it than before.

She sounded doubtful. "So Brent was married to a woman, someone who was a partner in his business?"

"Yes."

"And he's prepared to just suddenly *be gay* with all his friends and customers and everyone?"

River rubbed a hand over his face. He didn't like the implication, which was that he was being naive, even though he couldn't deny he'd thought the same himself. "He says he doesn't care about that. And he does seem to be pretty… self-directed."

"Men say a lot of things." She huffed. "Look, ordinarily, I'd say that if you like it there in Seattle, and you're enjoying this relationship, stay another three months. What could it hurt? But I think you know this Rome opportunity is rare, or you wouldn't be so tempted by it. Correct?"

He thought about that. "True. But it's not just Rome. It's the fact that I was supposed to leave in September. That was the plan. My house-sitting gig is up then."

"You could live with this Brent for a while, couldn't you?"

River tensed up. "I don't want to do that. I don't want to mooch off him and lead him on, make him think it's serious, then bug out."

No, that was his mother's MO. Brent didn't deserve that.

His mother was quiet for a minute. When she spoke her voice was dull, like she'd lost interest. "Well, you'll figure it out. You always do.

Just let me know if you'll be in Rome, hmm? I would like to see you, lambchop."

River felt disappointed. But that wasn't exactly a new feeling when it came to his mother. "Yeah. That'd be great."

"And it's only the start of July. You still have the rest of the summer in Seattle. By the time that's up, you'll be dying to get back on the road!"

She had a point. He still had the summer.

"Just remember. We're not like normal people, River. Stuck in some horrid small town, never seeing or doing anything, bound to a relationship long after it has any spark of life in it. That's your grandparents. Your dad. Not you and me. We're dandelion puffs, floating wherever the breeze takes us, light as a feather. Rome, darling! Look at all the exciting things ahead of you. There's no reason to feel blue. I hope to see you there. Kisses. Gotta go."

After he hung up, River sat and watched the city lights for a long time, until the nightly breeze had turned frigid. He went to reach for his phone and realized it was still in his hand. The time said 10:00 p.m. Not too late. He placed the call.

"Harrison? It's River. I'm in. We're going to Rome."

Chapter 25

Brent

Brent opened his eyes to see a spill of gold hair on the pillow next to him. A cold nose poked his back through the covers. He smiled and turned his head.

"Yes, good morning, Lily."

She barked, an urgent sound, and wagged her tail madly.

Brent nudged River's leg. "Hey. Someone has to go out."

River gave a groan, which told Brent he'd already been awake. He sat up, covers falling to his waist, and stretched.

Brent gave a little hum of contentment. He would never have imagined he'd be here, with two dogs staring at him from beside the bed and a gorgeous young man sleep-warmed next to him. He was so grateful. He was a lucky guy.

He leaned over to kiss River's bicep, then shoulder.

River quirked an eyebrow at him. "You always wake up so happy."

"Not always," Brent said, thinking of darker days.

River smiled at the implied compliment and got up. He was exuberantly, delightfully nude, his cock a little plump with morning wood. Then he tugged on a pair of sweatpants, which was a shame, really.

"Come on, you savage beasts." He left the room, Lily bounding after him and Beauchamp waddling as fast as his little legs would take him.

"Mmm." Brent flopped back on the bed and folded his arms behind his head. He spread out his legs like he was making a snow angel, just because he could. The warmth that lingered in the sheets from River's body gave him a little thrill.

Lily and Beauchamp had taken to Brent's house with nary a doggie grumble. Within an hour on their first visit, Beauchamp had been asleep on the old Indian blanket Brent spread out on the couch, his tongue sticking out adorably. Lily had settled at River's feet on the deck as he worked, her head on his foot. Clearly, she'd missed him during the days.

It was so obviously better for them to be at Brent's house that River never brought up doubts again. They'd spent the whole of last weekend at Brent's house with the dogs. River had introduced Brent to the dog-park experience. They'd walked the pooches around his neighborhood too. It was very couple-y, and Brent loved it. When some of his neighbors did a double-take, he just waved and called hello.

River came back into the bedroom, the dogs padding after him, looking much more relaxed. He was carrying two cups of coffee from the espresso maker downstairs. He handed Brent his, made with oat milk, just the way he liked it. River sat on the edge of the bed carefully with his own cup so as not to spill. "So what's up for today?"

"I'm meeting the contractor at the cafe to go over the remodel specs. He thinks he can have it done in two weeks. I can't wait to see it."

"That's fantastic."

"Good thing too. August thirty-first will be here before we know it. And the invitations to the grand opening are being printed next week. After that, we can't push it back even if we want to."

"Um," River agreed, sipping his coffee.

"Why don't you go over there with me? When I'm done, we can take the dogs to the park."

River glanced away. "That's okay. I need to get the first batch of test recipes off to Rene this morning."

Brent sat up and brushed River's hair off his shoulder. "How long will that take? I don't meet the contractor till eleven. Can you be done by then? Or you can finish it up when we get back from the park."

River gave Brent a look he didn't know how to interpret. "Aren't you sick of me yet? Or, if not of me, of Lily and Beauchamp?"

Brent laughed. "Never. Anyway, it's Saturday. I just thought it would be nice to go to Discovery Park and take a little walk. I hate that our entire weekend is about work."

"Well, that's what happens when you're opening a cafe in seven weeks."

"I know. But we're on schedule. No need to kill ourselves." He kissed River's shoulder.

River sighed. "Okay. I should be able to finish up what I need to do this morning."

By one o'clock, they were walking high up on a seaside trail at Discovery Park. The July day was a little too warm for Beauchamp. He walked along enthusiastically at first, but by the time they'd gone a mile, he just wanted to find a spot of shade and lie in it, panting hard.

"I'm sorry." River squatted down to give Beauchamp some water. "He really doesn't go far. We should have left him at home."

At home. Brent liked the sound of that.

"No worries. It's just nice to be out. There's a bench over there in the shade."

They coaxed Beauchamp to the bench, where he promptly fell asleep under Brent's outstretched legs. Lily sat watching birds with avid fascination. The day was mostly cloudy and unusually muggy, but spots of blue appeared here and there in the sky.

Brent put his arm behind River on the bench, feeling very comfortable with everything. Just... everything in his life right now.

"So how does the grand opening work?" River asked. "Do you just put out a sign and open the doors to the public?"

"No." Brent's hand found its way to River's shoulder and his thumb traced River's ear. "It's a Big Fucking Deal. We'll invite the press, food critics, restaurant people I know. All the AJC staff who aren't working that day. I want to make it a company-wide celebration. This store is something special, and it deserves to have a true launch."

River smiled. "It's going to be surreal to see it actually open and serving real customers after all the time we've spent thinking about it. Watching you make this happen—it's been impressive, Brent McKay."

The compliment sank into Brent like a warm hug. He wanted to impress River, wanted him to see he wasn't just the depressed basket case he'd been when they'd met. "It helps to have a great partner."

River licked his lips, something hesitant in his eyes. He looked as if he was going to say something, but he didn't. He just leaned back against Brent's arm and gazed out over the Sound.

On the drive home, Brent said, "I need to stop by the First Hill branch. Justin had a question about a supplier. Do you mind?"

"No problem."

Brent found a parking spot in the shade not far from the store. When he stopped the car, River said, "Maddy's probably working today. I haven't had a chance to thank her in person for house-sitting for me. Crack the windows a few inches for the dogs, and I'll go in."

Brent put the back windows down a few inches, and they left Lily and Beauchamp snoozing.

The First Hill AJC was quiet when they walked in. There were a dozen patrons, all seated and looking at phones or laptops. Justin was at the register. Maddy and a new girl were at the coffee station.

"Hey, Mr. McKay!" Justin called out. His gaze darted to River as he walked over to Maddy, and a frown appeared between his brows.

Brent went up to the register. "Hey, Justin. I got your email about Rainier Foods."

Justin grimaced. "Yeah, um, they've been weird lately. Like, some days they'll make a delivery and then, like last week, there were three days when they just didn't show up. When they do deliver, the milk smells off."

"Off, how?"

"C'mere. I'll show you."

Justin moved behind the counter to the coffee station. Brent followed along on the customer side till he was standing next to

River. Justin opened one of the under-counter fridges and pulled out a carton of whole milk, opened it.

"Smell this," he said, turning. He froze, a look of shock on his face. Maddy's mouth fell open.

For a second, Brent couldn't figure out why they were staring at him. Then he realized that he'd done what came naturally whenever he was near River. He'd put an arm around him, hand on the back of his neck.

River stared straight ahead, his expression neutral, but he tensed under Brent's hand.

Brent chuckled. "Yeah. Um... didn't mean to spring it on you. But River and I are dating." He moved his hand down to River's shoulder and squeezed, looking at him with affection.

River looked at him and smiled, but it didn't reach his eyes. Brent felt a ping of doubt. He probably should have checked with River first. River had worked with Maddy and Justin, after all. They were his friends.

"Oh, wow. I mean... congratulations, Mr. McKay," Maddy stammered.

Justin just stood there, his face red, holding the carton of milk.

Brent took a step away from River and held out his hand. Justin looked at him blankly. There was something like hurt in his eyes.

"Justin? The milk?"

"Oh." Justin thrust the milk carton out.

Brent took it, opened it, and sniffed. It definitely seemed strange. Smelled like garlic.

He held it out to River. "What do you smell?"

River took it and sniffed it. "Garlic."

Brent sniffed it again and nodded. "Good nose. Maybe some of their herd got into garlic plants. Or maybe it's in their storage tanks. And they've been unreliable too?" he asked Justin.

Justin nodded, his face now very red. The rosy flush clashed with his orange-red hair. "Very. I've, um, had to go get stuff at the supermarket."

"Okay. I'll call my contact at the distributor. If they can't clean up their act quickly, I'll find someone else. Thanks for calling it to my attention."

Justin nodded dumbly as Brent handed back the carton.

"Was there anything else?"

Justin's gaze flickered to River. "Nah. Wouldn't want to bother you. Guess you're pretty tied up with the, um, *new cafe*."

He sounded resentful, and Brent felt lost. He'd obviously missed something in the dynamic here. But the thought just made him feel stubborn. He was the goddamn owner. If Justin didn't like him dating River, that was his problem, and he could keep it to himself.

"Yes, River and I are both busy getting Harmony Tree Cafe ready to launch," Brent said tersely. "But if you need something, email or text me. As usual."

They said their goodbyes, which were awkward, and got back in the car.

River was quiet as Brent drove over Capitol Hill and headed down toward Madrona. The tension in his body, the grim set of his face, was new. He was angry. Brent had never seen River angry. He was normally such a chill guy. It scared Brent.

"Hey. I'm sorry if I was out of line. I should have asked you if you minded me outing us as a couple to Justin and Maddy. That was inconsiderate."

River looked at him finally, his eyes snapping. "It's not about *me*, Brent. It's about *you*. You just came out to your entire staff. Justin will tell all your managers. You might as well have hired a skywriter."

Brent blinked and focused on the road. "Okay. Well. I don't care if people know I'm bisexual. I don't have anything to hide."

"And yeah, you told them you were dating *me*. Which is a really big...." River stopped, his hands clenched in his lap.

"Really big what?"

River frowned and didn't answer.

Shit, Brent couldn't have this conversation while driving. He made a quick left and drove a few blocks to a small park. He pulled into a parking space and shut off the car.

Brent felt a twinge of dread that was far deeper than he wanted to admit. River had been a little distant this week. There'd been times when Brent thought he was holding back. But then again, he'd spent most of his time at Brent's house, and their tantric sex continued to be incredible. River had to feel the connection between them, right?

"Do you not want this?" he asked, his voice rough. "I guess I'm old-fashioned. I figured I should treat you the way I would treat anyone who was important in my life. The way I'd be with a woman I was seeing. Is that wrong? I'm not ashamed of you. Of us. I'm proud to be with you."

River was quiet for a moment, looking down at his hands.

"Am I crowding you? Am I…" He sighed. "Am I being overbearing?"

River shook his head. He let out a long sigh. "No. No, you're great, and I love being with you. I'm sorry I got angry. I guess I'm worried about you. *For* you. We haven't discussed it for a while, but… you remember I'm leaving in September, right? So I'm not sure how much you want to let everyone know about this relationship when it has a definite shelf life."

Brent's heart plummeted and cold seeped through his veins. "Oh."

He looked out the window at the green park. A mom pushed a little girl of about three on a swing set. There was a lump in his throat that felt too familiar from days gone past, days when grief had been a constant companion. "I know you said that a while ago. But I thought… thought you might decide to stay. You could manage Harmony Tree. Or not. Whatever you want."

"I've already made plans, Brent." River gave him a firm look. It was not unkind, but it left no room for argument either. "I've arranged a place to stay and signed up for classes. I'm going to Rome with a friend. It's all set."

"Oh. Okay. I see." Brent didn't know what to say. He felt crushed, stupidly so. He'd always known River was just passing through. But he'd let himself forget, to believe that them getting together would change things, that it would mean as much to River as it meant to him. As if his magic penis would make River forever devoted. Stupid.

Brent's eyes stung, and he swallowed down bile.

River's face softened, and he reached over and rubbed Brent's arm. "I'm sorry." His voice was rough and filled with regret, as if he really was sorry.

Brent just nodded.

"Hey. We've still got the rest of the summer. I told my friend I couldn't leave until September twenty-fifth, so that we'd have more time together. And we've got a cafe to open. Do you think we could just enjoy being together for the time we have? I'd really like that."

He cupped Brent's neck, tugging him a little, and Brent willingly leaned over the console for a hug. He held River close, burying his nose in River's neck.

At least River wasn't pushing him away right now. It wasn't over. Everything was all right. He'd been too clingy, that was all. Even as inexperienced at dating as he was, he knew that was the worst thing you could do, smother someone. He was gaga over River, but he had to cool it.

River was going to leave—he'd *always* been going to leave. Brent could be okay with that. He had to be okay with it. He didn't own the guy. River was a free spirit. Wasn't that one of the things that made him so appealing? You couldn't change someone. Brent knew that.

"I want to be with you as long as you're here," he said.

River sighed and hugged him tighter. "Me too. I just want to be fair with you, not lead you on. You're important to me."

But not important enough for you to stay. And that hurt, too, so Brent did the only thing he could to feel better. He kissed River, focused on the smell and taste of him. In the here and the now.

Chapter 26

August, 2019

River

Brent kept insisting the taste-testing party was supposed to be casual, but it didn't feel that way to River. The housekeepers came and did a major overhaul of the house. A ramp was rented and installed at the front stoop to make the party wheelchair accessible. Elaborate floral arrangements were delivered. River took Lily and Beauchamp over to the houseboat so they'd be out of the way, and when he got back, Rene, the chef who'd been working with River on the menu, was there with a staff of three in formal-looking white chef's tops. They were setting up large silver covered trays of food on the dining room table and crates of beer, water, and soft drinks.

River had busted tail to get the kombucha ready in time. He had about two hundred bottles of his homebrew in five different flavors, which Rene had artfully arranged in ice buckets on a white-linen-covered table out on the deck, as if they were fine champagne.

River fussed with them, making sure all the labels faced up.

Brent came up behind him and placed hands on River's shoulders. "They look great. I'm excited for people to taste them."

"I should have had real labels printed. At least computer-made ones. I didn't realize we were being fancy."

"Are you kidding? I love seeing your handwriting on them. Makes them more authentic. And we're not *being fancy*. I told you, this party is–"

"Casual. I think you and I have different definitions of the word." He laughed and waved a hand at the large vase containing a selection of ferns, white carnations, and purple orchids that sat next to River's homebrew.

Brent smiled. "I just wanted it to be nice. It's the interior designer in me. Doesn't mean it has to be high-pressure."

River leaned back, letting himself be wrapped in Brent's arms and taking a moment to let his anxiety go. Why was he so freaked? It wasn't his nature. But this party was important. Rene had been tweaking the recipes, and River trusted his expertise. But the kombucha… the homebrewed kombucha was all River and also the entire point of the new cafe. It had to be a smash.

And still, River would be chill about it if this was just a job. But this was the first big event where it would be him and Brent, together, as a couple. Brent's parents were coming, his best friends, along with business people Brent knew. People from AJC were coming. And River had invited the folks from Expanded Horizons.

He was still conflicted about being "out" as a couple. They'd been together now for six weeks, and they were practically joined at the hip. River had never been this close to anyone in his life. But Rome loomed in the distance like the iceberg lying in wait for the Titanic. That unsettled him in ways he didn't even fully understand and made things so much more complicated. Brent's parents might just smack him. And he wouldn't blame them one bit if they did.

Brent gave him a squeeze. "Hey. This is supposed to be fun. You've worked hard to get to this point. And trust me. If there were any problems with the recipes, you or I would already know it. Rene would know it. We like them, and so will everyone else."

"Yeah. You're right."

"Is it… us you're worried about? I can play it cool if you prefer."

That was thoughtful. Brent was a thoughtful man. But River shook his head. "Everyone already knows. You told your family, right? And Justin probably told everyone else in Seattle. I don't want you to feel guarded. That's not cool. Let's just be ourselves."

Brent kissed River's neck and held there for a moment, his breath in River's ear. "You're important to me. And you'll always be important to me, no matter where you are. I want my friends and family to know you."

River had no words for that, so he turned in Brent's arms and pulled him into a deep kiss. And damn the caterers, or anyone else who might be around.

Since they'd had the discussion about River leaving September twenty-fifth, River had tried hard to make everything all right. He spent all his time at Brent's with the dogs, only going over to the houseboat every few days to collect the mail, water the plants, and make sure it was secure. They spent hours making love, and River gave it everything he had, wanting to show that his care and affection were true. He'd kept the surrogacy stuff out of Brent's face as much as he could, booking his weekly appointments back-to-back so they had minimal impact on his work on the cafe or his time with Brent.

It had been obvious that Brent was trying too. He touched River every chance he got, took him out to nice dinners and held his hand, made casual remarks about Rome that were encouraging, even though River could tell he hated the idea. The sadness River saw in his eyes at times was quickly blinked away.

They were both doing their goddamn best to make the most of the situation. River told himself he was lucky and should be grateful. He was lucky to have this here and now, and he was lucky to have Rome ahead of him. Most people would kill for the opportunity. But although the doubt and regret might be out of sight at times, it never fully went away.

Brent pulled back from the kiss. "Mmm. We should get ready. People will be arriving in about forty-five minutes."

River gawked and checked his watch. "Oh. Shit! Why didn't you tell me?"

Brent laughed as River ran inside.

"So you're River." Sean sipped kombucha from a bottle and eyed River with a wary expression.

"I am. I've heard a lot about you, Sean."

Sean grinned. "Oh, yeah? What did Brent tell you about me? He told you I'm great, right?"

"Let's see. He said you've been friends since high school, that you were a huge support to him during Kathy's illness. Oh, and that you're the king of crude."

"Fuck yeah, I am!" Sean enthused. "Brent told me about you too. Well, not about, *you know*, the dirty deets or anything. Just in general. When he saw you through Expanded Horizons. And stuff." Sean blushed.

River raised his eyebrows and sipped his beer. "He said you encouraged him to go to Expanded Horizons. So thank you for that."

Sean wiped his forehead. "Yeah. Never expected *you* to come out of it though. You were a bit of a surprise, being a guy and all. Never saw that coming, but guess maybe I should have? Brent's not your typical football-and-sweats kind of bro."

"Yeah, not really," River agreed.

"Honestly, though, I've never seen Brent this into anyone."

River blinked in surprise at that. "Really?"

Not even with Kathy? River wanted to ask, because Sean had known Brent in high school. But it seemed out of line to ask Sean to compare him to Brent's late wife.

Sean stared into River's eyes. "Never. I mean, maybe it's a midlife thing. Or maybe when you've been through what Brent's been through, you appreciate the good stuff more."

River nodded thoughtfully. "That's an interesting observation, Sean."

Sean puffed out his chest. "I know, right? Brent told me you're into the deep stuff. So I'm making an effort. How'm I doin'?"

River laughed. "Gold star, you."

Sean looked around and lowered his voice. "So you studied tantra, huh? Like, officially?"

Sean was a funny guy. And fairly openminded. River could see why Brent liked him. "Yes, Sean, I studied tantra. Officially."

"Huh. You should consider offering a class for couples. After Brent told me about it, I was curious. So me and Sharon watched some videos. We tried some stuff, but I'm not sure we're doing it right? I thought there might be a class, but there's nothing regular in Seattle. Bet a lot of people would be interested."

River nodded enthusiastically. "Couples work is awesome! I know people who've taught couples' classes. They say it's really rewarding, helping people reconnect with someone they've been with for a long time, discover a deeper intimacy."

Plus, River thought, when you worked with couples you weren't a participant yourself, you just guided them verbally. That had a new appeal now that he was... in a relationship? Yeah, of course he was. At least for now. Brent had been good about not asking about his surrogacy clients, but he still acted tense when he knew River had an appointment.

"You should totally do it!" Sean nudged River's arm. "Hey, maybe you could tie it in with the new cafe somehow. Like, Harmony Tree could offer classes and stuff."

"Maybe," River replied vaguely.

The comment dampened his mood again. He wouldn't be here long enough to establish a couples' tantra clinic or anything else.

Sean seemed to realize it. His face grew serious and the wariness in his eyes returned. "You should know—Brent's the best guy on the planet. I mean that. He's a really, really good human being. The best."

"He is."

Sean shook his head, as if River wasn't getting it. "What he went through with Kathy.... The way he stuck through it, and was always so good to her, no matter how bad it got. He's one in a million. And he deserves to be happy. You know? He deserves someone who will appreciate what a great person he is."

Someone who will stick around. Sean didn't say it, but the words were implied.

"I couldn't agree with you more," River said steadily. He gave Sean a soft smile even though his stomach ached. "So what do you think of that kombucha?"

Sean looked at the bottle in his hand. He had the cranberry flavor. "It's pretty damn good. I always thought it was sort of fru-fru or somethin'. And Brent's been telling me all about the kombucha-on-tap thing, and I'm down with it, because I trust his opinion, and he's so excited. But damn, I see it now. Love the fizz. Good flavor. Not too fruity. It's not alcoholic?"

"Just a little bit. Like one percent."

"Cool." Sean took another swig.

Brent walked up and put a hand on River's shoulder. "Sean, are you embarrassing me?"

Sean gave a fake aghast expression. "Moi?"

Brent rolled his eyes. "Hey, babe, my folks just got here. They'd love to meet you."

"Sure." River managed a parting smile at Sean even though his heart was pounding.

He felt like such a fraud, being presented as Brent's boyfriend. He hid his unease, though, and Brent's parents were lovely. His mom had kind eyes and a gentle spirit, and she reminded River very much of Brent, down to her dark hair and green eyes.

She pulled River into a long hug immediately. "River, we're so glad to finally meet you. I knew Brent had someone special in his life. He's been so happy. I bugged him until he told me about you."

"I'm honored to meet you, Mr. and Mrs. McKay. You raised a beautiful human being, inside and out."

Brent's dad stuck out his hand. "I'll have to agree with you there. Brent's been through a lot, and he's handled it better than I ever could. I'm Jim, by the way."

"Hi, Jim." River shook his hand.

"And please call me Brenda," Brent's mom said.

Jim McKay had a crew cut of silver hair, wore glasses, a red plaid shirt, and shook hands with a soft grip. Brent had said his mom had been a secretary in a dental office and his father a pharmacist.

Brent slipped an arm around River's waist. His parents didn't blink an eye. "I told River you guys are recently retired and might be looking for some travel tips."

"That's right," Jim agreed. "We're living the good life now. We've been looking at travel companies, but there're so many options, it's hard to nail something down. We'd love to hear about the places you'd recommend."

"Sure, I'd be glad to."

"Why don't we grab some plates and kombucha first?" Brent suggested. "This way, Mom."

Brent got his parents loaded up with food and drink and then left them seated on the deck with River. They spent the next half hour talking about the recipes and about travel. Jim and Brenda asked River a lot of questions about his work. He skimmed over the tantra details—because *parents*—but talked about some of his interesting experiences with reiki, and his studies in Eastern religions. It ended with River massaging Jim's neck, which was really painful and stiff. River sent some reiki energy into his chakra there, and Jim swore it felt better.

Brent was busy with any number of guests but looked at River and his parents with an amused smile whenever he came out onto the deck to lead another person to the kombucha.

There might have been some regret in that smile too.

River liked the McKays very much. While they chatted, Jim often touched his wife—a hand on her arm, a caress of her shoulder, or brushing back her hair. It was easy to see how Brent had managed to escape toxic masculinity given their example, and where his steadiness and curiosity came from, his security in who he was. Some people found River's discussion of reiki weird and woo-woo, but the McKays had a genuine intellectual curiosity about it.

At last the McKays went to refill their plates, and River wandered into the house. He saw Michael Lamont and his husband, James, in his wheelchair. They were at the front door, and River went over to greet them.

"It's great to finally meet you," River told James, shaking his hand. "I read *Sentimental Cyanide* after Michael told me about it. What a gorgeous story. I love the way Lamb represents the highest attribute of love that humanity is capable of, yet he's android. And the whole healer aspect was near and dear to my heart. I feel like I could read it a dozen times and not catch all the meaning in it."

James smiled and reached out for Michael's hand. "This one here inspired it. You can thank him."

"But only you could have written it, babe. Sorry we're late. James was on a phone call about a *very* exciting new project." Michael gave River a wide-eyed stare meant as a hint, River was pretty sure.

James gave Michael a warning look. "NDA, my treasure."

"I know, I know. But it's so *exciting*."

"Hmm. Might I see you two at the Oscars sometime soon?" River guessed.

"Maaaaybe," Michael said leadingly.

James sighed. "The guy is irrepressible, I tell you. No more hints. This is a taste-testing party, right? I saved my appetite especially."

"Well, the opening of a new cafe can hardly compare to your news, but come try the food. There's homebrewed kombucha flavors too. We'd love to get your thoughts."

River showed them the way to the buffet table. While they got their plates, River grabbed them a couple of kombucha bottles from the deck. They met up again in the family room where a group from Expanded Horizons was hanging out. River hadn't even seen them arrive since he'd been talking to Brent's folks. He handed James and Michael their bottles, took requests, and went out to grab another round.

After he passed out the bottles, he grabbed a chair from the dining room and joined them. Jack Halloran was there with his husband, Tony, and Dr. Trudy Kaplan had brought her wife Sydney. Brent came over and there were introductions all around. There were no seats, so Brent plopped down on the carpet at River's feet. River made room so Brent could sit between his legs, back against the seat. Brent, chatting with Jack, raised his hand and River took it.

He'd told Brent he wanted him to act natural, and he certainly was. It was so boyfriend-y, more so because James and Michael, Jack and Tony, and Trudy and Sydney were also openly affectionate. River tried to enjoy the moment, the closeness, the camaraderie, despite the pain in his heart.

Nothing was permanent. You could only count on this moment. Anything else was illusion.

Jack gave Brent a smile. "Why am I not shocked you two ended up together? You saw something in River the first time you laid eyes on him. I remember it well. I showed you that brochure in my office, and you couldn't stop staring at his picture."

"Really?" River asked, smiling.

"Yup. He was resistant to the idea of seeing a surrogate at first, but even then, he couldn't keep his eyes off you."

"Aw, I love that," Michael gushed. "It was love at first sight."

"I might have been curious about him," Brent admitted, looked up at River with a smile.

"I'm just glad you waited until you were no longer a client to start seeing each other," Jack added.

Jack's husband, Tony, guffawed. "Yeah, because you and I were so mature that way."

Tony was a lively Italian from New York. He told the story of how he and Jack met. He was a private investigator who'd been looking into a woman's death. She'd been a client at Expanded Horizons, so he'd gone to see Jack undercover. He admitted he couldn't keep his hands off Jack, even while he was posing as a patient.

That lead to Michael and James talking about how they'd met at a book signing. James had always been Michael's favorite author. And Trudy and her wife talked about how they'd met in medical school.

It was all so very domestic, and everyone seemed so in love. River felt the weight of Brent's hand in his, down in his very soul. Maybe he imagined the deep sadness and want he felt in Brent's energy, the wish that they could be a "real" couple too. Or maybe River was projecting, and those feelings were his and his alone.

Later, Michael caught River alone on the deck and looked at him with concern. "Are you all right?"

"Sure. Why?"

"When we were in there, you seemed troubled. Is everything okay between you and Brent? Sorry if we were a bit much. I know you guys are new."

"No, it's fine." River gave Michael a reassuring smile. Then he sighed. "Well, not quite fine. I'm moving on in September so it's, um, it's... it just is what it is."

Michael frowned. "Moving on?"

"I'm moving to Rome. I was only ever supposed to be here for a year. I'm house-sitting for someone, and that's up September tenth."

"Oh." Michael bit his lip. "Geez, we really put our foot in it, huh? Feet? Whatever. Anyway, that's a bummer. Everyone loves you here. I know you're a great addition to the clinic. And you and Brent, you feel..." He hesitated.

"We feel what?"

Michael shrugged. "Like you belong together."

River looked around at the beautiful house, the fancy party. Kathy McKay belonged here. River? Not so much. "That's sweet, but this isn't me. I'm more of a backpack-and-hostel kind of guy."

"This isn't the stuff that matters," Michael said seriously. His eyes were kind. "Hey, if you ever want to talk, we can do lunch. We can swap Expanded Horizons stories. It'll be fun."

"I'd like that. After the next staff meeting?"

"Let's do it! Tuesday." Michael held out a fist.

"You're on." River bumped it.

Michael went back inside, and Maddy came over and gushed to River about the kombucha. She fished around about openings to work at Harmony Tree, and River promised he'd suggest it to Brent.

He smiled and chatted with her, but his heart wasn't in it. He liked Michael. He wanted to have lunch with him. He sensed Michael could become a true friend. And Maddy. And Jim and Brenda McKay. Even Sean. But at the same time, he didn't want to get any closer to any of them.

He didn't think he could stand the weight of one more cherished thing left behind.

Chapter 27

Brent

Brent was drying his hair from the shower when the familiar clink of dog collars sounded in the bedroom. River was back with the hounds. Brent tugged on flannel PJ bottoms and left the bathroom, smiling.

"Congratulations. I'd consider tonight a huge success."

Beauchamp shimmied his butt at the sight of Brent, and the dogs ran over to get their due in pets and kisses.

"Do you think so?" River pulled off his white tunic shirt and dropped it on a chair. "It seemed to go well."

"Absolutely. I heard only good things about the food. Especially the curry stew and the sweet and sour tofu. Sean said he could live on that alone. And everyone raved about the kombucha."

River stepped up to Brent and traced a water droplet down from his shoulder blade. "It's a relief. I want this to be successful for you." His smile was a little sad, and it made Brent's chest ache. But he refused to give in to that now. Tonight was a night for celebration.

"I hope you didn't feel too bombarded by Sean or my folks. It was nice of you to spend so much time with them."

Brent had been so proud of River. He'd looked gorgeous tonight in a white tunic shirt that was a bit of Far East, dark blue jeans, and sandals. He'd freshly washed and blow-dried his hair, somehow pulling it very straight, and he'd worn it down. It looked like gold silk. And, as always, his intelligence and gentle, radiant nature had shone through. Even if Brent had noticed a moment or two of sadness.

"They're nice people. You're lucky. My dad would have freaked if I'd always been straight and suddenly showed up with a boyfriend. My mom... she likely wouldn't have made an appearance at all."

"I'm very lucky," Brent agreed.

River's smile was melancholy, and Brent hated to see it. Not his beautiful River, who normally lit up the world. Or at least, Brent's world. So he pulled River in for a long, slow kiss.

He hardened against River's hip. With River, his dick responded embarrassingly fast. Hell, a smile could do it. Or the way River's bare legs in shorts looked when stretched out on the sofa. Brent thought maybe his libido was making up for lost time.

River thickened in his jeans too. His fingers crept under the elastic at the back of Brent's sleep pants, and he made a yummy noise.

Brent broke the kiss. "Uh, that reminds me. So tonight when Sean and Sharon and I were talking with another couple, Sean brought up tantra—not in relation to you, just as a thing he and Sharon had been researching. And this other guy, Steve, was also interested in it. He mentioned something you never told me about."

"Something I never told you about? What?" River looked bemused.

Brent felt his cheeks heat. "He said that some tantriks do, um, a prostate massage? It was funny, actually. You should have seen the horror on Sean's face. But I never knew that was a thing. So.... Is it a thing?"

River smirked. "Oh, yeah. It's a thing."

Brent felt a little hysterical bubble of laughter in his throat. But he didn't want to offend River, so he kept it to himself. "Like... is there a purpose to it? Or is it just a feel-good thing, or...."

River ran a finger along Brent's crack. "Oh, it has heaps of benefits. Think of it like an engine tune-up on your car. An occasional deep stimulation of the prostate reduces the risk of prostate cancer and bladder infections. And it's good for clearing the sacrum chakra, allowing more intense orgasms and stronger erections. Plus, you know...." River looked up into Brent's eyes. "It's a feel-good thing."

Brent's face grew hotter. "Oh. Yeah. That sounds...." He swallowed.

"At the ashram, even straight men enjoyed it. But it's cool if you don't want to try it. Some people aren't comfortable with anything anal." He shrugged, as if dismissing the idea.

River was teasing him—a little. It was reverse psychology, and it worked. "I'd be open to trying it. Only with you, of course. Because

I trust you. Kathy said it didn't hurt when she and I tried it. Me on her, I mean. She never... No one's ever stuck anything up there."

"Not even yourself?"

Brent shook his head. "Never really thought about it. But I liked anal sex. A lot." He smiled ruefully. "Guess that might have been a clue."

"Not necessarily. I think lots of hetero couples enjoy it."

"I guess." Brent toyed with River's hair. "We went through a period where we tried a lot of different stuff to spice things up. Not that our sex life was ever bad, but we let it get routine. With work and everything."

"That's common. That's why tantra is so great. You focus on touch, on appreciating each other's bodies and the connection, not on orgasm." He gave a confused little frown. "Sean was talking to me about couples' tantra tonight. That's something I'd like to do—someday."

"You'd be so great at that. What you and I do... I can't ever imagine it getting stale."

River's expression softened at the compliment, his eyes going warm. "Me neither. The way we connect.... It's really unique."

"Is it?" He was fishing, but Brent couldn't help it. "You don't feel that kind of connection with others? Clients or... past lovers?"

"No, Brent. Not with anyone else. Never have."

River's words were very serious and the look in his eyes was almost too much. Too much like love. Brent couldn't let himself think about that. "So. About the prostate massage thing...."

"We could do it tonight if you're not too tired?"

Tired? After getting a taste tonight of what it would mean to have River in his life forever, as his true partner, to see him interacting with his friends and his mom and dad.... Brent wanted to be with him in every way possible while he still could. But he made a lighthearted reply.

"Baby, please massage my prostate. I'm dyin' for it!"

River laughed. "Oh, you are so on."

*   *   *

When Brent came back upstairs from getting them glasses of wine, candles flickered on both bedside tables, incense burned, and River's little oil-warmer pot was set up. The familiar sights and smells made Brent's dick, which had softened on his kitchen journey, swell and plump. God, he loved that warm oil. The idea of River using it *there* was surprisingly arousing.

River straightened from placing a large towel on the bed. He was naked, his cock hanging—not at full mast, but definitely not limp either.

He sat on the bed on the towel, cross-legged, his gaze inviting Brent to join him. Brent put the wineglasses next to a candle and sat on the bed, mirroring River's pose, their knees touching.

They always started sex this way, holding hands and gazing into one another's eyes. The deep breathing created an altered state that put Brent in another time and place. If all you cared about was getting off, this would seem like a terrible nuisance, just staring into someone's eyes for five or ten minutes. But Brent loved it. It created a space away from the thoughts of work and his endless to-do lists, a space in which all that existed was himself and River, and time was measured in soft caresses and the heartbeats of his beloved.

He'd never felt as deeply integrated with another person in his life. In this space, the trappings of who he was, who River was, fell away, and they were just two human beings, literally and emotionally naked in front of one other, joining in a union that went beyond the flesh.

Soul to soul.

It was hard to imagine ever again having sex the way he had before. It was hard to imagine having sex with anyone but River ever again. But he didn't want to think about that now, didn't want anything sorrowful or negative to intrude, not now.

He let the thoughts drift away on his breath and focused on River's eyes.

Breathe in, breathe out, until River's exhales became his inhales, until his head spun and energy hummed through his body while his muscles relaxed.

River leaned forward and kissed him softly—a gentle, suckling kiss.

Brent placed his hands on River's bare shoulders. He could go for a lot more kissing. But River pulled away and smiled. "Let's start with you on your back."

Oh God. Were they really doing this prostate thing? A flush of heat went through Brent and a twinge of nerves too. But he trusted River. If he said it felt good, then it did. River moved aside, and Brent lay on his back, making sure he was on the towel.

Was he gonna love this? Hate it? He had no idea.

River propped Brent's knees up on pillows, opening him up. Something about the position never failed to get Brent rock hard, maybe because it was a signal to his genitals that they were about to get lots and lots of attention. His dick skated up his belly until it was pointing at his chin and bobbing just a little to his heartbeat. Subtle. But River never made him feel self-conscious, either of being hard or not being hard.

He began with massage—Brent's feet, calves, belly, chest, arms, neck. His breathing was deep and loud, reminding Brent to stay with his tantric breath too. He melted deeper and deeper into the mattress, and his eyes closed.

God. He never wanted this to end. Wanted River. Only River.

River understood that when you loved someone, it was worth taking time for them, taking lots of time, every day. He understood that *love* was the only thing that really mattered. A few years ago, Brent hadn't understood this. How had River gotten so mature so young?

River got more oil on his hands and massaged Brent's inner thighs, pulling him open a little more with his thumbs. Brent's dick jumped on his stomach. Sexual energy pooled in his belly.

River's massaging fingers moved inward until River's thumbs brushed over Brent's pucker. Brent made a peculiar noise and raised his hips.

Jesus. He wasn't really that interested in this. Was he? Apparently he was.

But River didn't hurry. He massaged Brent there for what felt like a long time, using his fingertips and lots of oil, while the heel of his hand rubbed behind Brent's balls. Slowly, all sensation seemed to focus there, around his anus, in a way it never had before. Brent couldn't believe it felt so nice. Sexy as fuck.

"Can you…" His voice croaked. "Are you gonna… do more?"

He could swear River grinned, even though his eyes were closed.

"Impatient, hmm? I'll start with one finger. If you don't like it, I'll stop."

Oh, hell no, Brent didn't want him to stop. After all that massaging, he needed to feel something push and prod there.

"Just relax." River placed one hand over Brent's cock and pushed it gently down against his belly, holding it there, while the fingers of his other hand slid down from his balls.

"Breathe," River reminded him. Gently, River pushed the tip of one finger in.

Oh.

Brent froze, focusing on the sensation.

"Try not to tense up. Imagine pushing your breath into this space, expanding it. This is your *muladhara,* or root chakra." River rubbed his thumb gently against Brent's perineum and Brent relaxed his muscles. The finger went in another inch.

Oh. Okay.

Brent's balls drew up tighter and his dick throbbed against River's palm. Energy sparked in his groin. He wasn't sure he could stand the sense of anticipation, of it being too much and not enough.

"Keep going," he muttered, his tongue thick.

River withdrew his finger and replaced it a moment later slick with more hot oil. Brent had one instant to think that the heat felt nice, and then, in one smooth move, River slid it all the way in.

Brent's hips arched up. "River!"

"Shhh. Relax."

River left his finger inserted but not moving. With his other hand, he gripped Brent's penis loosely and gave it a few strokes.

Oh God. Okay. Yeah. That works.

"You're so sexy, Brent," River said, his voice rough. It was the first time he'd ever said that during tantric sex, and it made Brent's heart chakra bloom with pleasure. "Can you relax your hips back to the bed for me?"

Brent was surprised to find his hips raised, his ass gripping River's finger. He forced himself to relax back onto the towel.

River pumped him a few more times, twisting his finger gently. Then he did something in there that made hot, electric tingles explode inside him. Brent gave a little cry.

"Mmm. That's your prostate." It felt like River gently rubbed it. "Does that feel okay?"

"Oh *fuck!*" Brent said on a sob.

"Oh *fuck*, good? Or *oh fuck* bad?" River sounded amused.

"I have no idea," Brent said, half laughing, half crying. "Do it again."

"First breathe. Relax and unclench for me."

Brent did both, forcing his body to become loose and focusing on his loud tantric breath. River slid his finger out, then back in with more warm oil. That felt... nice. Weird, but nice. He gently rubbed that spot, and the sparks flew like a garden of fireflies in the night. His dick strained against River's palm. It felt harder than it'd ever been before. Scarily hard.

"Oh my God," Brent whispered.

"Keep going?"

"Hell yes. Maybe... another finger?" For some reason, Brent thought more pressure would feel good.

River withdrew, then pressed two fingers inside him. And fuck yeah, it did feel good. There was something about the feeling of being forced open that was hot. Sort of the way it felt when River filled his mouth with cock. There was no pain at all, which was unexpected. But then, River had been so careful.

River gently rubbed Brent's prostate with two fingers. The other hand circled his dick with one finger and a thumb, jerking him loosely, lightly, maddeningly. It felt incredible, as if both of River's hands were plucking his pleasure zones—one in a way he knew very well, and one in a way that was totally new. The two zones fed each other, nerve endings meeting and sparking fire deep inside him. Brent used what he'd learned of tantra to push those waves of pleasure up and up until they filled his entire body, to surf on the delight, without chasing an orgasm. But the feeling was so overwhelming. It felt like he had no control. His body shook with the intensity.

"I might come," he said, his breath and words raspy.

"That's okay. A prostate orgasm is different. You should experience it."

Oh, yes, he was going to come. But all of a sudden, Brent knew what he wanted.

"Stop," he said, tensing up.

River stopped immediately, removing his hands.

Brent opened his eyes and pushed up onto his elbows. He looked at his lover. River was sitting back on his heels, and he was visibly aroused. His chest was flushed, his nipples peaked, and his penis was fully erect, standing proud from a blond nest of curls. Brent couldn't help but be pleased that touching him aroused River so much.

River's brows knit together. "Are you okay? Did something hurt?"

Brent swallowed. "I'm perfect. But could we... is anal sex allowed in tantra?"

"Love, we can do anything that feels good. Nothing is taboo." River's eyes sparked hot, and his penis gave an eager bob.

"Then would you? I've kind of been curious about it, and I'm so ready right now... I want to feel you inside me when I come. I want it."

God, he did. He wanted to experience River fucking him. Only fear of pain or that he might not like it had held him back, and now that was gone. Everything River had done so far felt amazing. And he wasn't ashamed to ask for this. With River, he wasn't ashamed of anything.

River took a hitched breath. "Okay. But, uh, I don't have a condom."

"I have some. They're probably still good."

River hesitated. "The massage oil doesn't go great with latex."

Brent nearly growled. "Then do we need a condom? I've been tested and you said you have. I've only been with you. I only want to be with you."

River met his eyes for a long moment. Something flickered in those stormy depths, something like sadness, but maybe Brent imagined it, because River nodded and leaned forward to kiss him.

His lips were soft and tender, and he kissed Brent as though he were precious. He pulled back and rested his forehead on Brent's. "You want me inside you?"

Hearing River say the words sent a thrill down Brent's spine. "Yes. So much."

River kissed his cheeks sweetly. "And I want to be inside your beautiful body."

Brent swallowed something hot in his throat. *I love you*, he thought, and nothing about that felt wrong.

River rested back on his heels again. He rubbed Brent's thighs and seemed to consider. "Are you okay to stay on your back? I want to see your eyes."

"Yeah. Me too."

River's eyes burned into his for several seconds, as if pinning this moment in his mind, as if acknowledging it. And him. Acknowledging what Brent was offering.

Christ, the things River made him feel. He never thought he'd want something like this, to be covered, to be fucked. But he did want it, and being with River somehow freed him to want it, freed him to trust in all forms of pleasure, of exploring his body's limits and all the ways the two of them could express their care for one another.

Their love? Yes. Their love.

River poured more warm oil from the pot and rubbed it on himself, his hand doing a corkscrew motion over his own dick that Brent wouldn't mind seeing a lot more of—some other time. Then River leaned forward on one arm, his face above Brent's. As beautiful as his eyes were, Brent couldn't help but look down his body to watch as River took his dick in his hand and leaned forward. He wished he could see everything, but his genitalia were in the way. He felt it, though, felt the smooth, blunt head against his hole, where he was suddenly aware of how empty he felt, how raw and sensitive.

River carefully pushed in and Brent gasped.

His head thudded back to the bed, and he stared into River's eyes. He felt... everything. River's penis was much different than his fingers. More rigid. Bigger. There was a little burn and a lot of fullness. It felt... weird? Weird. And kind of amazing, as if his body was doing something he had no idea it could do.

"Breathe. Relax your muscles," River whispered, watching Brent's face intently.

He inhaled deeply, and Brent mirrored him. They both exhaled, loud tantric breath, and Brent's body relaxed. River went in another inch, as if Brent's body was pulling him inside. Again. Again. And then Brent realized he was in as far as he could go.

River stopped, not moving. He bent down to kiss Brent briefly, though the angle was challenging. He went back up on one elbow and smiled. "How does it feel?"

How did it feel? Indescribable. He had another man's penis inside him. Maybe there should have been a sense of shame. But nope. It was River, his beautiful River with his beautiful soul, who made everything feel so natural and right. And Brent wished he could hold him inside forever.

Brent took a shaky breath. His eyes stung. "Feels good. Really full."

River smiled. "I know. Let me know if it starts to sting. I can add more oil. Or stop."

"No. No stopping. Please."

River circled his hips, rocking gently inside him, and just that much pressure on his prostate, which River had made him feel for the first time in his life, sent waves of heat through his groin. His dick bounced once on his belly. "Right there."

"I've got you." River pulled out and thrust in. Brent gripped River's waist, urging him to do it again.

River thrust—hard and steady, not teasing. And thank God. Brent tried to focus on the feeling, the friction and pressure and the way it all seemed to tie directly into his balls. And River above him, gazing into his eyes, watching the tightening of River's pleasure in his face. The way his eyes got that almost pained look. The way his upper lip trembled. And it wasn't just the physical sensations. It was the idea of it, of surrendering to River, of being taken, that was erotic on a level somewhere under the skin of Brent's heart.

So good. Even... familiar?

Why did this feel so familiar? Had River made love to him like this before? In another life? Brent might have scoffed at that idea normally, but at this moment, he enjoyed the fantasy that River had penetrated him many times before, that their bodies had been joined like this in decades past, maybe always. *Yin* and *yang*. *Yang* and *yin*. Maybe they'd been different genders at different times. Maybe they were both genders. Or none at all.

Brent threw back his head, arching his back and giving in to the images of him and River that flooded his mind. He clung to River's waist, urging him to thrust harder, faster. The pleasure wound and wound and wound, tighter and tighter, a snake winding up his spine.

"Brent, look at me."

Brent forced his eyes open. River's face was red and tense in a way Brent had never seen before. He was close, breathing hard, thrusting fast. The sexual energy was already flooding Brent's body, but looking into River's pleasure caused it to surge. Brent felt it in his heart chakra and exploding from the top of his head. He felt like a damned light bulb.

River propped himself up on one arm and with the other reached between them, grasped Brent's dick, and just *squeezed*.

Brent gave a strangled cry and came. He couldn't have held back the orgasm, didn't want to. It felt like it was coming from his balls, but also from inside him, from his prostate, a strange wavery thrumming that heightened and extended his orgasm so that it felt like water was gushing out of him.

Somehow he kept his eyes open, fixed on River's face. And in the midst of the waves of pleasure, he watched River come. His hips slammed home and stayed there, deep as he could get, his lips trembled, his eyes burned. Deep inside Brent, his dick jerked and pumped three, four times.

They stared at each other for a heartbeat that felt like eternity.

River collapsed beside Brent, breathing hard. He lay against Brent's chest, his heart thumping wildly. Brent petted River's back, which was slick with sweat, as his own body slowly calmed down.

A heaviness stole over him, and a quiet satisfaction. He smiled. "You decided to ejaculate?"

River nodded. "I wanted to be with you in that moment." River's hand stole up to interlace fingers with Brent's.

"I'm glad." Brent kissed the top of River's head. Even though he had gotten quite good at internalizing orgasms himself, he felt foolishly proud that River had ejaculated inside him. What a weird buzz of satisfaction that gave him!

"Your *yin* energy is so pure," River said. "You're amazing. You can be so masculine and driven. But you have this feminine side that is just as strong. It's beautiful. I love that you can express both sides so freely."

Brent gave a dazed laugh. "I never even knew I had that side until you."

River was quiet for a moment, and then he said, "You've taught me things about myself too."

Brent wanted to ask what, but he was a little afraid to hear the answer. He didn't want to talk about River leaving. So instead he said, "Shall we sleep?"

"Yeah."

They managed to get under the covers. Brent used the towel they'd had on the bed to wipe an obscene amount of ejaculate off his belly and then they entwined their bodies. Chest to chest. Curled around each other like *yin* and *yang*.

Chapter 28

River

"Caesar salad, please. Dressing on the side." Michael handed the waiter his menu.

"I'll take the orange tempeh bowl," said River, handing his over too.

The waiter left and River stirred his tea. "Not hungry?"

Michael gave him a knowing look. "Don't worry. I'm not anorexic, just small. James has been on a cooking jag lately, so I like to go home with a healthy appetite. I think it's lasagna tonight."

"Ah, the things we do for love." River smiled, but his heart wasn't in it.

Michael watched him for a moment, his eyes kind. "So. You've got this crazy-exciting year in Rome coming up, but you're torn about it, huh?"

"Pretty much." Wasn't River just wishing for someone he could talk to a few weeks ago? And here was Michael, offering to lend an ear. He was sweet. "I know it's for the best long term. And it's all arranged. But it's... hard."

"Hmm. First things first. How is it all arranged? You can't change it?" Michael leaned forward and sucked on the straw in his iced tea, his dark eyes curious.

River shook his head. "I'm staying with an eighty-year-old who was a client. Yeah, I know, bad idea. But he's a really interesting guy, and it's not like that. He just wants to see Rome again and can't take the trip on his own. He has an Airbnb there, and he already took it off the market. And booked our flights. That's thousands of dollars right there. Plus, I enrolled in a tantric yoga course in Rome and had to put down a deposit. It's all set."

"It sounds idyllic," Michael mused. "Let me ask you this—if it weren't for all of that, would you want to stay? At the party, you and Brent just seemed so... grounded. Really close."

River sighed. "I love Brent. But even if I could stay, for how long? I can't see myself giving up traveling and learning indefinitely. And it would never work between us anyway."

"No?"

River shook his head. "No. For lots of reasons. The one you can probably relate to is that I'm a tantrik healer. Brent's been very patient about it, but I worry that eventually he'll resent it, my seeing clients, touching them. I'm just not sure how I can commit to long-term monogamy with anyone."

"You're right. That's not easy."

"How do you make it work? Doing surrogacy and being married. It doesn't bother James?"

Michael leaned forward, his expression sympathetic. "All surrogates have to deal with the issue sooner or later. I know of a few surrogates who quit when they met that special someone. Some partners are okay with it. I'm lucky that James is, but we established really specific boundaries."

"Oh yeah? Like what?"

"I don't do anal with clients. Ever. And I involve James. I don't tell him my patients' names or anything, but I'll describe in general what the client's issue is and how we work on it in a session. I know it's frowned upon. Confidentiality and all that." Michael played with his straw. "But my relationship with James is the most important thing in my life. And I think it helps him think of it clinically, you know? And knowing what I'm doing exactly puts his mind at ease. Like, he's not imagining things are worse than they are."

"That's interesting."

Michael nodded. "It works for us. And if a client starts pushing past the professional boundaries, we're done. Honestly, though, the cases Jack involves me in are usually pretty severe. James and I both really want to help them."

River thought about James's book, the way his character, Lamb, began as a sex robot and ended up being so much more, embodying the highest form of love.

"James seems like a kind man."

Michael laughed.

"What?"

"Oh, he is. Only he has such an acerbic tongue. He'd find that description of himself hilarious. He'd probably tell you to fuck off."

River smiled. He thought he would like to know James better. If there was time.

"Brent strikes me as a good man too," Michael said leadingly.

"He is. He says he understands that I help people. But I generally avoid talking about my surrogacy clients with him. I guess I figure, 'don't ask, don't tell,' right? I mean, he knows when I see clients, but it's not like, 'Hey, honey, how was your day?' 'Fine. This guy with premature ejaculation lasted for two minutes this time before coming all over me!'"

River shook his head and went on. "The thing is, he was married for nineteen years and never cheated on his wife. He's very loyal. It's not that he complains about my work, it's more like I *feel* he couldn't possibly approve. And I'm a healer. That's my path. Eventually, it will come between us."

Michael nodded thoughtfully. "I get that you feel you can either follow your calling *or* have a relationship. I totally felt that way for years. But it doesn't have to be black or white. Just because Brent and his wife had a certain kind of relationship doesn't mean it has to be that way with you."

River grimaced. "Maybe. I admit, I have a bit of a *Rebecca* syndrome. You know, thinking the wife was perfect and I can't measure up."

It sounded whiny to admit it, but it was true. Kathy was the perfect business partner, the perky Doris Day wife to Brent McKay. River was... a strange choice by comparison.

"River, he loves *you*. I know he does. I saw it at the party. And you and he have your own thing. It doesn't have to be like the relationship he had before."

River thought about that. "You're right. I shouldn't worry about what it *should* be. I should just let it be what it is. But then it keeps coming back to me. Ultimately, I'm just not the settling-down type.

I don't know if I'll ever stay in one place. So even if Brent could embrace my tantrik self, and we could figure everything else out, it's…" He sighed. "Kind of moot? Ugh. I'm sorry. You're sweet to listen to me, but there's not much that can help. It's just… hard."

Michael leaned forward and rubbed River's arm. "I'm sorry. It's tough to have to make a choice between two things you love. And I get the appeal of the traveling life. Personally, I could never hack it. I own too many books, and you'd have to pry them from my cold, dead hands." He laughed. "But I can see that it would be super-rewarding and exciting. Jack said you studied tantra at an ashram in India? Tell me about that."

The conversation moved on from Brent McKay. Which was just as well.

As a surrogate, Michael was quite interested in tantra, and they discussed it for a long time. River gave him some good books to check out.

Who knew? Maybe Lamb of *Sentimental Cyanide* would one day become a tantric master too.

Chapter 29

River

The rest of August went by fast—bullet-train fast. The cafe was set to open on August thirty-first, a Saturday. Brent did a press release and sent out cool-funky invitations that were specially printed with the cafe's new logo. *Harmony Tree Cafe & Kombucha Bar.*

And suddenly, it was real.

The weeks leading up to the opening were frantic. The furniture arrived from the wholeseller, and Brent spent two days on site with a couple of burly movers, shifting things around until he was satisfied. Security cameras and the iPad-driven order system were installed. The kombucha tap system and coffee station were put in place. The Wi-Fi was hooked up and the final menu given to the woman who did the fancy blackboards. Brent had hired a brew master to recreate River's kombucha brews in large batches. River was a little sad about that. The kombucha was his baby. But what did he expect? He was leaving. Someone had to fill the hole he was leaving behind.

Somebody else's life.

River and Brent didn't talk about River leaving anymore. They *never* talked about it.

They didn't have time for five-hour tantric sessions, but they made love every night, and the intimacy was always profound. Staring into Brent's eyes as they teased each other's cocks, or joined together in sixty-nine, the energy flowed between them in an endless circle. Sometimes River filled Brent, and a few times Brent filled River, seamlessly moving between push/pull, give and receive.

Sorrow and elation.

On the day before the grand opening, Sean dropped off a copy of the *Seattle Times* at their doorstep in the morning. At the top of the Local section was a story entitled, "Next on Tap for Brent McKay."

There was a photo of Brent in front of the retro kombucha taps with their names like "Happiness" and "Soother." The newspaper had sent out a professional photographer, and Brent looked so handsome. The article discussed his past success with Adrenaline Junkie Coffee and was very complimentary about the new concept and menu. It called Brent "one of Seattle's best foodie creatives."

"What a great piece," River commented after reading it at the breakfast table. "You should frame it and put it on the wall in the cafe. Our first rave review." He couldn't help but feel proud.

Brent looked pleased, but he shook his head. "It's fantastic but… Christ. With a feature like this, we're going to be overrun tomorrow. I need more staff. And I should have Rene double the food order." He was out of his seat making calls before he'd finished talking.

It was all sort of twisted up. River knew Brent had set the grand opening for August thirty-first in deference to his very early remark that he would be leaving in September. Which made everything rushed. Which, in turn, gave them less time to just be together. They could have moved the date back since River wasn't leaving now until September twenty-fifth, but the opening involved so many moving parts, and the schedule was set. Besides, River was looking forward to having a few weeks before he left that weren't consumed by the cafe.

Saturday dawned like a benediction—clear and sunny and slated to be a perfect seventy-five degrees. River and Brent got to the cafe at 6:00 a.m. to help set up. Rene brought all the food, which went into the cold case, soup pots, and large fridge in the kitchen. The kombucha taps were all working—River tested them all, and the brews tasted just as they should. The coffee bar was stocked with everything they needed. River made a chai for himself and coffee for Brent just to test them out.

The staff arrived. Justin was working the register today, there were two on food, experienced people from elsewhere in Brent's empire, and River had requested Maddy help him with drinks. Brent told River he didn't have to work behind the counter today. He could be more of a meeter and greeter. But River wanted to serve the kombucha, chai, and other drinks himself. Besides, he preferred being busy so he didn't have to schmooze or stress about how things were going.

When the doors opened at eight, there were only a few people waiting outside. But by ten o'clock, there was a line down the block. The tables filled up so people stood at the counters along the window. And then even that was too crowded, so people got stuff to go and hung out on the street outside. It was a scene. River just kept making drinks, absorbing compliments, and sending out happy, welcoming vibes with his smile and cheerful attitude.

There was finally a bit of a lull around two. Justin wandered over to the kombucha taps trying to look casual. River knew what was coming, but he gave Justin a smile. "Hey. How do you like the new place?"

"It's awesome." Justin looked around, his expression envious. "I love the kombucha on tap idea, the décor..." His gaze skimmed the abstract tree painted on one wall. "The art. The logo. The colors. It's all perfect. Mr. McKay is a genius." He glanced at River. "Oh. And I know you helped a lot too."

"Thanks."

"So... You and Mr. McKay, huh?"

"Yup. Me and Mr. McKay." River kept his expression neutral. His instinct was to give some excuse. Something like, *We were working together all the time, and it just happened.* But he didn't owe Justin anything.

Justin tsked. "If I'd have known he, like, *at all*, swung my way...." He shook his head. "Man. I would have been all over that like white on rice."

River didn't say anything. Brent wouldn't have been into Justin. Would he?

"Are you guys serious?" Justin asked, crossing his arms over his chest.

River huffed a laugh and gave Justin a raised eyebrow.

"Sorry. Sorry. I know it's none of my business." He sighed. "Hope springs eternal."

River was not going to tell Justin that he was leaving in September and therefore, no, it wasn't serious. That would be like throwing a ball up in the air at the start of a volleyball game. The thought of Justin and Brent together made his gut tighten. He thought for a moment he might actually be sick.

But, again, what did he expect? Someone else would fill the void he left. If not soon, then eventually. Probably not Justin, but someone.

Someone else's Brent McKay.

"Two bowls of veggie curry coming through!"

Chapter 30

"Want to go down to the lighthouse?" River asked.

"Sure."

They managed to walk side by side on the hiking trail. Brent held River's hand. Very little on Earth could make him let go. It was their last weekend together, and Brent had surprised River with a two-night stay at a beachfront B&B on San Juan Island.

The September days were still long, and the light was golden during this after-dinner hike. River's hair was down and silky from a recent shower. His beard looked soft. He wore green cargo shorts and a white, gauzy pullover shirt that was the epitome of summer.

And Brent's heart ached.

It was a familiar pain. It had been growing for the past few weeks. After the launch of Harmony Tree Cafe, which had been wildly successful, there was less to distract Brent's brain from the reality of what was coming. Their time together was running out like the last sands in an hourglass. Yes, he'd had plenty of business calls to field. There was an investor in New Jersey who already wanted to open up a Harmony Tree Cafe there and another guy in California. There were tweaks to make to the menu and staff. But Dani had taken over as manager, and she had it well in hand. And even though he was staying on top of Adrenaline Junkie Coffee much better these days, those branches pretty much ran themselves.

That was good because Brent was suddenly very selfish of his time. Selfish of River's time. Now that the Reynolds had returned from London, River lived at Brent's house. If only Brent could keep him there. Lock River away. But that wasn't how life worked. He couldn't make River want this life. He couldn't change his lover's soul.

There was a saying Brent had come to absolutely loathe—*If you love something, set it free.* It was the worst saying of all time. And Brent struggled with following its advice every single day.

"It's so cute," River said, as they walked up to the lighthouse.

It was cute—a small, square structure with a pointed red roof. It looked like a fairy house. The lighthouse tower clung to one side like an afterthought, overlooking the rocky promontory the lighthouse guarded. From leprechauns, perhaps.

River tried the door. It opened. Inside were boards telling the history of the place. The Lime Kiln Lighthouse was its name. River took his time reading the information, but Brent didn't have the patience for history lessons right now.

"Can we go outside and sit in the sun? I want to talk." Brent's heart pounded. But he meant to have this conversation while they were on the island, and suddenly he knew it had to happen right now.

River gave him a curious look. "Okay."

They left the building and found a large flat rock to sit on. The water stretched out blue, blue, blue for miles. The navy mounds of distant mountains looked like filigree on the horizon.

Brent half turned to face River and took his hand. "River."

River's eyelids fluttered and he got a slightly wary look, like he didn't want to have this conversation. And yeah, they'd been avoiding it. But they were out of time.

"Yes, Brent," River said quietly.

Brent took a deep breath. His heart hurt. It hurt so damned bad. "There's something I want to say. Because if I don't say it, I'll always wonder *what if*."

River visibly swallowed. But Brent went on.

"I know you already have all these plans in place for Rome. And I get that it's an exciting opportunity. I don't want to hold you back. But."

"Brent—"

"No please, just let me say this." He looked River in the eyes, laying his soul bare. "I love you. I've fallen head-over-heels in love with you. This is not a passing fancy for me. I want you in my life. I want to be with you, grow old with you. And I didn't want you to leave and not know that... this is how I feel about you. That's how I see *us*. I thought Kathy was the love of my life. And she was. But you are too. The two of you are like... like bookends. Only you, River, you're part of my soul."

Brent had to take a deep breath to go on. "And if you really want to go to Rome and take this class, I'll wait. I'll wait as long as there's a chance you'll come home to me."

River's eyes grew damp. Brent had never seen him cry. He suddenly looked so broken. "Brent... I tried to tell you from the start. I'm not the stay-put type."

"I know, but...." Brent's breath hitched, and he closed his eyes for a second. "I know that you've traveled a lot, and that's your lifestyle. I'm not trying to change you. I just needed you to know that you have this choice. This other choice. This life with me. If you want it. Live with me. Work with me. Or focus on your clients. I know healing is important to you, and I want you to be true to that. Whatever you want. It's all on the table."

Tears rolled down River's cheeks, and he pulled his hand away to wipe them. He covered his eyes, his shoulders tight. And Brent's heart sank further. *Please.*

"That's not fair to you." River's voice cracked, his expression resigned as he dropped his hands. "I don't know what will happen after Rome. But I know it will be something. There will always be something. I don't want to be like the wild and crazy mom—or aunt—who comes back into your life now and then before running off to something new. Believe me, I know what it's like to be on the other end of that. You deserve better. You deserve someone who will be with you, love you, be devoted to you, every day of your life. And I do love you. I love you more than I've ever loved anyone."

Heat clogged Brent's throat as his hope failed. He clenched his fists on his lap. "But."

"*But* what you're talking about, that's just not me. I've got my own path to follow. I told you, dedication to a spiritual path is selfish. I can't limit myself to one place or to one... one person."

Brent flinched. "You wanted the white picket fence once upon a time."

River blinked at him. "Are you talking about when I went to live with my dad? Brent, I was fourteen. And I learned my lesson, believe me."

Anger sparked. "Just because your attempt at living a so-called normal life with your dad wasn't great, doesn't mean it can't be. We could be so amazing together. And you can still take classes and practice here in Seattle. What is it you think you'll find out there that you can't find here?"

River's jaw clenched and his words got more adamant. "That's just not who I am! I... I need to keep moving. See new things, experience new places. I don't expect you to understand, but please try to respect my feelings."

Brent deflated. For a while he watched the water, and it occurred to him how small he was, how small they all were, compared to the ocean. Yet this was his life, and if it mattered not a whit to God, it mattered to him. And he'd fought for it. And failed. "I respect your feelings, babe. And you're right. You warned me from the start. I built up dreams and... and I shouldn't have. That's on me. But I just want to say one more thing." He swallowed.

River looked wary, like he just wanted this intensely painful conversation to end. But he sighed, and said, "Go ahead."

"I want to say that it's possible to surprise yourself. It's possible that you—and by that, I mean the universal you—are not a hundred percent what you think you are. You once told me that other people's expectations can be a prison of the mind. Well, your own can be too. I never thought I'd fall in love with a man or have an interest in Eastern philosophy. Or kombucha." He smiled sadly. "Just consider—as you go on with your life—that maybe you're not the rolling stone you think you are. That maybe, someday, you'll want forever too."

A breeze came up that was cool on his face, making him aware of the tracks of his tears. He held out his arms in a kind of apology, and

River embraced him. They held each other, clinging hard, for a long time.

It was goodbye. There was a deep, hollow pain in the vicinity of Brent's heart that he knew would not go away quickly. Maybe never. He'd lost Kathy, and now River too.

He wanted to ask River what happened when your heart chakra suffered a mortal blow. He did not.

He simply cried. And River cried too.

Chapter 31

Rome was everything River could have imagined and more—the bridges over the river, the grandeur of the Vatican City and St. Paul's Square, the quaint oh-so-European shopping streets, the unbelievable food, Trevi fountain, the ruins. In Rome, you stood on the foundation of antiquity. Of sacredness. And, with the superb nightlife, of sin.

Harrison's apartment was up three narrow flights—which River had to help him up and down. It had high ceilings, a kitchen that was small but serviceable, and a pull-out couch that River insisted on sleeping on, despite Harrison's many ploys. The location could not have been better. River could walk to everything, including his classes.

And despite all that, he was absolutely, *extravagantly* miserable.

He tried to shake it off. He went out to dinner with Harrison and his friends—all seniors, and all vibrant theater people. River liked them. But he didn't feel like he belonged, especially given the hours of old stories, half told in Italian, the cigarettes, and the wine. The jokes were often insulting to one minority or another. Or to women. They were from a different era.

Every night, Harrison tried to wheedle River into his bed, "Just to sleep, dear boy." Every night River said no. Harrison's attempts at seduction were annoying, but, honestly, River's head was too distracted to pay it much mind.

He thought things would improve once he started his classes. Tantric yoga. He'd been so looking forward to it.

But... he didn't love it. Of course, he always enjoyed yoga, and it felt great to stretch his muscles and calm his anxious brain. But the tantric aspects felt rudimentary compared to the ashram, and the whole discipline felt shoehorned together. The lessons were redundant to other things he'd studied and, at times, simply wrong. The teacher was an Italian yogi in his forties, and he came across as a narcissistic dick, more interested in helping the women in the class with their "form" than he was in any real spiritual practice.

River told himself he was being harsh. Maybe he was cynical after his experience with Shri Agontha. He didn't want to be. He *wanted* to believe, to be generous and openhearted.

So River tried.

He called his mother. Not shockingly, her trip didn't materialize. She'd left Francois and was "stuck" in Paris with a new friend she "couldn't abandon right now." Of course, she had no trouble abandoning her plans with River. River didn't bother to tell her that. It was pointless.

The fifteenth of October came and went. Three weeks since he'd left Brent. Three weeks of feeling like he wanted to die. And then, day by long, painful day, it was Halloween.

"A bunch of us ex-pats are taking a Dark Rome walking tour on Halloween night. You should come!" Wendy was a tall, lanky New Yorker who'd lived in Rome for five years. She was a local yoga instructor and was taking the Sacred Tantric Yoga class to add to her repertoire. She seemed nice, but River had turned down her invitations before. He couldn't keep doing that. He needed to try to make friends in Rome. He was about as low as he'd ever been in his life.

"Sure, I'll go. Thanks for asking."

"Great! Give me your number, and I'll text you the time and place. Halloween night, okay?"

"I didn't know they celebrated Halloween here."

Wendy shrugged. "Yeah, not so much. But more Italian families are letting their kids dress up and taking them around their piazzas to collect candy from neighbors. Some of the clubs have themed parties, but they're a scene. I thought this sounded like a fun alternative."

The tour was fun. Six of them from the tantric yoga classes showed up and a few dozen strangers. The guide was an exuberant and hot Italian with perfect English. Harrison would have drooled over him, River thought. They visited piazzas where heretics were burned at the stake and were said to still roam. They went past a building from the fourteenth century where an executioner had lived, the place still haunted by his victims. They went underground and saw a huge pit of human bones where the bodies of plague victims had been sealed away.

"How are you liking Rome?" Sergio was a lithe, doe-eyed Italian from his class, very clearly gay. He'd stuck close to River on the tour.

"It's an incredible city."

I wish I could appreciate it more. I need to appreciate it more, River thought.

"Yes. I was born here. If you like, I could show you around. Maybe next weekend? I have heard that you are a tantrik already, and I would love to... to do some practice with you." Sergio's limpid eyes were filled with longing. He seemed very gentle, and normally River would be up for a tantric session with him. But.

River gave him an apologetic smile. "I'm sorry, but I'm...." *What?* "I'm... sort of getting over someone."

"Ah, it is the heartbreak, yes? I see this in your eyes." Sergio's expression was sympathetic. "Sometimes it can help, being with someone new."

"I feel you. But... I'm not ready."

"Okay. Maybe in some months. We will be in class together, yes?"

"Yeah. Maybe." River sighed. Sergio was sweet. And River knew he had to make an effort. "I wouldn't mind getting some local tips though. Tell me what I definitely need to see in Rome."

They talked as the group tour wandered through the streets, and Sergio pointed things out as they went.

On the Ponte Sisto, the guide had them imagine a ghost carriage containing the only female pope fleeing Rome. Supposedly it was still seen to this day. But all River could imagine was Brent McKay—being on this tour on Halloween night with Brent would be *a blast.* He could imagine how delighted Brent would be, how his eyes would sparkle, how he'd soak everything in like a sponge. He'd hold

River's hand and treat him like he was the most important person in the world.

You could invite him to visit you here. One phone call, one email, and he'd be on a plane tomorrow.

Yes. But what about next week? What about when it came time to move on to the next destination? River couldn't offer Brent a fraction of his time, his life. A vacation relationship. It wasn't fair.

He'd planned to look for work in Rome, maybe a part-time massage or barista gig to earn some cash. But he didn't have the energy. He didn't care. He stopped going out with Harrison and his friends. He went to his classes and that was all. His appetite deserted him.

One night, he cried in the dark on the sofa bed until he realized that, like a persistent tickle in the throat, if he let himself indulge in tears, he'd never stop.

It was ridiculous! He had nothing to cry about, feel sorry for himself about. He had to get over this. He went to a beautiful little stone church a few blocks from Harrison's apartment and prayed and meditated for a long time. It did help for a while.

A few weeks after Halloween, Harrison met River at the apartment door as he came up the stairs from class. He wore his long black wool coat and made a shooing gesture. "Turn around. Come, Mr. Larsen. We're going for a walk."

"But I just got home. I wanted to take a–"

"No! I sprayed for bugs, so we can't go in there right now."

River tried to push past him through the open doorway. "I don't smell anything."

"Out!" Harrison shut the door and locked it as if he were hiding a cardinal sin. "Now, will you make me go down those stairs by myself? I'm liable to break my ankle. Not that you should trouble yourself over lil' old me."

With a sigh, River resigned himself to a walk. He helped Harrison move slowly down the stairs. The old man had a cane, but he preferred to lean on River. Out on the sidewalk, it was chilly and the midafternoon street was busy with young children and their parents, and mobs of teenagers, just out of school. With Harrison's arm in his, they made their way the few blocks to Piazza Navona with its gorgeous marble fountain, the Fontana dei Quattro Fiumi.

Harrison found an empty place to sit on the fountain's lip. Naturally, it was close to the enormous, naked male Triton figure. Harrison glanced over it admiringly before they settled.

"Ah, Rome," he said with a contented sigh.

Chapter 32

River

"If I were casting Hamlet, you'd be perfect for the role," Harrison began, his tone arch. "I never thought I'd see a real, live human being as morose and conflicted as that damn Dane. You've proven me wrong, dear boy."

River wanted to laugh, only it really wasn't funny. "I'm sorry. I know I haven't been good company. And that's the whole reason you invited me."

Saying the words, he realized how true they were, and guilt assailed him. What a raw deal this was turning out to be for Harrison "I can pay you rent. I earned good money while I was in Seattle, and I stuck almost all of it in savings."

Harrison looked heavenward as though for patience. "Oh, please. This isn't about money. I'm *worried* about you. You've lost weight. You're depressed. I thought you needed time, but we've been here almost two months, and it's not getting any better."

River leaned forward, elbows on his knees. "It feels... it feels like my heart is being ripped in two. I thought it would fade. But...." He shook his head.

Harrison clicked his tongue. "Love can be so cruel. You're up to your ears in it, dear one. So what exactly is the problem? Does he not feel the same?"

"He does. He asked me to stay."

"So why are you here?"

River rubbed his chest. "Brent... he wants it all. I don't think he can do partway. And that's not me."

Harrison's eyes glittered. "Because...?"

River blew out a breath. "You can't put your faith in people. You can't *need* people, rely on them. That only leads to heartbreak in the end. Buddha says desire is the cause of suffering. If you don't expect anything, *desire* anything, pin your hopes on anything, you can't be disappointed. You need to let things flow through your life. Just let things be what they are."

Harrison made a thoughtful sound. "Sounds to me like you've known some crap people."

River gave a sharp laugh of surprise. "What?"

"Is your Brent unreliable?"

River hesitated. "No. But that's not the point."

"Then explain it to me. *Slowly.*" Harrison made a theatrical flourish with his hand, as if offering River the stage.

River sighed. He honestly wasn't sure anymore. But he tried. "Say I agree to stay in Seattle indefinitely. Live with Brent. What if it doesn't work out? Then I've made a huge mistake. Or what if I really need to go do something else, like if there's a teacher I want to study with in another country or I get a chance to do a retreat in Tibet or something? But I can't because I've made promises to someone. I want to experience the world. To settle down forever in one place... that's simply not me. Ultimately, I'm a dandelion puff. You know?"

"You're a what?" Harrison sounded incredulous.

River gave him a sad smile. "It's something my mother always says. She says we're like dandelion puffs, her and I. Light as a feather. Floating wherever the breeze takes us."

Harrison stared at him, a frown of confusion between his brows. "River..." He spoke slowly. "What is a dandelion puff?"

River blinked. "You mean, metaphorically?"

"No, I mean literally. What, literally, is a dandelion puff?"

"Um...." Did Harrison really not know? "When a dandelion flower goes to seed it turns into a puff ball that's so light—"

"Yes. Yes. But you said the key word in there."

River didn't get it.

"The word is *seed*, River. A dandelion puff is a seed pod."

"Okay?"

Harrison spoke with exaggerated patience. "So a seed, dear boy, cannot fulfill its purpose until it lands somewhere and takes root."

River straightened in astonishment. He laughed. "Okay. Wow. Guess my mother didn't really think that through."

Harrison gave a thoughtful hum. "Listen, I made those same excuses for most of my life. What if someone comes along I want to fuck, but I can't, because a lover expects me to be *monogamous*?" He said the words with mock horror. "What if I get the opportunity to direct a production in London? I need to be free as a bird. My career always comes first." He waved a hand. "Etcetera, etcetera. So I fucked my way through half the gay men on the East Coast and a few straight ones too. I never let anyone tie me down."

He put a hand on River's thigh and squeezed. "And here I am, a lonely, pathetic old goat at eighty-fuck-all-years-old who can't even get it up. And I'm still trying to seduce beautiful young things like you."

River didn't know what to say.

"You're not like me, River. You're not driven by ego. You're a kind man. And I dare say you are infinitely capable of love."

River felt so torn. His stomach ached and his throat stung. Hamlet, indeed. "Love, yes. Of course. But there's universal love, love for everyone. And then there's love for, dependence on, a specific person."

"Mmm. Loving amorphously is safer, I suppose."

Is it? Am I just a coward?

"It seems to me," Harrison mused, "if you want to do something that's spiritually difficult, loving one person, working things out with them, trusting them enough to put your heart in their hands, and be responsible for theirs in turn, is much more challenging than loving *mankind*. But what do I know? I was never willing to even try."

River watched the couples and families in the piazza and thought Harrison was probably right. Loving a partner, children, was infinitely harder. And scarier.

"I do know one thing for certain," Harrison went on. "Your heart is telling you what it wants, my boy. Do you really intend to just go on ignoring it?"

"I don't know what to do!" River wanted to go back. His heart wanted it. Even his body was rebelling against him. But was it the right thing in the long run? "The whole white-picket-fence thing. Can it ever be real?"

Harrison nodded his chin at a stooped old Italian couple who were strolling arm in arm, elegantly dressed. He had a bright red rose in the breast pocket of his gray coat. It matched the scarf on her head. "It is for some people. I never believed in it myself. I guess that's a choice I made. You'll have to make that choice for yourself."

River suddenly remembered something he'd said to Brent in India. That believing in life after death, in faith itself, was a choice.

Sounds a lot like marriage, Brent had said.

And finally, River got it. Loving someone was a leap of faith.

Chapter 33

River

River stuffed everything he owned into his two giant duffel bags and gave Harrison a final hug.

"I can fly back and escort you home. Just let me know when you're ready to go."

Harrison waved a hand in dismissal. "That won't be necessary. I want to stay. More of my friends are still in the land of the living here than in Seattle. And Antonio lost his partner a few years back. Maybe, if I'm lucky, he'll consider me."

Antonio was a short, very dapper Italian actor only a few years younger than Harrison.

"That would be fantastic," River said sincerely. "You'd make a great couple."

Harrison almost looked shy. "We'll see. But you've inspired me, dear boy. Maybe there's hope for both of us, hmm?"

River hurried down the stairs. He'd managed to find a flight to Seattle that was leaving soon. That was great except it was leaving *very* soon.

He hailed a taxi, which would be faster than public transportation. It dropped him at the airport, and he made it to the gate with twenty minutes to spare.

As he sat there, he thought about calling Brent, letting him know he was coming. But his phone wasn't registered for international calls, and WhatsApp just didn't cut it when it came to *I'monmywayhomeiloveyou* messages.

Instead, he brought up Facebook and looked at Brent's personal page. It hadn't been updated since he'd posted reviews and articles about the Harmony Tree Cafe in early September. Apparently, he hadn't felt much like being online.

On a whim, River checked out Justin's twitter posts. Justin posted about everything. Maybe he'd mentioned Brent.

The top post sent a chill through River's veins. *Wish me luck, babies. Hot date tonight @rondo with a daddy I've been pining over forever. Aphrodite, do your thang.*

No. No, no, no, no, no. It couldn't be. Was Brent going out with Justin?

River didn't want to believe it. But why not? It had been two months since he'd left Seattle. Maybe Brent was trying to move on, find some comfort. And he was such a good guy. Justin had had two months to worm his way into Brent's affections by fair means or foul.

If Brent started seeing Justin, *slept* with him, that would be it. He was so damn loyal.

River had fifteen long hours to be tortured by the possibility on his flight from Rome to Seattle via Dublin. There wasn't anything he could do while he was in the air except hope that it wasn't too late. If this was really their first date, surely Brent hadn't given his heart to Justin yet. There was still time.

His flight landed at SeaTac just before 7:00 p.m. River had no idea what time their date was, but he figured he might as well go right to Rondo, an upscale restaurant on Capitol Hill. It was on the way. If they weren't there, he'd go on to Brent's house in Madrona and hope to catch him before he left.

He grabbed a yellow cab outside the terminal—faster than an Uber—and gave the driver the name and the address of the restaurant. God. He couldn't be too late!

He'd fucked up. But there still had to be a chance to turn it around. The universe wouldn't be so cruel, even if he'd almost discarded the greatest gift life had ever given him.

"You in a hurry?" the cab driver, a man in a turban, asked him, glancing in the rearview mirror.

"That obvious? Yeah, I am." He hesitated. "Gotta put a stop to something."

"It's life or death, huh?" The cab driver had a half-teasing smile.

"Of my heart, maybe."

The cab driver nodded. "Been there. We'll get you there as fast as possible."

"Thanks. Could you wait outside while I go in and check something?"

"Sure. It'll be on the meter though."

"That's fine."

They pulled up outside the restaurant. River threw a few twenties over the seat so the driver wouldn't think he was ditching him. "Just wait here."

"You got it."

River ran inside.

Rondo had small, intimate tables running along the window. River scanned the room, heart in his throat. God, he was about to see Brent again. His heart wanted to be happy about that, but what would Brent think? Would he be pissed that River barged in on his date? After Brent had offered him everything, and River had said he couldn't, wouldn't, settle down? God, he'd hurt Brent so much. Maybe Brent hated him now.

His gaze scanned past a lone figure next to a window, bounced back. Justin. He looked different in an expensive purple shirt, his hair slicked back and face glowing with moisturizer.

The seat opposite him was empty, and he watched out the window avidly. Had Brent not arrived?

River hurried to the table and plopped into the seat opposite Justin.

Justin gawked. "R-river? What are you doing here?"

River tried to control his racing heart. He had no rights here. None. He could only plead for mercy. "Hey. Um. Sorry to just show up like this, but I saw your tweet."

Justin frowned. "Uh... so? It wasn't an open invitation. I thought you were in Rome. I mean, Rondo's good, but it's not *that* good."

"Look..." River sighed. "I love him. I love him so much. And he loves me, or he did. I know I left, but I'm back, and I want to make things work. Sometimes you just have to have faith, you know? And I didn't, but now I–"

“Justin?”

River looked to his left. A man stood there with a perplexed look. He had a silver buzz cut, youthful skin, and a gold turtleneck. He looked between Justin and River questioningly.

“Oh,” River said as the world shifted back into place.

“Oh?” Justin crossed his arms and glared at River. “How do you know Carl? I mean, what the fuck!”

“I’ve never seen this guy before in my life,” Carl declared.

“No! No, I thought you had a date with Brent. Your tweet....”

Justin’s face relaxed, and he laughed. “Oh my God! You thought...! Ha-ha! I am so going to hold this over you, River. Like *forever*.”

River scooted out of the booth. “Sorry. I’m really sorry, you guys.”

Before he could leave, Justin grabbed his arm. His smile was gone. “Look, if you came back for him, you’d better fucking mean it.”

River nodded. “I do.”

“Because he’s been a fucking wreck.” Justin scowled. “*Again*.”

River nodded again, silently, before turning and leaving the restaurant.

Chapter 34

Brent

Brent's eyelids were heavy as he tried to focus on the page. The Cold War thriller he was reading was usually a reliable escape route. Anything to take his brain offline for a while.

Outside the tall glass windows in his family room, it was dark and rainy. He could only make out a little of the rain-soaked deck. The lake had vanished entirely, as if it weren't there at all.

The thought made him shiver. Things could vanish so easily.

He checked his watch. Eight thirty. Too early for bed. Did he really care?

Yes. Yes, he did care. He'd been sleeping too damn much lately. He'd done that after Kathy died, and he wouldn't allow himself to go back there. He wanted to hold on to the positive things River had brought into his life, not wallow in self-pity.

Back to the spy stuck in Berlin....

He'd just managed to get back into the story when the doorbell rang. Who'd stop by at this time of night? Without calling or texting first? Sean maybe. Brent got up and went through the house to the front door, shuffling in his slippers like an old man. He opened it.

River stood on the front stoop in the rain. He wore several layers of coats, and duffel bags and a backpack were at his feet. His hair was up and messy, and there were circles under his haunted eyes. He looked like he'd just gotten off a plane. He looked like a shadow of the man who'd left Seattle two months ago.

Brent's hand seized around the doorknob. "River?"

River's face did something complicated. "Funny thing happened to me in Rome. I hated it. My heart was kind of broken? And I realized it didn't mean anything. The classes. The history. The food. Nothing meant anything without you. The whole world means nothing without you." Tears welled in his eyes and joined the rain on his face as he struggled to get the words out. "So I was wondering… if it's too late… for me to come home?"

This couldn't be real. It was more than Brent had even dared hope for. And maybe he should pinch himself, but instead he threw the door open and had River in his arms before he could form one single rational thought. Rain pelted down on them both as they clung together. It was fresh and cold, and River was there, real and smelling a bit of plane air, and for the first time in months, Brent could breathe.

River clung to him so hard. He kissed Brent's cheek, lips warm against cold skin. "I never should have left. I was just so used to moving on, I didn't know how to stop. Can you forgive me? Can I come home? I love you so much."

The relief and joy and leftover sadness were so big in Brent's chest that he thought he might explode. And there was River's energy, pouring into him like the sweetest drug. "You will never not be welcome in my life, baby. No matter how far away you go, you're still a part of me. That will never change."

Twenty minutes later, they were dry and in bed, both wearing one of Brent's thermal shirts against the November chill. They were on their sides, legs entwined, but with enough distance between them so Brent could look at River's face. He thought he could stare at River forever.

River's blond hair was loose and damp, frizzed from the rain. Brent smoothed it back. His thumb traced the dark half-moon under one blue-gray eye. "You look so tired, babe. Are you okay?"

"I haven't been. But I will be now." River cupped Brent's neck, his face serious. "I meant what I said. Everything about Rome, as great as it was, it didn't matter without you. I just wanted to come back here the whole time."

Brent swallowed a lump in his throat. "Really?"

River nodded.

"That's funny, because I'd reached the conclusion that none of *this* mattered without you. I was thinking I'd sell everything and join you on the road. If you'd have me. I was gonna ask you if I could come to Rome to talk about it."

River tried to laugh and cry at the same time, and it was amazing to see. "Oh God. We're so stuck with each other."

Brent smiled. "I guess we are. Just call me *Sticky Man*." His smile faded. "After Kathy, I was so depressed. I couldn't find a way to get interested in life again. Then you came along with your... your vitality and peace, your light. You taught me to feel joy, to see beauty in the world. I want you in my life, however that works for you. I don't want to change you."

River cupped Brent's neck. "This works for me. For the first time in my life, I want roots. I want a house that is really mine, not a temporary room. Somewhere I can put up drawings I like and hoard used books. Experiment with cooking. Use my own things. Have a towel that I like. And a pillow."

"You want your own pillow?" Brent teased, but his heart melted. He never thought he'd hear River say those words. But it was so, so welcome. "You want to live here with me, then? Everything I have is yours. Though we can buy you your own towel and pillow, if you insist."

River rolled his eyes at Brent's lame humor. "I would love to stay here. I'll pay rent. I want to carry my own weight."

"If that's important to you." Brent took River's hand from his neck and kissed the palm. "Do you want to manage Harmony Tree?"

River's eyebrows furrowed. "I'd like to stay involved with it, but I don't think that would feed my soul, you know? I'd love to build my massage and reiki practice here. Maybe start a tantra class for couples." He flushed. "I won't go back to seeing individual clients."

"You can if you want to."

River shook his head. "It never felt right after we got together. I felt conflicted. I know you're okay with it, but I'm not."

Brent felt a throb of relief. He'd tried hard not to be jealous of River's surrogacy work, but it hadn't been easy. "I'm sure you could build a practice fast here, with word of mouth. You're so gifted."

River smiled. "Thanks. Building a healing practice sounds so good to me." River sighed. "Something that will last. I don't know why I resisted staying put for so long."

He kissed Brent. And it was heaven. But Brent couldn't help smiling through the kiss.

River pulled back. "What's so funny?"

"Just thinking that all this *roots* stuff is ironic since now I want to travel."

"We can do both, can't we? Have our home here in Seattle, and take some killer trips once in a while." River grimaced. "God, I used to think that sounded like half living. Now it sounds perfect. What did you do to me, Mr. McKay?"

A bubble of joy rose up Brent's spine. "Love you, maybe? Yeah. I think I just loved you. With everything that I am."

River breathed out a shaky sigh. "That course in Rome made me realize... whatever it is I've been searching for, it's not out there. It's not with some guru. What I've been searching for... is you."

PART V: UNION

"Never judge people by their past. People learn, people change, people move on." – Buddha

Epilogue

One year later

River

"Now take your partner's hands and look into their eyes. Hold their gaze. Tantra is about forming a deep connection to your partner, staying present with them in the moment, creating a space, a bubble, where only the two of you exist. In this space, you return to the root of who you are as individuals and a couple, outside of all the worries and minutiae of your daily lives."

River sat cross-legged at the front of the rented yoga studio on his mat, his spine straight, voice soothing. The couples in the room sat facing one another, hands clasped, looking into one another's eyes.

It was a bit strange to have such familiar faces in this class. There were six couples today. Jack and Tony, Michael and James, Trudy and Sydney were there. The clinic's other surrogates—Andrea, Emily, and Philip—were also there with their significant others.

River wanted this trial class for Expanded Horizons to go well, but he felt no worry about it. He was confident in the value of the offering, and that things would go the way they were supposed to go.

Last year after returning from Rome, River put all his energy into creating his own healing practice—Harmony Moon Touch. He offered a range of sessions from regular massage to intense reiki healing work. At first he hadn't added tantra, and he didn't go back to work at Expanded Horizons. He wanted to honor his and Brent's relationship by reserving all of his sexual energy for them. But Sean kept bugging River about doing a tantric class for couples, with the doggedness that only Sean could employ.

Last spring, River and Brent attended a tantric couples retreat in Oregon offered by a lovely blonde yogi named Sandra. River loved the setup and the way Sandra kept the focus on the spiritual. In their group sessions, she taught the ideas and concepts behind tantra and led the couples through the early stages of a tantric session—the gazing and breathing, light touches and kissing. The couples had then been given assignments to do back in their room which, obviously, went a lot further.

River returned home inspired, and he immediately set up his first couples class. He put up flyers at Harmony Tree Cafe and sent word out to his growing email list of massage clients. His first seminar, which took place on a weekend at a local hotel, had ten couples. His second one hit capacity at twenty couples and had a wait list. He'd done one a month since, and they were always full.

Now Expanded Horizons was interested in adding tantra couples therapy to their offerings. Jack said they'd been getting more couples who wanted help improving their sex lives. So they'd set up this sample session. River was excited about the possibility of working with Expanded Horizons again. He missed being a part of their group and their mission. They were all focused on the same thing—sexual healing. It made sense to work together.

River quietly got up from his mat and walked around to see how everyone was doing. Tony and Jack were seated in perfect tantric pose, but Tony made funny faces at Jack, crossing his eyes and poking his tongue into his cheek to simulate a blowjob until he noticed River was nearby. Then his expression went serious and utterly innocent. River just shook his head and smiled.

James, whose legs were paralyzed from a childhood bout with polio, sat on a mat with a blanket over his lap. Michael had had to talk James into this because, Michael said, he was self-conscious about his body and was reluctant to do a group thing. But River and Michael discussed how it could be done, with the two of them arriving first and getting James onto the mat before anyone else arrived. There was no actual nudity in the class and nothing too explicit.

In the end, James had clearly thought *fuck it*, because when he'd arrived there'd been a half dozen people in the room, and before

River could clear it, James had told Michael to simply lift him to the ground. He'd settled his own limbs and blanket with minimal fuss or self-consciousness. The pride on Michael's face was unmistakable, and River felt he'd witnessed something private and meaningful.

River strolled past them. Michael and James held each other's gazes with a clarity and strength of connection that was beautiful to see. River let his heart chakra be fed for a moment before moving quietly back to the front of the room.

"The next step is tantric breath. Deep, loud breathing from your belly activates and energizes the chakra along your spine. In each tantric session, you'll build up sexual energy and then use your breath as the engine to spread it through your body, again and again, all while keeping a deep, mindful connection with your partner."

"That sounds easy," James quipped, and everyone laughed.

River grinned. "It's not easy. It takes a lot of focus. But the more time you spend in tantric practice with your partner, the richer the experience will become, and the longer you'll be able to sustain it."

"So how long do you and Brent go for?" Tony asked, keeping his gaze on Jack.

"When we have time, we can go all weekend." The bliss in River's voice was a little embarrassing, but hey.

"Oh my God, we are so learning this!" Tony exclaimed. "Focus on me, Jack, honey. Come on!"

The light-heartedness in the class was fun, but it fell away after River got everyone doing tantric breath. Gradually, an intimate bubble manifested in the room, as if the world outside didn't exist. The couples followed River's directions to touch each other lightly—hands, arms, faces, legs—and to use slow kissing as an exploration and form of communication that didn't have to lead to anything.

The energy was so strong and beautiful, River teared up once or twice. These were good people, and the couples were very much in love. He only wished all of his classes were as open and receptive as this one. But then, at least one person in each couple had dedicated themselves to sexual healing and were open-minded and eager to learn. It was awesome.

When the session was over and most people in the class were resting on their mats, Trudy pushed to her feet and approached River.

"Okay, we're in," she said in a low voice. "This is glorious, River. How many hours a week can you give us?" Her neck was flushed and her eyes bright.

"Um…. Fair question." River was thrilled, but logistics were a real challenge.

Harmony Moon Touch's calendar was currently booked a month out. But working with Expanded Horizons was important to him. It wasn't a matter of money. He had plenty of that. He'd found out after he got back from Rome that Brent had made him co-owner on Harmony Tree Cafe. And not only was the business booming in Seattle, but they were franchising it in other cities as well. Brent had insisted that the concept was as much River's idea as his, and River hadn't protested too much. He knew it was part of Brent's nature to want to give him things and secure his future. River had never felt so loved and cared for in his life.

"Did you want me to do group classes or work with couples one-on-one? If you want one-on-ones, I could maybe do two sessions a week. If you like the group classes, I'd recommend the full seminar. It's two days with a morning and afternoon session each day, and the couples do exercises on their own in between."

Trudy shook her head. "I had my doubts about the group classes, but this was perfect. You handle it beautifully. It's intimate but not too intimate."

River smiled. "Thanks. Honestly, I borrowed ideas from a number of other teachers."

"We all do, River. That's the advantage of being part of the human species." She winked. "Could you do one couples seminar a month? Depending on demand, we might eventually add more."

"Perfect." River smiled.

Trudy was so enthusiastic about the therapy, and everyone else came up to say how much they liked it. River left the yoga studio on a high of optimism and joy.

It was still astonishing to him. He'd spent his entire adult life taking classes and trying to learn the skills to help people. But it wasn't until he settled in one spot—Seattle—that he flourished as a healer.

Harrison had been right. Being a dandelion puff floating on the breeze was all well and good. But in order to fulfill his purpose, River had to land and allow his roots to grow.

He was so grateful he'd found Brent, and that their love had been so deep he'd had no choice but to settle down in Seattle. He might easily have gone through his whole life always moving, always searching, and always, ultimately, being left half full. But his heart had known what he needed, even though his head had been stubbornly resistant.

When River returned home from the studio, he found Brent on the deck with their shelter dog, Mumsie. She was an older girl, part Australian shepherd and part god-only-knew, who was submissive and sweet and grateful for any and all attention thrown her way. She got up from her bed at Brent's feet to greet River. She didn't have the rambunctious energy of a puppy—or of Lily—but her impressive tail wag made her pleasure known all the same.

"Hey! How'd it go?" Brent smiled up at River. The reading glasses perched on his nose were too adorable. He took them off and tilted his head up. River answered the silent request, leaning over his shoulder for a kiss.

"It was fantastic. Everyone raved about the class."

"Of course they did." Brent reached up to capture River's neck and pull him down for another long kiss. When they parted, Brent sighed happily. "Mom and Dad sent a postcard from Delphi. It's on the dining room table."

"I saw it. They're so sweet." Jim and Brenda seemed to love River, and he returned the sentiment. "They're becoming quite the world travelers, your folks."

"I know. I'm jealous as hell." Brent raised his eyebrows in an accusatory look.

River just smiled. "You say that, but you're the one who can't stop creating new cafes. I don't know how you'd do that if we were bouncing all over the world right now."

"I might as well use my time in Seattle wisely, since you're so in demand here with your clientele."

"Ha! Yes, one of Seattle's *best foodie creatives* is only whiling away his time. Hence the three new Harmony Tree branches in the past year and now White Picket Fence."

White Picket Fence was Brent's newest cafe. It was slated to open in December and would serve down-home comfort food. The theme and decor were pure American small town.

Brent pulled River down into his lap with a growl. "Can I help it if you unblocked my *Svadhishthana* chakra a bit too well? The creative energy is flowing, baby."

"Mmm. I'm not complaining."

"And don't forget, you promised me a three-week trip in April, and I'm holding you to it, No matter what. Swear!" Brent narrowed his eyes in warning.

River laughed. "If you think I'd miss my own honeymoon, you're crazy."

"But we still haven't figured out where we're going," Brent pointed out.

"Anywhere you want, love," River said sincerely. "Egypt. England. Spain. I'd go anywhere with you."

They got distracted making out for a while. Long, lazy kisses, wandering hands, and the occasional grind and squeeze. It was lovely to allow arousal to build and simmer. There'd be time later for something more serious. There was always time for lovemaking.

Mumsie's cold nose prodded River's leg, and when he looked up, she gazed at him hopefully, her tail wagging.

"Mumsie says it's time for our evening walk," River announced.

"Well, Mumsie can hold her horses for a moment."

"She's a dog. She doesn't have horses."

Brent gave River a wry look. "*Because* I have something to say to you, River Larsen."

River softened in Brent's arms. Hearing his name on his lover's lips always turned him to jelly. "What?"

Brent took River's hand and kissed his fingers, one by one. "I just wanted to say that I love you. More than anything in this world. That's all."

Warmth spread through River, expanding his heart and filling his veins. He breathed in the moment, heady and sweet. "And I love you too. *My* Brent McKay."

THE END

Dear Reader

Thank you for spending time with myself, River, and Brent. I planned a 4th installment of the Sex in Seattle series, one featuring a traveling tantric guy who worked for the clinic as a surrogate, but it spent years on the back burner. After taking some time off this past winter, I decided it was time to tackle River's story. I've always been interested in Eastern philosophy and took a few courses in college, though I am far (far) from an expert on the subject. That is to say, I'm more Brent's level than River's! I hope I intrigued you enough to do some searching on these topics on your own.

As always, I very much appreciate my readers posting recommendations for my books on social media and reviewing on Amazon and Goodreads. Thank you! Your reviews truly make a difference in drawing other readers and that helps me continue writing full time.

I appreciate my readers so much. It is awesome to hear from you and to know that I made someone smile or sigh. Feel free to email me: eli@elieaston.com.

You can also visit my website: www.elieaston.com. I have first chapters up for all my books and some free stories too. And you can sign up for my newsletter to get a monthly email about new releases and sales. (https://www.subscribepage.com/ElisNewsletterSignup)

My facebook group is a place to chat about Eli stories and get opportunity to read ARCs, excerpts from works-in-progress, and other goodies. (https://www.facebook.com/groups/164054884188096/)

Follow me on Amazon to be alerted of my new books. (https://www.amazon.com/Eli-Easton/e/B00CJUKM9I/)

I can promise you there will always be happy ending and that love is love.

Eli Easton

The Sex in Seattle series

Check out the rest of the books set in Expanded Horizons, a sex clinic in Seattle.

The Trouble with Tony – Private Investigator Tony DeMarco is hired to investigate the suspicious death of a young woman. She'd been seeing Dr. Jack Halloran at Expanded Horizons sex clinic, so Tony goes undercover there to see if the doc is a suspect. The last thing Tony expects is that Jack can help him with his own sexual healing!

The Enlightenment of Daniel – Daniel is a high-powered business man who's an expert in hostile takeovers. His father's imminent death shakes Daniel to his core, prying loose feelings for his very male business partner that Daniel had no idea were there. After doing "due diligence" by seeing a professional at Expanded Horizons sex clinic, Daniel decides to go after what he wants.

The Mating of Michael – When sex surrogate Michael Lamont meets his author hero (and unicorn) at a book signing, he knows James needs him in his life. But will prickly James, wheelchair-bound thanks to a childhood bout with polio, ever let Michael close?

Read more about these books and check out the free first chapters at: https://www.elieaston.com/sex-in-seattle-series

Also by Eli Easton

From Dreamspinner Press
A Second Harvest (Men of Lancaster County #1)
Tender Mercies (Men of Lancaster County #2)
The Stolen Suitor
Snowblind
Boy Shattered
From Eli Easton
Angels Sing
Superhero
Puzzle Me This
The Trouble With Tony (Sex in Seattle #1)
The Enlightenment of Daniel (Sex in Seattle #2)
The Mating of Michael (Sex in Seattle #3)
A Prairie Dog's Love Song
Heaven Can't Wait
The Lion and the Crow
Five Dares
Robby Riverton: Mail Order Bride
How to Howl at the Moon (Howl at the Moon #1)
How to Walk like a Man (Howl at the Moon #2)
How to Wish Upon a Star (Howl at the Moon #3)
How to Save a Life (Howl at the Moon #4)
How to Run with the Wolves (Howl at the Moon #5)
Before I Wake
Blame it on the Mistletoe
Unwrapping Hank
Midwinter Night's Dream
Merry Christmas, Mr. Miggles
Desperately Seeking Santa
Christmas Angel
Family Camp (Daddy Dearest #1)

www.elieaston.com

About Eli Easton

ELI EASTON has been at various times and under different names a preacher's daughter, a computer programmer, a game designer, the author of paranormal mysteries, an organic farmer, and a profound sleeper. She has been writing m/m romance since 2013.

As an avid reader of romance, she is tickled pink when an author manages to combine literary merit, vast stores of humor, melting hotness, and eye-dabbing sweetness into one story. She promises to strive to achieve most of that most of the time. She currently lives on Puget Sound with her husband, dogs, and lots of very large trees.

Her website is http://www.elieaston.com.

You can e-mail her at eli@elieaston.com

Twitter is @EliEaston

Facebook: https://www.facebook.com/profile.php?id=100008994061782